T0029517

Also by Katherine Kovacic

True Crime
The Schoolgirl Strangler

The Alex Clayton Art Mysteries
The Shifting Landscape
Painting in the Shadows
The Portrait of Molly Dean

JUST
MURDERED

JUST MURDERED

A MS. FISHER'S
MODERN MURDER MYSTERY

KATHERINE KOVACIC

Poisoned Pen
PRESS

Copyright © 2021, 2023 by Every Cloud Productions
Cover and internal design © 2023 by Sourcebooks
Cover art by Jeffrey Nguyen

Sourcebooks, Poisoned Pen Press, and the colophon are
registered trademarks of Sourcebooks.

All rights reserved. No part of this book may be reproduced in any form or by
any electronic or mechanical means including information storage and retrieval
systems—except in the case of brief quotations embodied in critical articles or
reviews—without permission in writing from its publisher, Sourcebooks.

The characters and events portrayed in this book are fictitious or are used
fictitiously. Apart from well-known historical figures, any similarity to real
persons, living or dead, is purely coincidental and not intended by the author.

Published by Poisoned Pen Press, an imprint of Sourcebooks
P.O. Box 4410, Naperville, Illinois 60567-4410
(630) 961-3900
sourcebooks.com

Originally published in 2021 in Australia by Allen & Unwin, NSW, Australia.

Library of Congress Cataloging-in-Publication Data

Names: Kovacic, Katherine, author.
Title: Just murdered : a Ms Fisher's modern murder mystery / Katherine Kovacic.
Description: Naperville, Illinois : Poisoned Pen Press, [2023]
Identifiers: LCCN 2022028811 (print) | LCCN 2022028812
(ebook) | (trade paperback) | (epub)
Subjects: LCGFT: Detective and mystery fiction. | Novels.
Classification: LCC PR9619.4.K68 J87 2023 (print) | LCC
PR9619.4.K68 (ebook) | DDC 823/.92--dc23/eng/20220617
LC record available at https://lccn.loc.gov/2022028811
LC ebook record available at https://lccn.loc.gov/2022028812

Printed and bound in the United States of America.
PAH 10 9 8 7 6 5 4 3 2 1

FOR ADVENTURESSES EVERYWHERE

ABOUT MS. FISHER'S
MODERN MURDER MYSTERIES

Just Murdered, written by Katherine Kovacic, is based on *Ms. Fisher's Modern Murder Mysteries* television series, Episode 1, written by Deb Cox.

The television series, *Ms. Fisher's Modern Murder Mysteries*, was created by Deb Cox and Fiona Eagger and inspired by *Miss Fisher's Murder Mysteries*, the TV series based on the Phryne Fisher mystery books by Kerry Greenwood.

Ms. Fisher's Modern Murder Mysteries are produced by Every Cloud Productions for Seven Network Australia, in association with Screen Australia, Film Victoria, and Fulcrum Media Finance.

PROLOGUE

Adversity and challenge were nothing new to the members of the Adventuresses' Club of the Antipodes, but disturbing events had plunged them deep into unfamiliar territory.

That morning a package had been delivered. This wasn't an unusual occurrence, and nor was this particular package entirely unexpected. Unwanted, yes, but not unexpected.

Samuel Birnside—honorary member and odd-job man— had answered the postman's ring and met him at the solid iron gate set precisely halfway along the perimeter wall. Having intercepted the package, he'd intended to take it straight inside but instead found himself unable to move, staring at the brown paper, the numerous stamps that identified its point of origin and the spidery black handwriting. The unfamiliar scrawl hit him like a punch to the stomach, and Samuel realised a part of him had been hoping to see the address written in the firm, flamboyant style he knew so well.

But no.

Giving himself a mental shake, Samuel pushed his glasses firmly up the bridge of his nose, rolled his shoulders, and tugged at the hem of his cardigan, settling it more comfortably. Then he turned towards the grandiose mansion and prepared to deliver the news.

He had hoped to make it all the way to the Camelot Room, the nerve centre of the Adventuresses' Club, but Birdie met him in the entry porch. Dressed in her customary jodhpurs and turtleneck, the club president's face was pale, the lines radiating from the corners of her eyes more prominent than usual. Today she seemed just as weighed down as the statues that supported the arch above her head.

She looked at the package and then at Samuel. 'So it's arrived.'

Meeting her eye, Samuel could only nod.

Without another word, she turned and preceded him into the house.

Inside the Camelot Room, Birdie moved to stand behind her assigned chair, gripping the backrest upon which was affixed a small brass plaque that proclaimed it the rightful place of *Adventuress Birnside.*

Samuel placed the package in front of her then retrieved a pair of scissors from the bureau. 'You'll want to open it first.' He passed her the scissors, and Birdie prodded the parcel with the tip of the blades, reluctant to discover its contents.

'She only took that case because of me.'

'Birdie! You can't blame yourself. Since when did Phryne Fisher do anything she didn't want to do?'

Birdie shook her head slowly, eyes glistening. If it had been anyone else, Samuel would have called them tears. But crying was not something Birdie tended to indulge in. Nonetheless, he moved a little closer, standing behind his sister's shoulder in silent solidarity.

'Right.' Birdie took a deep breath and slashed through the

string in a single motion. The outer layers of brown paper fell away, revealing a battered tin of the type that usually contained an assortment of chocolates or sweet biscuits. Placing the scissors carefully to one side, she prised off the lid and pushed back the banana leaves that had been used as padding.

Samuel and Birdie both leaned forward and peered at the contents of the tin. A revolver, its gilt barrel and pearl handle stained with mud.

Birdie slammed the lid back down with a dull clunk. 'Meeting. Here. Now,' she said.

Samuel nodded once and hurried from the room to summon the other Adventuresses.

Founded in 1900, while women in most parts of Australia were still fighting for the right to vote, the Adventuresses' Club of the Antipodes was variously home or home-away-from-home to a number of women from all walks of life: women of outstanding achievement, women of skill and talent, women whose courage and tenacity were beyond question. In short, women of vision—who pushed against the limits of 1964 society—found kindred spirits within the walls of the mansion on Greenwood Place.

Samuel traced a path through the building, opening doors, knocking discreetly, or raising his voice depending on the Adventuress he was trying to rouse. In the ballroom, two women were engaged in a fencing bout, almost dancing across the floor in a series of parries and ripostes. At the sight of Samuel, they stopped and raised their masks.

'Meeting. Camelot Room,' he said.

Leaning out a window, he spotted botanist Minnie Bell kneeling among the plants. 'Dr. Bell! Camelot Room.'

As word spread, Adventuresses began to appear, alerted by

their colleagues or by the atmosphere now filling the house: anxiety, anticipation, and a sense of foreboding.

Samuel knocked on one last door, swinging it open without waiting for a reply. Inside, Violetta Fellini was engrossed in an experiment. Not wanting to interrupt, he paused and watched for a moment. Violetta was a study in contrasts: a classic beauty with a strict Italian upbringing who had never married, a warm and generous personality disguised by a severe hairstyle, and a shyness that at one time had tended to hide a brilliant scientific mind. It was only when she found the Adventuresses' Club that Violetta had begun to be comfortable in her own skin. Now, in her state-of-the-art laboratory, every movement was deft and assured, and her face was continually lighting up with the joy of discovery.

A beaker of blue liquid bubbled over a Bunsen burner. Violetta drew a minuscule quantity of something brown from a test tube and, using a long pipette, carefully added two drops to the beaker. There was a whoosh as the liquid turned clear, and her face was momentarily hidden by a cloud of smoke. When it dispersed, she was smiling. But then she saw Samuel and the smile fell away.

'Has it arrived then?' she asked, replacing her safety goggles with a pair of glasses.

'Just now. Birdie's called a meeting.'

Violetta removed her white coat, then together they made their way through the building.

There were only two empty chairs remaining when they arrived in the Camelot Room. Violetta slid into the one bearing her name as Samuel softly closed the door and took up a position in the corner, shoulders resting against the gilt-embossed wall.

'This is all they found.' Birdie addressed the room as she

lifted the mud-smeared gun from the box and placed it gently on the table in front of her.

The air in the Camelot Room rippled with the collective sigh of the assembled women.

'But surely…' began one of the Adventuresses before subsiding, her question unasked.

'So they've given up,' Violetta said.

Birdie held up a hand in a gesture that was half calming, half resigned. 'Officially, the search for the crash site is over. However, Tribal Chief Kabui said he is eternally grateful that his son's murder was solved, and he assures us he will never stop searching the highlands of Papua New Guinea for Phryne Fisher.'

'And if anyone could survive a plane crash in the jungle, it's Phryne.' Samuel's consoling words did nothing to raise the spirits of the assembled women.

'But without her gun…' someone murmured.

'Even without a gun—and regardless of the situation—Phryne Fisher would have plenty of resources at her disposal. And, above all, she has her ingenuity.' Birdie placed both fists on the table and leaned forward.

Around the room, heads nodded: there were murmurs of approval and even a faint, 'Hear, hear.'

Out in the hallway, the grandmother clock began to strike, and the gathering fell still as the Westminster Quarters rang out and the hours tolled. The ensuing silence was heavy with portent.

Finally Violetta cleared her throat. 'Has a letter already been sent?' she asked.

'Yes,' Birdie replied. 'Once six months had passed with no contact from Phryne, I spoke to her solicitor. She'd left detailed instructions in the event something should happen,

and following her wishes, a letter—worded in a suitably...
enticing manner—was dispatched weeks ago.' Birdie swallowed hard.

'However'—Samuel came to her rescue—'we could only
send it to the last known address, and as you're all aware, past
attempts at communication have been unsuccessful.'

'But even if we do get a response, what then? Without
Phryne, who will expose the corrupt? Champion the under-
dog? Challenge the bullies and bigots? Who in this town will
protect the vulnerable and fight for what is right?' Violetta's
voice cracked with emotion.

'As ever, each of us will have her part to play, but we also
need to remain hopeful, Violetta,' said Birdie. Her gaze travelled
round the room, taking in every Adventuress. Then it fell on the
single empty chair. A chair bearing the name *Adventuress Fisher.*
She stared at it for a long moment. 'We *must* remain hopeful,
because, God knows, we could scour the earth from pole to pole
and never find another woman like Phryne Fisher.'

One

'Are you trying to kill me?'

Peregrine's attention snapped back to the woman sitting in front of her. Outside the sun was shining brightly, but in the hair salon, storm clouds were gathering.

'Sorry, Mrs. Judd!' As she loosened the perming rod, Peregrine risked a glance in the mirror. The manageress, Mrs. Morgan, was staring straight back at her, lips pursed, one eye narrowed.

'Everything all right over there?' Mrs. Morgan asked, scissors poised mid-snip.

'Yes, thanks!' Peregrine forced a smile at her client's reflection, but Mrs. Judd wasn't fooled.

'You've only been here a few months, haven't you, dear? And before that it was...what were you doing before you started hairdressing?'

Peregrine blew a stray lock of dark brown hair from her eyes. 'Working at the bakery.'

'I thought it was the pharmacy.'

Peregrine had doused three-quarters of Mrs. Judd's head

in perming solution, but now she paused. Suddenly the frilly smock she was wearing felt unbearably hot and constricting.

'I've just been looking for the right job; somewhere I can express my creativity.'

Mrs. Judd opened her mouth to reply, but her words were drowned out by the revving of a powerful engine.

All heads turned towards the salon window. There was a station wagon idling just outside: a cream station wagon, trimmed with distinctive faux wood panels.

Peregrine set a record applying the rest of the perming solution, then tucked a plastic cap on Mrs. Judd's head. 'Do you have plenty of magazines there? This needs to process for a while.' She started towards the door, peeling off her gloves and smock as she went. 'Is it okay if I take my tea break now, Mrs. Morgan?'

'Fifteen minutes, Peregrine!' ordered the manageress, but all she got in response was the tinkle of the bell as the door closed on Peregrine's retreating figure.

In the car park, Eric Wild dangled an arm from the open window of his Ford Falcon Squire. Eric had been trying to look cool, but the moment he saw Peregrine a broad grin broke through the veneer of casual indifference, lighting up his handsome face.

'Eric!' Peregrine trailed a hand across the car's bonnet, then leaned in and planted a lingering kiss on his lips.

'Hop in.' He cracked the door for her, sliding across the bench seat as Peregrine climbed behind the wheel.

'I've only got fifteen minutes.'

'You can do a lot in fifteen minutes.'

Peregrine quirked an eyebrow at her boyfriend then floored it, squealing with delight as they peeled out onto the road. At the speed she was driving, it only took them a couple of minutes to get to the beachfront car park, which—at 11 a.m. on a Wednesday—was delightfully deserted. Peregrine saw her chance and, with Eric shouting encouragement, she put the wagon through its paces, fishtailing through the gravel, accelerating and braking hard as dust billowed around them. Finally she brought the Ford to a stop overlooking the ocean. Switching off the engine, Peregrine sat for a moment, hands on the wheel, savouring the feeling of power and control. A girl could get used to this.

'So what do you think?' Eric's arm slid along the backrest until the tips of his fingers rested lightly on the nape of Peregrine's neck.

'I love it. Where did—'

His hand brushed the edge of her jaw, cutting off the rest of the question.

'How much do you love it?' he asked, eyes never leaving hers.

Peregrine pressed her cheek into his palm and inhaled slowly, a feline smile curling the edges of her mouth.

'This much,' she said, pivoting towards him and pressing her lips hard against his.

The next few minutes were a tangle of limbs that came to an abrupt end when one of Peregrine's kitten heels, which had somehow come adrift from her foot, found its way to a point beneath Eric's shoulder blades. He sat up suddenly and their foreheads collided.

Peregrine put a hand to her temple, and the feel of her dishevelled hair reminded her of something.

'Oh, no! What time is it?' She straightened her top and began re-pinning her hair. 'Drive! I have to get back!'

'Peregrine…' Eric implored, walking his fingers up her long, bare thigh to the cuff of her short shorts.

Peregrine playfully slapped Eric's hand away and gave him a shove in the general direction of the steering wheel. 'Come on!'

Eric sighed heavily, but he knew when Peregrine meant business. Giving up, he got the car started and they drove back to the salon in comfortable silence.

—

There was always a chance her extended absence would pass unnoticed, but as Peregrine hurried—with as much nonchalance as she could muster—through the door of the hair salon, she found the manageress waiting for her.

'Peregrine Fisher!'

'Sorry I'm a bit late, Mrs. Morgan.' She ducked her head and tried to sidle past, but the manageress grabbed her by the arm.

'Just how long was that perming solution left on Mrs. Judd's hair?' Mrs. Morgan hissed. Her face, inches from Peregrine's, was white with fury.

Peregrine's eyes widened. 'Well, that depends.'

'On?'

'On...when you rinsed it off and applied the neutraliser?'

They both looked over at Mrs. Judd, her head now wrapped in a towelling turban, idly flicking through a copy of the *Women's Weekly*. Then Mrs. Morgan marched across and slowly unravelled the towel. As it came away, Mrs. Judd's nearly-dry hair was revealed: it looked like she'd stuck her finger in a power socket. Mrs. Judd glanced up and the smile of anticipation froze on her face, turning into a full-throated wail as she stared at the mirror in horror.

Mrs. Morgan rounded on Peregrine. 'That's it. Out!'

'But—'

'But nothing. I gave you a chance—against advice, mind you—because of your mother. She had her troubles, but she was a good woman who helped me when I needed it. Giving you a leg up seemed the least I could do, but this is the last straw. Now get your bag and get out.'

'I'm sorry!'

'Sorry won't fix this!' Mrs. Morgan gestured towards her client's head and, in response, Mrs. Judd let out another wail. 'The trouble with you, Peregrine, is you don't make an effort. How old are you now? Pushing thirty? You can't expect other people to look after you forever. I know you've had a hard time since your mother died, but unless you wake up to yourself quick-smart, you're going to end up just like her!'

Stung by the words, Peregrine began to slowly gather her things. She couldn't remember a time when she'd had someone to really look after her, least of all her mother.

'And here.' Mrs. Morgan thrust a pile of envelopes towards her. 'I won't be holding post for you anymore either.'

Peregrine took the pile of letters and crammed them into her tote bag. Mrs. Morgan jerked her head in the direction of the door then turned back to her distraught client, soothing and clucking even as strands of hair drifted slowly to the floor.

Squaring her shoulders, Peregrine left the salon for the last time, giving the door a defiant shove with her hip as she went. Needing something to boost her spirits, she stopped to buy a blue heaven milkshake before starting the slow walk home, the light breeze cool on her bare midriff. Her shorts and bikini top were far more suited to the beach than the centre of town, even if the entire business district was just a few sandy streets book-ended by a petrol station and a fish-and-chip shop. But Peregrine was used to ignoring frowning shopkeepers and tutting matrons. She had never been one to play by the rules—at least, not unless they suited her.

On the unfashionable edge of town, farthest from the sea-shore, Peregrine turned into the Paradise Caravan Park and slowly made her way past empty sites and deserted vans until she reached the section where the waifs and strays—the permanents—resided. The sun-bleached caravan she rented was hotter inside than out, so Peregrine took her milkshake and sat on the van's step, the pile of letters in her lap.

There were quite a few, and Peregrine flicked through them, seeing on most her mother's name and the familiar crossing out of one address after another. Annabelle had never liked to stay in one place for long and had been constantly on the move. Sometimes she had been fleeing a debt; at other times she'd expressed an urge to wake up to a different view. In hindsight, it seemed to Peregrine that Annabelle had in fact been trying to outrun her own personal demons. In the end the reasons didn't matter, but growing up, Peregrine had come to dread the moment when her mother would appear, empty suitcase in hand, and tell her to start packing. It meant her schooling had suffered, but she'd learned a lot of other stuff along the way, the sort of things you could never find in a textbook. Peregrine knew that now, but back then the only thing she'd felt was the agony of leaving friends behind and having to start afresh in a new school, a new town.

Her mother would have thrown most of the letters away unopened, and Peregrine was about to do the same when one at the bottom of the pile caught her eye. Addressed to her mother, it too had come via a roundabout route, crisscrossing Australia until finally someone had written, *Try Budgiwah*, and underlined the words heavily. But unlike the flimsy paper and onionskin of the others, this envelope was a thick, cream-coloured piece of stationery, and there was an elaborate shield printed on the upper left-hand corner. It looked expensive—and important.

Peregrine brought the envelope close to her face, trying to make out the tiny words on the shield.

'*Gloria in...Gloria in Con-spectus...Hominum?*' She wrinkled her nose and flipped the envelope over. The back was even more intriguing. A large blob of red wax sealed the envelope and there was also a return address: *Greenwood Pl., Melbourne, Victoria, C1.*

Peregrine stuck her finger under the flap and pulled it loose, then extracted a single sheet of paper. There was no salutation or signature, just the same crest and address at the top of the page, but this time with a name: *The Adventuresses' Club of the Antipodes.* Beneath that was a terse, handwritten message:

Please attend urgent meeting regarding inheritance.

'Inheritance? I wish!' Peregrine snorted and was about to throw the note away, but there was something about the heavy paper and elaborate writing that made her hesitate. She read the message a second time, turned the paper over to check there was nothing on the back, then returned to the front and read it again.

Peregrine dropped the letter into her lap and looked up, her gaze wandering over the faded and rusting caravans. Even if it was some sort of trick, what did she have to lose? And if it was real...

She stood abruptly, sending the remnants of her milkshake flying, and hurried inside. There she pulled out a flimsy suitcase, the only one she owned. Peregrine didn't really have much to pack, but the caravan rocked as she slammed drawers open and closed. The narrow wardrobe had room for just an armful of clothes, and she pulled them all out and dumped them straight into the case. Somehow Peregrine managed to make everything fit, although she did have to sit on the case to get it closed. Then she had to open it again and find something more suitable to wear. After some deliberation, she changed into pink stovepipe trousers and a patterned shirt, adding a mini-length coat to the outfit.

Before wrestling the suitcase closed for the second time, Peregrine realised there was one more thing she had to pack. Reaching above the narrow bed, she unpinned a photograph from the wall. The small snapshot, bleached from the sun, showed Peregrine and her mother, arms around each other and heads tipped together as they laughed at the camera.

'Time to move again, Mum,' Peregrine whispered, touching a finger to the faded image. She tucked the photo carefully inside the suitcase and thumped the lid closed.

Standing in the middle of the tiny space, Peregrine turned a slow circle. There was nothing left for her here, not in the caravan or in town. There was one last thing she had to do, however. Sitting down at the scratched Laminex table, she unfolded one of the envelopes from the day's post and exposed its unmarked interior. Then she used the stub of a pencil to write a note to Eric.

Five minutes later, Peregrine slammed the door of the caravan for the last time and tucked the note into the wire screen. She walked through the Paradise without a backward glance, tote bag slung over her shoulder, suitcase bumping against her thigh.

Out on the main road, she felt her resolve waver and pulled the envelope from her bag. Peregrine read the message one more time and ran a finger across the crest before carefully tucking the letter away again.

'The Adventuresses' Club,' she whispered.

Then, turning south, Peregrine Fisher stuck her thumb out and began to walk.

Two

Some days later—her limbs stiff from nights spent sheltering in barns and churches—Peregrine Fisher stood outside the Queen Victoria Market in Melbourne, waving goodbye to the driver of the fruit truck who had brought her the last hundred miles to the city. Despite having an opinion on everything—and sharing them all with her throughout the drive—he'd never heard of the Adventuresses' Club or Greenwood Place. They'd arrived in the city just as dawn was beginning to colour the horizon, so Peregrine spent several hours wandering the market sheds. She'd talked to numerous stallholders, gracefully accepted the occasional apple or orange, charmed her way to several cups of coffee and laughed off three light-hearted yet flamboyant proposals of marriage (all made by Greek and Italian gentlemen with an average age of sixty). Unfortunately, even though many of the market families had lived in Melbourne for two or three generations, each time Peregrine asked about the Adventuresses' Club, she got the same answer. No one had heard of it.

Once the sun was fully up, the trickle of customers rapidly

became a flood, and the market soon rang with the shouts of competing greengrocers.

'Broccoli! Best in the market!'

'Potatoes! Seven pence a pound!'

For a while, Peregrine watched, entranced by the theatrics of both the vendors and the housewives who first feigned disdain at the sight of the fruit or vegetable on offer, only to capitulate when the price was right. Her new acquaintances cast the occasional smile in her direction, but the time for talking had passed, so, sketching a wave to anyone who might notice, Peregrine picked up her suitcase and made her way out of the market.

On the street, she took a moment to orient herself, then began walking in the direction of the city centre, guided by the height of the buildings and the flow of pedestrians in their smart suits and demure dresses, hurrying to begin another day in the office. Surely one of them could direct her to the Adventuresses' Club.

'Excuse me.' Peregrine reached out a tentative hand as a man strode towards her, briefcase thrust forward purposefully.

He brushed past.

'Excuse me.'

Another one did the same, huffing with displeasure.

'*Excuse* me.' Peregrine stepped in front of a man in a brown suit, forcing him to stop and creating a near pile-up among the walkers behind him. 'I'm looking for Greenwood Place.'

'Never heard of it,' he snapped, stepping around her and away.

She walked a little farther, carried along by the crowd, before inspiration struck. Moving to the edge of the footpath, Peregrine watched the traffic then abruptly stuck out her arm. 'Taxi!'

A car screeched to a stop beside her.

'Where to, love?' the driver asked.

'Oh, well, I don't actually have any money, but I was hoping you could tell me how to get to Greenwood Place.'

The taxi driver gave her an incredulous look. 'Ya flamin' kiddin' me?' he spluttered.

Peregrine shrugged, smiled, and waited, while the driver stared. Then he gave a snort of disbelief. 'Top end o' town. Collins Street.' Still muttering and shaking his head, he wrenched the steering wheel and steered the taxi back into the stream of traffic.

'I guess that means this must be the bottom,' Peregrine said to herself. She pulled the envelope from her bag, more as a talisman than because of any need to check the address again, and struck out with renewed energy. At least she knew now that the street existed.

Peregrine walked slowly up one of Melbourne's main streets, thrilled by the energy and bustle, awed by the buildings, delighted by the trams, and excited just to be alive in the city. She was in no hurry as she dawdled past boutiques with alluring displays of clothes and shoes, cafés filled with steam and the aroma of coffee, and hole-in-the-wall cobblers, their tiny rooms piled high with leather. The letter had been chasing her for weeks, after all, so what difference would an hour or two make? She stopped to watch a girl dressed in a red-and-white Mary Quant-style mini striding along on the other side of the street, her arms swinging freely. In each hand the girl carried several shopping bags, all adorned with a bright pattern and the name *H. R. White*. Peregrine couldn't decide what was more attractive: the girl herself or the sight of those colourful bags, swaying back and forth. She kept looking until the girl disappeared around the next corner.

Trailing slowly along the footpath, Peregrine came to a series of elaborate windows, each one emblazoned with the name *Blair's Emporium* and all filled with a dazzling array of products. She lingered at each display and when she finally arrived at the door, Peregrine hesitated, tempted to dive inside and see if the store lived up to the promise of its windows. But she was on a mission and, besides, trying things on would be much more fun if she had an inheritance to buy them with. Peregrine stepped away from the door, squared her shoulders and, after asking a police officer for directions, made her way to Greenwood Place and the Adventuresses' Club.

Three

Inside Blair's Emporium, a fashion parade was underway. Today's spectacle was the crowning glory of the season: a bridal extravaganza featuring the gowns of the brightest star in the Australian fashion and design scene, Florence Astor.

Blair's Mural Hall was a fitting venue for a presentation of such style and elegance. Sitting on the top floor of the emporium, the Mural Hall was a sumptuous ballroom, regularly used to host functions for the crème de la crème of Melbourne society. The ten murals that gave the grand room its name each had a different theme, from *Opera Personalities* to *Sport Through the Ages,* and, although men appeared in some scenes, they leaned heavily towards a celebration of women and their achievements. While most of the figures depicted were historic, an astute observer could find several familiar faces among the illustrious sisterhood, including soprano Dame Nellie Melba, novelist Katharine Susannah Prichard, and Adventuress Phryne Fisher.

At one end of the hall, a pair of staircases swept down from opposite sides of the room, the perfect setting for Florence Astor's show. The landing where they converged was a few steps above the parquetry of the main floor, and today it had been extended out to create a catwalk where, one by one, the house models paraded. Just in front of the landing and suspended from the ceiling above, a ruched amethyst curtain hung in a perfect circle. It formed a dramatic backdrop for the cream, white, and ivory tones of the gowns and, just as importantly, concealed behind its folds the breathtaking pièce de résistance of Florence's show.

The catwalk itself was flanked by several rows of small gilded chairs, the majority occupied by mothers and daughters. The more mature women were dressed for the occasion in well-cut suits, while the younger generation sported hemlines that were fashionably short. Or as short as their mothers would allow. All gazed with rapt attention at the catwalk as each creation made its debut.

In the front row, Terence Blair, proprietor of Blair's Emporium, smoothed the silver hair of his temple and discreetly glanced at his watch. The highlight of the store's calendar of events, and they were late. He smiled as he caught the eye of a fashion columnist on the opposite side of the catwalk, but inside he was seething. Just as a burst of polite applause greeted the latest Florence creation—a tea-length dress with a boat neck and three-quarter lace sleeves—there was a murmured apology from Terence's left, and his wife and son appeared. Colin Blair, sharply suited and with his slicked, black hair shining in the light, was solicitous as he helped his mother into a chair and waited while she arranged herself carefully next to her husband. From her understated hat to the pointed toes of her colour-coordinated pumps, Maggie Blair was the epitome of elegance. Today, however, her classic features remained hidden behind large, black-framed sunglasses.

'Blair's most important show, Maggie!' Terence hissed, bending close to his wife's ear. 'I reminded you last night! Is it too much to ask you to conjure up a modicum of interest?' He smiled broadly and clapped for the model currently gliding past.

Leaning in from the other side, Colin placed a reassuring hand on his mother's arm. 'Not to worry. We're here now, Mother, and it looks like Florence Astor has outdone herself.'

Backstage, Florence herself was feeling far less confident. In honour of the occasion her bobbed hair had been styled to greater fullness, making her look like a blonde Jackie Kennedy. Her black shift—simple yet timeless—was, of course, one of her own designs. Florence had earned her fashion stripes in the ateliers of Paris and Milan before returning to Melbourne and launching her own eponymous label, so staging a fashion parade was something she'd done dozens of times before. But that didn't stop the nerves or sleepless nights. Each collection was a gamble, requiring just the right mix of the familiar with the bold design innovation that had made Florence Astor a household name. Today's bridal show in particular had to be perfect and, to her discerning audience, everything they had seen so far had exceeded expectations. But Florence knew illusion was everything, and behind the scenes, tension was increasing as the finale drew close.

'Keep it up, ladies. Remember, look triumphant! You're getting married!'

Florence sent the next model down the runway, watched for a moment to see how the bridal mini dress was received, then turned to the next girl, adjusting the ivory pillbox she was wearing to a more jaunty angle and fluffing out the bejewelled veil. Satisfied, Florence stepped away and surveyed the backstage area.

'Has *anyone* seen Barbie? Has she even had the good grace to telephone?' she asked.

Lewis Knox appeared from behind a rack of gowns. Employed by Blair's as a storeman and occasional window-dresser, Knox had made it his business to ensure everything—from shoes and stockings to hats and accessories—was where it should be for the fashion show. Now, slightly out of breath from his latest search for the missing model, he shook his head.

'Sorry, Miss Astor,' he said. 'I've looked everywhere, but there's no sign of her.'

Florence threw up her hands. 'I simply cannot believe this! So unprofessional. We've had to cover for her for the entire show. I'll be damned if I let her ruin the finale! Pansy!'

Pansy Wing emerged from the corner where she'd been perched on a stool, waiting for her last turn on the catwalk. Dramatic sweeps of heavy black eyeliner and long false lashes accentuated her already-stunning eyes, while cherry red lipstick enhanced the cupid's bow of her pout. She hurried over to Florence, working every one of her natural assets, fully aware of the intensity of Lewis Knox's gaze.

'The showstopper, Pansy, the final gown—it's yours. Hurry and get dressed,' Florence said, one eye still on the catwalk.

'Yes! At last!' Pansy whooped, her cool facade slipping as she rushed away. She'd been one of Blair's house models for several years, but, despite her poise and beauty, Pansy had always come second to Barbie Jones.

Florence clapped her hands. 'The rest of you ladies, find your places, check your teeth for lipstick, and get ready to roll!'

The models arranged themselves in order, straightening hems, tweaking veils, and resettling bustlines as necessary. Florence gave Pansy as much time as she could before sending the line of women sashaying down the catwalk, accompanied by the rustling of fabric and the sighs of the audience. Even so, the last model had completed her turn and the dramatic pause was becoming slightly awkward before Pansy stepped around the amethyst backdrop.

The dress was a triumph. Floor-length white silk with a full train, the strapless bodice and elegant straight line were transformed into something indescribably chic by the addition of an oversized bow, angling down from Pansy's shoulder to her opposite hip. There were gasps of delight from the audience and the polite applause swelled into heartfelt admiration for a designer at her peak.

Pansy, her black hair arranged in an elegant chignon, smiled radiantly as a male model stepped towards her and offered his arm. She and her escort advanced slowly along the catwalk, giving the audience time to appreciate every detail of the design and the brides-to-be a chance to picture themselves walking down the aisle in Florence Astor's gown of the season.

'Bravo!' Terence Blair's grin was all teeth. Beside him, Maggie Blair also applauded, though her smile was tentative and quick to fade.

Backstage, Florence Astor prepared to step into the spotlight while Lewis Knox, peering around a corner so he could see the main room, waited for the right moment. At the far end of the catwalk, Pansy stepped away from her escort and struck a pose.

Now.

Knox pulled a lever and the amethyst curtain at the back of the catwalk began to rise.

Bit by bit, the tiers of a gigantic faux wedding cake were revealed to the delighted oohs and aahs of the audience. Over eight feet tall—and with each layer festooned with swags and flowers crafted from strips of plaster-soaked linen—the cake had taken the Blair's window-dressers weeks to construct.

Florence Astor was moving around the base of the cake as the curtain rose the last few feet, exposing the topmost tier. As she stepped to the centre of the catwalk, she was conscious of the crowd's approval of her and the collection. Florence smiled graciously and watched as Pansy, one arm curved elegantly towards the sky, began to turn a slow circle.

A hush fell over the audience.

Then someone screamed.

In an instant, the room descended into chaos. Chairs scraped across the parquetry and fell, more screams and shouts pierced the air and one matronly woman slid to the floor in a dead faint, her Oleg Cassini suit in disarray.

Florence, glancing desperately left and right, realised the audience's attention was no longer focused on Pansy or the designer herself but on something behind her. Pansy's slow turn had become a shocked pivot, and now she stared at Florence, eyes wide. Then her gaze moved up and she let out a blood-curdling shriek before swooning into the arms of her handsome escort.

Florence spun around. The giant wedding cake towered above her in all its ostentatious glory, except for the top. Instead of the delicate tulle heart she had asked for, splayed across the top of the cake was the missing model, Barbie Jones. She was wearing a short wedding dress, but her staring eyes, protruding tongue, and blue complexion made it clear that Barbie was very, very dead. A long veil fixed in her copper-red hair had somehow become caught in the curtain's mechanism, which was still in operation. Florence watched in horror as the curtain continued to rise, pulling on the dead model's head and causing her stiff body to jerk about like a broken wind-up toy.

'Bring it down! Bring it down!' Mr. Blair was shouting, his stentorian voice finally cutting through the din.

But the mechanism had jammed and the amethyst curtain did not fall. Barbie Jones remained in full view. Flashbulbs popped as newspaper photographers, sent to capture the parade and its attendees for the society pages, found themselves on the scene of a far bigger story.

'Everyone out!' Having failed to shield his well-heeled clients from the appalling spectacle, Terence Blair had decided his best option was to clear the room as quickly as possible. 'Everyone out! Now! *Please!*'

He began trying to herd women towards the doors at the far end of the hall and gestured for his son to do the same. Maggie Blair remained seated in the front row, forgotten. Her sunglasses were still in place, masking both her expression and the direction of her gaze.

Florence took charge of Pansy and the other models, corralling them backstage out of sight of the wedding cake and helping them into street clothes. She sent Knox in search of hot tea, but before he returned, one of the girls produced a small flask which passed rapidly from hand to hand. Florence was tempted to take a decent slug herself, but the last thing she needed was to face Mr. Blair and the police with alcohol on her breath.

Closing her eyes, Florence tried to forget the sight of Barbie, dead, on top of the cake. *At least she's not wearing one of my creations*, she thought, then hated herself for thinking it. It hardly mattered anyway. The show was ruined. Suddenly it felt like the walls were closing in: she needed fresh air, and the police could find her outside. Florence snatched up her bag and ducked out through the nearest door.

Gradually, the sound of shocked voices and hurrying feet diminished as the staff and management of Blair's Emporium cajoled and soothed their customers while bundling them out of the Mural Hall and away.

—

The quiet was quickly replaced by the heavy thump of police boots. Terence Blair, standing off to one side with his secretary, watched morosely as the police photographer began setting up his camera, and pointed mutely when a couple of uniformed officers asked where they might find a ladder, in preparation for bringing Barbie down. He contemplated the scene in front of him. All the doors to his magnificent Mural Hall were now closed, and in front of each one stood a policeman, ready to deny entry. Or exit. The gilded chairs on which the cream of Blair's clientele had so recently perched were a scattered mess, as though someone had suddenly announced a sale in the shoe department. He glanced at his secretary. Behind her thick glasses, Joyce Hirsch's eyes glittered with tears, but she stood with notepad and pencil poised, just in case he had any orders to issue.

'Poor Barbie,' Joyce murmured.

'The customers!' Terence Blair groaned.

Colin Blair approached his father. 'Mother...'

'She's over there.' Blair senior gestured to where his wife now stood at the back of the Mural Hall, either fascinated by the goings-on or shocked into immobility. 'Get her out of here, Colin. Take her home.'

Colin opened his mouth to respond then snapped it shut again. Collecting his mother, he put a comforting arm around her shoulder then, after a brief discussion with one of the police officers, ushered her out of the nearest exit. The door had only just closed behind them when it was flung open again and a heavyset man pushed through, overcoat flapping. He paused to take in the room, settled his greasy hat more firmly on his head, then stomped directly towards Terence Blair.

'Blair? Chief Inspector Sparrow. Central Police.' He stuck out a meaty hand.

Blair hesitated a moment before shaking it. 'Did you say Central? I went to school with your superior. Had dinner with him just last week.'

Sparrow forced a tight smile then turned to survey the scene. 'Bit of publicity! This'll be front page in the evening edition. Congratulations! The whole town will be talking about your store.'

'You can't seriously think I want Blair's Emporium linked with a story like this? The only person who'll be happy about this is the competition. Harvey White will expect my customers to beat a path to the door of his second-rate store now! If this isn't cleared up quickly, and with a minimum of fuss, it'll be a disaster.'

Another man entered the Mural Hall in the inspector's wake. Tall, with a chiselled profile and conservatively cut brown hair, everything about his appearance screamed 'police,' but his approach was far more subtle than that of Inspector Sparrow. Detective James Steed had already taken statements from several witnesses, including Florence Astor, whom he'd found outside smoking one cigarette after another. Now he went straight to the wedding cake and watched as Barbie Jones was brought down and laid on a stretcher. He waited until a sheet was arranged over her lower body before bending in for a closer look at the angry red mark around her neck. After several minutes he stepped back and signalled to the ambulance attendants, then watched respectfully as they covered Barbie's face and slowly wheeled her from the room. Detective Steed made a slow circuit of the wedding cake, examining its construction while wondering how—and why—the victim had been placed on top. On the floor behind the cake, he was surprised to find a few items of women's clothing, dumped in a pile. Steed used the tip of his pencil to pick through them, lifting each garment and scrutinising it carefully.

'Steed? Steed!' The shout came from the other side of the cake and was followed quickly by Inspector Sparrow himself.

'Sir.' The young detective stepped forward smartly.

'Do we know how Barbie Doll died?'

'From the mark on her neck it looks like Barbie *Jones* was strangled with something—a cord or belt of some sort, perhaps—but there's no sign of the murder weapon. I'll organise some officers to conduct a thorough search of the hall and the backstage area.'

'What about when? Do you have any idea when she died, Steed?'

Detective Steed sucked in a breath and kept his voice controlled. 'I'll have to wait for the coroner's report and confirm her movements last night, but at this stage I'm working on the assumption that Miss Jones was killed in the early hours of the morning, before the store opened.'

'You're working on an assumption.' Inspector Sparrow rocked back and forth on his heels as he studied Steed's face.

'Until I can confirm more details, yes. Sir.'

'Right. Good. What about this morning after the store opened? Who was around?'

'Quite a few people actually. According to the witnesses I've spoken to so far, Miss Astor, the designer, was here early, as were Mr. Terence Blair and his secretary, Joyce Hirsch.' Steed consulted his notebook. 'The models were backstage in the dressing room, and the storeman, Lewis Knox, was mainly in the loading dock but was also up here on and off, attending to a few final details for the fashion parade.'

'What about Blair's missus? Saw her on the way in. She looks a bit...' Sparrow held out a hand, palm down, and waggled it. 'Rather him than me!'

'Maggie Blair and her son, Colin—who's the assistant manager—were running late. They arrived together after the fashion parade had started.'

Sparrow stared at him for a moment, but there was nothing missing from Steed's report, nothing to criticise. Instead, the inspector poked the scuffed toe of his shoe at the pile of clothing on the floor. 'What about this lot then?'

'Undergarments—slip, corset, and brassiere—that appear to belong to the victim, sir, but they're badly torn, as though they were removed with force.'

'So our killer ripped her clothes off, then dressed her like a fairy.'

'A bride, sir.'

'Bride, fairy...' Inspector Sparrow shrugged. 'Either way, whoever did it is clearly a fruitcake. Give me a straightforward shooting during an armed robbery any day.'

Sparrow took another look around, his gaze lingering briefly on Pansy Wing as she leaned in the dressing room doorway, a slim cigarette held between her fingers. 'Right. I'll leave you to it, Steed,' he said, 'but I'm expecting a report on my desk today.'

'Sir.'

'And I want to hear what that Astor woman has to say with my own ears. Get her to come into the station at her earliest convenience. Actually, forget the convenience part.' He pushed his fists deep into the pockets of his rumpled coat and turned away.

James Steed watched his boss depart then tipped his head from side to side, trying to get rid of some of the tension in his neck. He looked across and caught Pansy Wing's eye. She met his gaze for a moment, then abruptly stubbed her cigarette on the sole of her shoe and disappeared into the dressing room. By the time he got there, she was already putting on her coat.

'A few questions before you go, Miss…Wing, is it?' He pretended to glance at his notebook.

Pansy sighed and waved a hand at him to continue.

'Were you and Barbie Jones close?'

Pansy shook her head. 'Only in the sense that we've modelled together at Blair's for ages.'

'Can you tell me what happened?' he asked.

'All I can tell you is that she didn't turn up for the show. And then…' Pansy gestured towards the Mural Hall.

'And you took her place as star of the show?'

'Just what are you—' she began, hands on hips.

'Someone had to.' The soft voice came from behind Detective Steed and he spun around.

Lewis Knox emerged from among the racks of wedding dresses.

'You're the storeman, aren't you?' Steed asked.

Knox nodded as he moved to stand next to Pansy. 'Someone had to take Barbie's place. The show would have been ruined otherwise.'

The detective winced, but Knox seemed completely oblivious to the irony of his words.

'Did either of you see Miss Jones this morning?' Steed looked from one to the other.

'We were all busy getting ready for the show,' Pansy said.

'And you weren't concerned when she didn't turn up?'

'It wasn't a problem until about half an hour before the show, when Miss Astor started asking for Barbie. Models just come and go whenever they like.' There was a note of belligerence in the storeman's voice.

'I just thought she was running late…as usual!' Pansy shrugged. 'Barbie never cared about holding everyone up, and she loved to make an entrance.'

Steed's eyebrows rose and he stared at Pansy. 'I see.' He scrawled something in his notebook and let the silence stretch before asking his next question. 'Why didn't anyone notice Miss Jones on the cake until the end of the parade?'

'The curtain was in place, and after Miss Astor made her final adjustments at yesterday's rehearsal, she gave us all strict orders not to touch anything,' Knox said.

'Florence Astor is always very particular.' Pansy rolled her eyes. 'You should have heard the argument she had with Barbie yesterday!'

'Really? They were arguing? Miss Astor didn't mention that.' Detective Steed flipped his notebook closed. 'Is she still here?'

Pansy Wing and Lewis Knox looked at each other and shrugged helplessly.

'Never mind. I know where to find her.' Steed slapped the notebook into the palm of his hand and, with a nod, took his leave.

Four

Peregrine stood in front of the Adventuresses' Club. Or, rather, she stood in front of a solid metal gate set into a high brick wall. From the other side of the narrow street, it had been possible to see the tops of trees and the decorative roofline of a large building, but from where she was standing now, all Peregrine could see was the door, a buzzer, and a highly polished brass plate etched with the name *The Adventuresses' Club* and, beneath that, *Members Only*. Walking through the city, with the sun shining and bustle of people around her, Peregrine had felt excited and hopeful. But now, standing in the cool shadows of Greenwood Place, she felt suddenly alone.

Peregrine shivered, then, closing her eyes, she pushed the buzzer and waited.

Nothing happened, so she pushed it again.

Still no response.

She put her finger on the buzzer and kept it there.

Suddenly, a small hatch set in the door flew open and a man's face appeared.

'Yes?'

'Oh!' Peregrine gasped and put a hand to her chest. 'I didn't notice there was a little window there! Hello.'

'Good morning. Do you have an appointment?' The man had a pleasant, no-nonsense sort of voice.

'Well, not strictly speaking, except…'

'Who are you here to see?'

'I don't quite know, but…' Peregrine began patting down her pockets, trying to find the letter that had brought her there. 'I have it here somewhere.'

'Do you have an invitation for the lecture? If you're here for the lecture, you're late.'

'No. I'm not here for the lecture. Just hang on a minute!' She plunged a hand into her tote bag and rummaged in its depths.

The man on the other side of the gate pressed his face closer to the Judas hatch and looked at Peregrine more closely. His gaze fell on her suitcase.

'You're not an Avon lady, are you? We don't do Avon. They should have told you not to call here.'

'I'm not an Avon lady, but I—'

'Do you have the password?'

Peregrine stopped her rummaging to stare at him incredulously. 'Password? Are you serious?'

'No appointment, no invitation, and no password. That means no entry. Sorry.' He slammed the door of the hatch.

'Hey! Wait! I'm here for a meeting! Come back!' Peregrine pounded her fist on the door. 'Ow.'

She pressed the buzzer a few more times but the iron gate remained steadfastly closed.

'Not very welcoming,' she muttered to herself, then took a few steps back and sized up the wall. Clearly, she wasn't going to get in through the gate, but one thing Peregrine's mother had taught her was not to give up easily. And during her teen-age years, Peregrine herself had dedicated many a Friday and Saturday night to developing her skills in the complementary arts of sneaking out and sneaking in. It would take more than one officious man and his precious password to stop her.

The wall was too high to climb, but at least the top was smooth and free of anything sharp or spiky: clearly the Adventuresses were more concerned with privacy than security. Picking up her case, Peregrine walked farther along Greenwood Place until she found what she was looking for. At the farthest end of the wall that marked the boundary of the Adventuresses' domain was a neat row of galvanised metal garbage bins, their lids firmly in place. Peregrine looked back up the street, but she was entirely alone, and far enough away from the busy main road that she was unlikely to be seen. It only took her a few minutes to arrange several of the bins into a rough pyramid, high enough so that, with a small jump, she should be able to grab the top of the wall.

Peregrine slung her tote bag across her body and clambered to the top of the stack of bins. The suitcase went first. She grunted with the effort of throwing it up and over the wall, then listened, bracing herself for the crash or outcry when it landed on the other side. All she heard was the swish of branches and a dull thud. Peregrine grinned, wiped her palms down the sides of her trousers, then swung her arms up and sprang for the top of the wall. She managed to get her upper chest half across, but her legs flailed as she scrabbled to find a toehold. Behind her, the rubbish bins clattered in a heap, but Peregrine ignored the noise, all her attention focused on pulling herself up.

With a final determined heave, she managed to get one leg over the wide top of the wall. For a minute or two Peregrine stayed exactly where she was, legs either side of the wall, leaning forward so her forehead rested on the concrete capping: it was as much to catch her breath as to avoid being seen. While she was there, Peregrine took a moment to examine her red low-heeled mules: the toes were now so battered and scratched they were unsalvageable. She made a mental note to wear plimsolls next time wall-scaling was on the agenda. Then she sat up and surveyed her immediate area.

Her suitcase would be safe where it had landed, nestled in a clump of azalea bushes, but her more immediate problem was getting down. A few likely-looking trees stretched their branches invitingly towards the wall in various places, but Peregrine realised there was a far better option. From where she sat, she could see the entire facade of the mansion housing the Adventuresses' Club. The front door was over to her right, and there was no sign of the officious man who had refused to let her in. Peregrine's perch also gave her a view down one side of the property: there was only a narrow gap between the building and the perimeter wall. Easy. Smiling with satisfaction, she pulled off her mules and dropped them close to the suitcase.

Barefoot, she stood up, stretched out her arms for balance, then made her way along the remaining section of the front wall, eased past the stone ball capping the corner, and started down the side. Expecting at any minute to hear an outraged shout of discovery, Peregrine was surprised to find she was actually enjoying herself. The mansion and its windows loomed. She hurried the last few steps, past the edge of the building and out of the main lines of sight. Now she was standing directly across from the side of the first-floor balcony. The balustrade was low—only about hip height—but the gap between the wall where she stood and outer edge of the balcony was wider than it had seemed from across the garden.

Peregrine looked down. It seemed rather a long way to the ground, and the only thing to break her fall was a concrete path. So, before she had time to change her mind, she leaped for the balcony. One foot made the top of the balustrade, but momentum kept her going, sending her sprawling. Thankfully, a wicker chaise longue, laden with cushions, had been placed to catch the morning sun, and Peregrine fell onto it, sending it skating across tessellated tiles and into a small table holding a potted fern. The plant wobbled, threatening to topple. Peregrine grabbed for it, catching the ceramic pot and setting it upright again.

'What was that?' a woman's voice called from inside the mansion. 'Samuel, was that you?'

'Not me—I'm right here,' came the response. Peregrine recognised the voice of the man from the gate.

There was a moment's silence, then the sound of footsteps getting closer. Peregrine scrambled to her feet and looked around wildly. A number of large sash windows were open, but it was impossible to know which would take her to safety and which would bring her face-to-face with the mansion's occupants. And she wasn't quite ready for that.

Peregrine raced back across the balcony, flattening herself into a shallow niche in the wall. No sooner had she done so than a woman's head appeared from the nearest window. She turned towards the chaise longue, and Peregrine saw the back of her head, chestnut hair flecked with grey.

'Must have been a strong gust of wind,' the woman said. Her head disappeared and Peregrine heard the window slam shut, followed by the snick of a lock. The sounds repeated three more times as the remaining windows were closed and secured.

Peregrine waited a little longer then slowly peeled herself away from the wall and risked a lightning glance through the nearest window. The room was a study, tastefully furnished and lined with books, but devoid of people. She moved along the balcony, checking each window and a set of French doors but finding them all locked.

'Rats.' She bit her lip.

The decision to scale the perimeter wall had been impulsive and—Peregrine was beginning to realise—perhaps not the best idea. If she called out now and advertised her presence, stuck on the first-floor balcony, it would hardly be an auspicious introduction to the members of the Adventuresses' Club. If, however, Peregrine could get inside and simply stroll casually into their midst, surely a group of Adventuresses would recognise and admire her intrepid spirit, ingenuity, and tenacity?

Leaning over the edge of the balcony, a quick reconnoitre informed her that going down was out of the question, which only left up. It seemed like the sort of building that would have a widow's walk or some sort of roof access—all Peregrine had to do was get up there and make use of it.

It proved to be much easier than scaling the perimeter wall. Between the balcony's balustrade, a handy drainpipe, and the decorative caps on the building's columns, Peregrine was able to clamber up and over the roof's parapet with relative ease. She discovered the roof itself was almost as elaborate as the mansion's facade: a series of gables and flat areas, part slate tile and part corrugated iron, with a tall tower rising an extra two storeys above a back corner of the building. A narrow walkway ran between the parapet and the nearest gable, and Peregrine began to make her way towards the tower. She was hoping one of its windows would be unlocked, but the closer she got the more disheartened she felt. The tower seemed to be unused and in a state of genteel decay, bordering on disrepair. The window she could see was filthy, with deep cracks radiating out above the lintel and bird droppings caking the sill. And when she was finally within touching distance of the grimy glass, Peregrine saw at once that she'd never be able to open it, even if it was unlocked. Decades of paint had sealed it shut. It would take a hammer, chisel, and hours of work before there was any hope of getting in that way.

With a heavy sigh of frustration, Peregrine turned and stared out across the roof. The sun came out from behind a cloud and she squinted as a flash of sunlight struck her directly in the face, reflected off one of the roof's many surfaces.

Frowning, she changed her position slightly and raised a hand to her brow, shielding her eyes against the glare. A small window, hinged open, was set into the side of a gable right in the middle of the vast roof.

'This is getting ridiculous.' Peregrine looked at the series of peaks and valleys separating her from the only point of entry. Then she thought of the letter tucked deep in the bag she still carried slung across her shoulder, the words *urgent* and *inheritance*. She studied the lines of the roof, mapping out the easiest path to the window, then she wiggled her toes and stepped out, picking her way between two slate-covered gables to the iron roof beyond. Now the only way forward was straight down the middle of a roof ridge. At least this part was iron, giving her bare feet far more purchase than the smooth slate. Arms out, eyes focused on the horizon and with a foot either side of the ridge, Peregrine started walking, forcing herself not to rush.

A pigeon fluttered in front of her and landed directly at her feet, its head bobbing as it stared with first one eye then the other.

'Shoo! Get out of my way!' Peregrine tried to flap a hand at the bird but the action caused her to list sharply to one side. 'Move!' She stepped closer to the bird and it shuffled away, keeping the same distance between them. Peregrine kept going forward and the pigeon kept moving back until at last only a valley in the roof separated her from the open window.

It was smaller than it had looked.

Peregrine edged her way across and carefully lowered herself down until she was sitting just next to the window. She listened but could hear nothing from within. Cautiously she eased her torso around and peered inside.

'You've got to be kidding,' she muttered.

She'd assumed the window would open into a small room, tucked up among the eaves of the vast mansion. The sort of space a maid would have occupied in years past, with a sloping roof that only allowed the occupant to stand fully upright if they were in the centre of the room. She'd expected it would only be a few feet from window to floor. She hadn't expected to be staring into a void.

The window was, in fact, set in the vaulted ceiling above a stairwell, its opening mechanism controlled by two thin ropes which dangled against the wall: one for pulling it open, the other to haul it closed. About ten feet below and slightly to Peregrine's left, a suit of polished armour stood at the point where stairs reached the first-floor hallway. She could see its companion across the landing, guarding a similar place at the top of a matching staircase. The two flights of stairs swept down and met beneath a stunning stained-glass window, before a single grand stairway continued to the ground floor. From her vantage point, Peregrine could see the entire magnificent stairwell laid out beneath her: the richly patterned wallpaper, the polished wood of the banisters, the worn red carpet on the stair treads and, suspended in the centre of the space so that its bulk sat level with the floor of the upper hallway, a magnificent brass chandelier, its hundreds of crystal teardrops reflecting the colours of the stained glass.

Peregrine sat back and considered her next move. She'd have to go in feet-first, that much was obvious. If she could lower herself carefully, it would only be a short drop of four feet or so directly onto the carpet of the first-floor hallway. And even if she lost her balance, there was room enough that she was unlikely to tumble down the stairs.

'I can do this.' Peregrine took one last look, fixing the geography of the landing in her mind, then eased herself around on the roof so she was on her stomach, with her feet poking through the window. Slowly she slid backwards. Lower legs, hips... The window was really quite small—actually only half a window, bisected by the hinged pane—and she had to wriggle a bit. Then Peregrine's entire lower body was through, her stomach on the lip of the window, torso and arms stretched out across the roof.

'Land soft, bend knees, roll,' Peregrine muttered. The words had been drummed into her years ago when, as a small, skinny little girl, a jackaroo on a station had taught her how to ride a horse. And how to fall off.

Now Peregrine let the weight of her own body pull her inside, her hands trailing, ready to grab the edge of the window. She felt her shirt ride up then fall back into place as she slid across the sill, and she braced for the coming jolt.

It came sooner than she expected, before her hands had even touched the windowsill. Part of the tote bag, which was still slung across her chest, had snagged on something. Now her fingers gripped the edge of the window frame, the bag still outside. The strap pulled up under her arms as she hung, but the bag was stuck fast. Peregrine tried to swing just a tiny bit, hoping the movement would shake things free. Her tote bag refused to yield. She looked down at her landing place, a patch of red carpet, only a few feet away. There was only one thing she could do.

Peregrine let go of the window ledge, catching hold of the bag's strap with both hands as she fell. It was a cheap canvas bag, and certainly not designed to do anything more than look stylish, so when Peregrine's full weight hit the strap there was a tearing sound, and the bag fell free. However the sharp jerk altered Peregrine's trajectory. Instead of dropping straight to the carpet, she swung to her right, straight into the suit of armour.

Instinctively, she grabbed at it, wrapping her legs around the metal torso as though ready for a piggyback ride. The armour wobbled on its pedestal then began to tip over. For Peregrine, the next few seconds seemed to happen in slow motion. She was aware of the cold metal and the sensation of falling, but, most of all, she was aware that the suit of armour was toppling directly towards the polished banister of the landing and the vast stairwell beyond.

Metal suit hit wooden banister with an almighty crash, the sound reverberating through the Adventuresses' Club. Peregrine shrieked as she was flung out into the void. The chandelier rushed up to meet her and she snatched at it, her hands somehow finding the thick rope of cord and wires and latching on. Her legs pedalled wildly for a moment before she was able to bring them up so she was almost sitting on the topmost brass ring. There was a cracking sound from high above, and the chandelier dropped a few feet, flakes of plaster drifting past her.

Peregrine held her breath, waiting for the whole thing to give way and carry her to the ground in a shower of crystal. But it held.

Doors slammed and feet pounded as Adventuresses came from every corner of the house. Peregrine watched as they gathered below: all staying at a safe distance, and all staring up at her with a mixture of shock and incredulity. She saw the man from the gate arrive, closely followed by a tall, brown-haired woman dressed in jodhpurs, boots, and a turtleneck. The crowd of women parted and the newcomer strode through their ranks, coming to a stop just beyond the range of any falling debris. Her brow furrowed as she stared up at Peregrine.

'Who the hell are you?' she asked.

Peregrine stared back defiantly. 'I'm Peregrine Fisher,' she said, trying to look as though she was perfectly comfortable where she was.

'Did you say Peregrine *Fisher*?'

'That's right.' Peregrine glanced down at her tote bag, which was somehow still hanging from her shoulder. There was a ragged tear in the canvas and a piece of paper poked through the gash. She plucked it free with two fingers.

Looking down, she saw the man who had turned her away was now standing next to the officious woman. Peregrine smiled sweetly and caught his eye. 'Here's the letter I received: I believe that's the information you wanted. It really would have been easier if you'd just waited a moment and let me in the front gate.' Peregrine opened her hand with a flourish and the letter fluttered to the ground, the eyes of a dozen women charting its progress. To Peregrine's delight, it landed right at his feet.

He picked up the letter, glanced at it, then passed it to the woman standing next to him with an apologetic shrug. 'Sorry,

Birdie, I was only following your instructions. You explicitly said no password, no admittance. She didn't know the password.'

'Never mind, Samuel,' came the reply. 'I still think having a password is a good idea and I can hardly blame you for—'

'Ahem.' Peregrine cleared her throat. 'Sorry to interrupt, but if you don't mind…'

Birdie and Samuel stared up at her.

'A ladder would be nice.'

Five

Once galvanised into action, Samuel and the Adventuresses moved quickly, and it wasn't long before Peregrine was in the Camelot Room, seated in a shabby velvet armchair. A bespectacled lady knelt in front of her, dabbing Peregrine's grazes with Mercurochrome, while at least a dozen more women milled about, filling the room and spilling into the hallway beyond. The women were clustered in small groups, all feigning disinterest in the newcomer who had made such a spectacular entrance. By contrast, Peregrine looked around with open curiosity, occasionally managing to catch someone's eye as they cast a sideways glance in her direction. Each time it happened, she smiled and called out a friendly hello, but every greeting was met with a stiff nod and a quickly averted gaze.

Peregrine leaned forward. 'Sorry, no one told me your name. And who are all these women?' she whispered.

'I'm Violetta Fellini and these women are Adventuresses,' Violetta replied. 'Most of them are just here for my lecture on women in the American and Russian space programs.'

'Oh! Sounds interesting! When is it?'

Violetta looked up from the cut on Peregrine's elbow, a smile playing around the edges of her mouth. 'Actually, I was in the middle of it when you…arrived.'

Across the room, Birdie clapped her hands. 'Ladies, I'm sorry, but under the circumstances we won't be resuming today's lecture. Samuel will see you out, but remember to sign our petition for women serving in the air force to be trained as pilots, not just auxiliary staff. We've shown the men how to run a signalling corps—now let's show them how to fly fighter jets!'

The room cleared quickly while Violetta packed up her first-aid box. Soon only four other women remained, sitting quietly on the other side of a large table. Peregrine heard the front door close, and seconds later Birdie and Samuel were back. She watched as Violetta joined them and the three held a whispered conference, passing her inheritance letter between them. Then Birdie stepped forward and studied her, eyes roaming over every part of Peregrine's face until it started to become uncomfortable. Peregrine reached up and tucked her hair behind her ears.

'Sorry I haven't had a chance to freshen up,' she said.

'So you're Annabelle Fisher's daughter.' Birdie made it sound like an accusation; it was a tone Peregrine had heard a thousand times before. 'Do you have any proof?'

Without taking her eyes from Birdie's, Peregrine rummaged in her bag then thrust a handful of papers at the other woman. 'My birth certificate, plus Mum's birth certificate and…some other stuff.'

Peregrine watched as Birdie scanned the top document, catching the quick flicker of eyes when she reached the part marked *Father Unknown*. She raised her chin and waited.

Birdie passed the papers back. 'And where is your mother now?'

'Under a lemon tree,' Peregrine said, and for the first time in a long and difficult stretch, she felt like crying. 'She died last year. The death certificate is in here.' She tapped the pile of papers in her lap.

'I'm sorry for your loss.' Violetta put a comforting hand on her shoulder.

'Thank you.' Peregrine sniffed hard as she bundled her documents away. 'Now would someone please tell me why I'm here?'

Birdie, Violetta, and Samuel exchanged looks.

'Tea?' Samuel asked no one in particular. 'I think this calls for tea.'

He disappeared and an awkward silence settled over them. Violetta pulled a chair close to Peregrine's and sat down, but Birdie couldn't keep still, prowling the perimeter of the room, occasionally stopping to stare up at a decorative banner trumpeting the achievements of *The Adventuresses' Club of the Antipodes*. After a few minutes that seemed like an eternity, the rattle of crockery announced Samuel's return. But instead of getting on with things, everyone waited while he took his time pouring tea, offering biscuits, and fussing with side tables. Peregrine remembered to say please and thank you, sipped her tea politely, and inwardly seethed as she waited for a response to her question. Finally Birdie set her cup and saucer aside.

'I have been instructed by your aunt, Phryne Fisher, and her solicitor to distribute her estate to her next of kin. It would seem that's you.' Birdie forced a tight smile that failed to reach her eyes.

'Aunt Phryne is dead?' Peregrine exclaimed.

'No!' Birdie snapped. Then, more quietly, 'No. She's merely missing. We have no body, no witnesses to her hypothetical demise, nothing. So as things stand, Phryne Fisher is missing.

However, she left explicit instructions that if six months passed with no contact and no signs of'—Birdie swallowed—'life, I was to track down her heir.'

'Me?' Peregrine squeaked.

'So it would seem,' Birdie replied. She walked over to a small writing bureau and extracted a lacquered box from the top drawer. Lifting the lid, she pulled out a set of keys and handed them to Peregrine.

'The keys to your house,' Birdie said.

'My house? I have an actual house?' Peregrine's mouth fell open.

'You have *use* of your *aunt's* house until such a time as she returns.' Birdie looked as though she wanted to snatch the keys back, but instead she pulled another key from the box. 'Your car keys.'

'A car? It's not a Hillman, is it?'

'No!'

'What kind of car is it?'

'Why? Will you be giving it back if it's the wrong sort?'

There was a moment's silence.

'Probably not,' Peregrine mumbled, gripping the keys tightly.

'And, finally, the keys to the safety deposit box at your aunt's bank. There's also a letter of introduction for the bank manager, but you'll no doubt need me to accompany you there.' Birdie looked into the box again and hesitated. Her hand seemed to hover for a moment and she glanced at Peregrine before slamming the lid closed.

'Wow.' Peregrine looked from one face to the other and stood. 'Thank you.' She extended her arms as if to embrace Birdie then thought better of it, converting the move into a sweeping gesture that took in the entire Camelot Room. 'What about this place? Am I a member now? Do I get to sit in this chair?' As she said it, Peregrine crossed the room and placed her hand on the shaped headrail of a Chippendale carver chair, her thumb brushing the brass *Adventuress Fisher* nameplate.

A collective gasp went up and hands reached forward to stop her. 'No!' shouted Birdie.

'Okay, jeepers!' Peregrine held her hands up in surrender and backed away from the chair. 'I just thought...'

'Sorry, but that is still your aunt's chair until... In any case, that's not how the Adventuresses' Club operates.' Birdie's face was white. 'You have to earn a place. Every Adventuress is remarkable in her own right—her achievements outstanding.' She looked around the room. 'Ineke Horchner, the first woman to conquer Mount Kilimanjaro.' Birdie pointed and a blonde woman inclined her head solemnly. 'International fencing champion Michiko Sato. Minnie Bell, botanist, and the world's foremost expert on the flora of the Northern Territory. Professor Violetta Fellini: chemist, microbiologist, and the youngest-ever recipient of Melbourne University's top science prize. Florence Astor, liberator of Australian women's fashion, champion of the trouser suit and... Where's Florence?' Birdie looked around at the assembled women.

'She's late,' Samuel said. 'The bridal show would have finished a while ago, so it's probably something to do with the line she's designing exclusively for Saks in New York. She should be here soon.'

'What about you two?' Peregrine looked between Birdie and Samuel. 'Why are you here?'

'Samuel is our gadgets expert, and he keeps the place running smoothly,' Birdie said.

'Well, that's a matter of opinion.' Peregrine raised her

eyebrows at Samuel, causing a blush to spread from beneath his cravat and advance rapidly up his neck.

'And my sister, Birdie,' he said. 'During the Second World War she played a vital role in—'

Birdie stopped him with a hand. 'The point is, Ms. Fisher—'

'I get the point.' It was Peregrine's turn to interrupt. 'What about my aunt? What did she do that was so amazing? Apart from being amazingly rich?'

Birdie stared at her in shock.

'You mean you don't know?' Violetta asked, her surprise mirroring that of everyone in the room.

Peregrine shrugged. 'How would I? I never met my aunt, and Mum never talked to me about that side of the family, except to say they'd all turned their backs on her and she wanted nothing to do with them. If I ever asked, Mum would just say they'd treated her badly then forgotten about her and I should act as though they don't exist.'

Birdie shook her head. 'That's so wrong—poor Annabelle! Your aunt, Phryne Fisher, did not forget your mother. She only discovered she had a sister five years ago, when her philandering father confessed on his deathbed. From that moment, she was desperate to find Annabelle, but every single letter she sent was returned unopened. Whenever she managed to track her down, your mother would disappear again. Phryne tried to respect Annabelle's decision to live her own life, but she couldn't let it go: she wanted to know her sister.'

Birdie crossed back to the bureau and pulled open another drawer, this time extracting a thick stack of letters, tied together with a velvet ribbon. 'Here.' She thrust the bundle forward, but Peregrine didn't take it, simply looked from the pile of unopened envelopes to the sadness and hurt on Birdie's face.

'You mean…my aunt never even knew I existed?' Peregrine's voice was small, and her lower lip quivered.

Violetta put her arm around Peregrine's shoulder and squeezed comfortingly. 'If Phryne Fisher had known she had a niece, she would have combed every corner of the earth until she found you. And you know what? I'm fairly certain she would have liked you.'

Peregrine suddenly felt exhausted. It had been a trying day and now the emotional impact of Birdie's words was threatening to overwhelm her. 'This is a lot to deal with. I really need some time to think about it all.'

'That sounds like a good idea,' Birdie said, her voice filled with relief. 'Samuel will organise a taxi to take you home.'

It took Peregrine a moment to realise Birdie was talking about her aunt's house, Peregrine's new home. 'Perhaps we could talk again tomorrow?' she ventured.

'Of course.' Birdie waved a dismissive hand. 'We still have a lot of details to square away, but nothing that can't wait another day. Or two.' She caught Samuel's eye and nodded towards the hall, where the telephone sat.

He hurried out of the room but came straight back again, a blonde woman in a black dress close on his heels. She shouldered past him and made straight for Birdie.

'Birdie! Thank goodness you're here! My bridal show was a complete disaster!' the newcomer wailed.

'Oh, come on, Florence, it can't have been that bad! It's only real weddings that are a disaster—for any right-thinking woman who has the misfortune to find herself walking down the aisle dressed as a bride.'

'My star model was murdered! Barbie Jones is dead, and she was laid out in a wedding dress and on display in front of the cream of the fashion industry and Melbourne society.'

'Murdered?' Birdie gasped.

'How awful,' Violetta murmured, crossing herself.

A group of Adventuresses immediately surrounded Florence, ushering her to the sofa, fetching tea and water, and offering an assortment of soothing platitudes and outraged exclamations as the designer described what had happened. Peregrine, listening with undisguised interest, edged closer to Samuel and plucked at his sleeve. 'Barbie Jones?' she whispered. 'Wasn't she the model arrested last year wearing—or almost wearing—a teeny-tiny red bikini? The one kissing the lifeguards at Bondi?'

Samuel swallowed and edged a finger under the knot of his cravat. 'I'm sure I have no idea.'

She rolled her eyes at him and moved closer to hear what the designer was saying.

'I just don't understand why anyone would want to kill Barbie!' Florence's voice trembled. 'She was young and beautiful; she had her whole life ahead of her!'

'That would be plenty of reason for some people,' Birdie said ominously. She sat down next to Florence, who regarded her with some consternation.

'The police were everywhere,' the designer continued, 'asking all sorts of questions. And even when I arrived *here*, there was a detective waiting out the front. Can you believe it? He told me they had *more* questions and I needed to present myself at headquarters!'

'Maybe you're a suspect!' Peregrine had edged her way into the group and now all eyes turned to her.

'Me? Why on earth would they think I did it?' Florence frowned as she looked Peregrine up and down. 'Who are you, anyway? Birdie'—she turned to the woman next to her—'who is she?'

Violetta stepped forward, pulling Peregrine with her. 'This

is Phryne Fisher's niece. Florence Astor, meet Peregrine Fisher.'

Florence regarded Peregrine again, this time with open fascination tinged with a hint of speculation. 'Really? Phryne's niece? Well, I never!'

'Believe me, none of us have ever,' Birdie said, folding her arms.

'Now that I'm looking at you properly...' Florence stood up and took Peregrine's hands in her own. 'Oh! You are so much like your aunt! I wish she was still here: God knows I could use a good detective right now!'

'A detective! Is that what she was?' Peregrine's eyes lit up at the thought of her aunt wielding a large magnifying glass.

'I don't suppose it runs in the family, does it?' Florence's tone was light, but her grip on Peregrine's hands told a different story.

'I don't know.' Peregrine shrugged. 'But I'm happy to give it a red-hot go!'

Florence sighed with relief, and Peregrine beamed at her, but suddenly Birdie was on her feet, stepping into their space and forcing Florence to release her grip on Peregrine's hands.

'You'd be happy to give it a "red-hot go," would you?' Her voice was disdainful, and the Adventuresses looked at her in shock. 'This is not a game, Ms. Fisher. We're perfectly capable of looking after our own without your assistance. Perhaps you should just be satisfied with everything your aunt has already given you!'

'Birdie...' Violetta began.

'I was only offering to help,' Peregrine said, stung by Birdie's tone.

'Thank you, but I'm sure we can contrive to muddle along without you. If you ever do manage to prove yourself to be half the investigator your aunt was, feel free to come back and restate your offer then. Good day, Ms. Fisher.' Birdie pushed through the stunned Adventuresses and stalked from the room.

'I might just do that!' Peregrine called after the retreating figure.

Somewhere deep in the house, a door slammed.

There was a moment's stunned silence.

'She hates me,' Peregrine said. 'Why?'

'Ah, it's not you,' Violetta said. 'What she hates is the thought that Phryne Fisher might never return.'

'Give Birdie some time,' Samuel added. He extended an arm, ushering Peregrine towards the door. 'Come on. Your shoes are here and I've got your suitcase just outside as well. I've called for a taxi—it'll be at the gate in a few minutes—so here's money for the fare. Oh, and I've also written down the address for you.'

Peregrine could tell Violetta and Samuel believed what they were saying, but she wasn't convinced. She put on her shoes, taking more time than necessary to settle them on her feet, then straightened up and took a deep breath.

'Just make sure you keep my seat warm,' she said, then walked from the room, collected her suitcase from the hall and kept going, out through the front door of the Adventuresses' Club and straight down the path.

Aware that Violetta and Samuel were watching, she kept her shoulders straight and strode confidently. It was only when she reached the gate that Peregrine looked back. The main door was closed now, but she could still see through the window of the well-lit Camelot Room. Birdie had returned and joined Violetta, Samuel, and a group of Adventuresses clustered around Florence Astor. Care and compassion were evident in the tilt of Birdie's head and the way she rubbed Florence's hands between her own. In fact, Peregrine was struck by how close all the Adventuresses seemed. A tear welled in her eye and she dashed it away, but she couldn't push aside the overwhelming feeling of loneliness that enveloped her and, despite the warmth of the afternoon sun, Peregrine shivered.

Beyond the high brick wall, a car horn tooted impatiently and, after a final lingering look, Peregrine passed through the metal gate and let it slam behind her. She climbed into the waiting taxi and handed the driver the address, written in Samuel's immaculate hand. She hadn't bothered to look at it herself: she didn't know her way around Melbourne, so it didn't really matter. The only thing that mattered was that wherever she was going, it was away from here.

Six

In the back seat of the taxi, Peregrine turned her head away from the Adventuresses' Club and closed her ears to the perky Doris Day song playing on the radio. Her eyes were open, but as they drove smoothly out of the vibrant city and into the more sedate suburbs, Peregrine registered none of it.

After a short drive, the taxi cruised slowly down a quiet residential boulevard, swung into a wide concrete driveway, and came to a stop. Peregrine was oblivious. The driver looked at her in the rear-view mirror, cleared his throat, jingled a pocketful of change, and finally said, 'We're here, miss.'

Peregrine started, then leaned forward and peered through the windscreen at the house in front of her.

'Are you sure?' she asked.

The driver shrugged. 'This is the address you gave me.'

Peregrine paid the fare with money Samuel had given her and got out. She thanked the driver for hauling her battered case from the taxi's boot and watched as he reversed out into the street and pulled away. Then she simply stood and stared at the house. Peregrine didn't know what she'd been expecting.

Perhaps a nice Victorian house of red brick with iron scrolls, lacy curtains and tidy hedges, the sort of thing a maiden aunt would inhabit. But this…

It was like nothing she'd ever seen. It must have been built in the 1950s—certainly not more than five or ten years ago—and it rose above her, two storeys of modernist glass and concrete balanced on a stone pedestal. A tarpaulin-draped car sheltered in the undercroft and Peregrine skirted past, keys in hand, to stand in front of a blue door. Through the clear glass panel to one side, she could see open stairs leading to the house above. She closed her eyes, touched her fingertips lightly to the rough stone wall, then fitted the key into the lock. It turned smoothly.

Suitcase in hand she climbed slowly and, as her head rose above the decorative planter at the top of the stairs, a sunken lounge came into view. Peregrine had to stop and catch her breath. The floor-to-ceiling windows were covered with sheer white curtains, allowing light to flood the room, casting shadows on the pale green walls. She took in the television, the pair of Danish teak chairs—upholstered in a nubbly yellow wool—and the curved white sofa, built into the edge of the sunken area.

'Oh, wow,' she whispered.

Peregrine dropped her case, stepped out of her shoes, and shed her cardigan, then descended the steps set between two sections of the sofa. She dug her toes into the thick carpet as she moved towards the main feature of the room: a white chimney suspended over an open concrete fireplace, the whole thing set against yet another stone feature wall. A bespoke drinks cabinet ran along one side of the room, modern paintings were dotted about, and every item she could see—from the lamp in the corner to the triangular coffee table—somehow blended with its companions, proclaiming the taste of the woman who had collected each piece.

Peregrine wandered from room to room, running her hands over cushions, opening cupboards in the kitchen, and turning on taps in the mint-and-white powder room. The top of the vanity was bare, except for a cake of soap in a scallop-shaped soap dish. Peregrine lifted it to her nose and inhaled the scent of lily of the valley, then replaced it carefully. She looked at her reflection in the mirror and was surprised to see that the brown-eyed, brown-haired woman looking back at her was the same one she had seen yesterday and the day before. She didn't feel the same.

Opening the next door, Peregrine stepped into the main bedroom. It was the most beautiful room she had ever seen. Decorated in shades of pink and green, the space was dominated by a large four-poster bed, watermelon-pink curtains tied back at every corner, and the pale pink brocade counterpane piled high with pillows and cushions. Off to one side, and separated from the main room by gauzy curtains of mint-green chiffon, stood a decadently deep bath, clearly designed for luxurious soaks, and beyond that she could see a dressing room with vast wardrobes, their doors firmly closed.

Peregrine sat on the edge of the bath and rubbed her eyes, half expecting the magical room to vanish. But when she looked again it was all still there, waiting for her. Glancing down, something under the bed caught her eye. She dropped to her knees and, leaning forward, picked up a pair of black velvet slippers, delicate, narrow, and embroidered in gold across the toes with a monogrammed *PF.* She stroked the nap of the velvet and hugged the slippers to her chest.

'Thank you,' she whispered.

In that moment, the aunt she had never met felt very, very close.

—

Somewhere in the house, something hit the floor with a dull thud. Peregrine jumped to her feet, eyes wide, all her senses alert. There was a crash of breaking glass. She hurried from the bedroom, bare feet silent in the plush carpet. Back in the sunken lounge, Peregrine looked for anything she could use as a weapon. Her eyes fell on a small statue sitting on a corner of the cocktail cabinet: a figure of a woman with an elaborate headdress and flowing robes. Peregrine hefted it in her hand; it wasn't as heavy as it looked, but there was enough weight to do damage if necessary. Gripping the statue tightly, she crept towards the rear of the house, following the sound of a series of muffled thumps and bangs.

Peregrine sprang around the corner, brandishing the statue in front of her like a knife.

'Stop!' she yelled. 'Who are you and what the hell do you think you're doing?'

A man was standing on the other side of the room. He stared at her, a slow grin spreading across his face. Of average height, he wore a gabardine coat over a shabby suit, with a battered trilby clamped on his grey hair. He was holding an open, leather-bound book in one hand, which he snapped shut and tucked under one arm.

'I could ask you the same question, girly,' he said, completely unfazed by her sudden appearance.

Peregrine's eyes darted around the room. Other books— similar to the one the stranger held—were tumbled onto the floor, drawers were pulled open and a tangle of tape spewed from a reel-to-reel recorder.

'Give that back.' Peregrine used the statue to gesture at the book he held. 'It belongs to me.'

The man laughed. 'Possession is nine-tenths of the law, which means it's mine now. I'm an associate of the late Miss Fisher. Just had to deal with some unfinished business now she's gone.'

He turned his back on Peregrine and left the room by another door, moving through the rooms along the back of the house while Peregrine mirrored his path at the front.

'Hey! Stop!' she shouted as he strolled through the galley kitchen and she hurried through the lounge room.

He crossed the corner of the lounge in front of her and started down the stairs. Peregrine realised she'd lost the book, but for the moment she was just glad the man was leaving.

'Get out now, or I'm calling the cops!' She brandished the statue again.

The man paused, his torso still visible over the top of the planter.

'What a good idea. You should definitely do that.' He raised his hat and smirked, then continued down the stairs.

Peregrine waited to hear the door slam, peered over the edge to make sure he'd really gone, then slumped, letting out a breath she didn't know she'd been holding. She gave herself a shake, trying to get rid of the impression of slimy menace the man had left behind.

She hurried back through the house, desperate to work out exactly what he'd taken. The small room between the kitchen and the lounge wasn't one of the ones she'd already explored: it seemed to double as both breakfast room and study. A drop-front desk sat open, its contents in disarray and covered with shards of coloured glass: scattered writing implements suggested the broken item had been a pencil holder. But as Peregrine scanned the room, she could see that a lot of things appeared to be untouched. Cotton gloves were draped carefully over one end of a chrome shelving unit, binoculars and a camera were undisturbed... The stranger had only been interested in books and papers. Peregrine put the statue down and knelt in front of the shelves. She studied the volumes in front of her, scanning the spines and picking up a couple from the floor. They looked like diaries or journals of some sort, all identically bound in the same red Morocco leather and numbered sequentially. Peregrine replaced the fallen copies and ran her hands over the books, counting them off until she came to the empty space where number twenty should have been.

'That bastard,' she murmured, angry with herself for letting the man simply walk out with the book under his arm. Peregrine decided to make good on her threat and report the break-in to the police.

But first she needed to change. It wasn't that she thought her purple trousers and red shirt were inappropriate for a police station, but they bore the marks of her long and somewhat strenuous day.

In the main bedroom, Peregrine tipped the contents of her suitcase out and selected a pleated blue skirt, white blouse, and tangerine cardigan. Twenty minutes later, dressed, hair tidied and carrying one of the journals, Peregrine trotted down the stairs and shut the front door firmly behind her, giving the handle a jiggle to make sure it was properly locked. Then she turned and contemplated the tarpaulin-draped car. The shape told her it was something low to the ground, and after the revelation of the house itself, Peregrine knew her aunt would have chosen something special. She put down the book and, moving to the back of the car, took hold of the tarp and whipped it away.

Peregrine stared at the car and felt her heart beat a little faster. 'No way,' she breathed. It was as though her unknown aunt had chosen the car with Peregrine in mind.

She ran her hand along the side of the baby-blue Austin-Healey 3000, admiring its sleek, curved lines and the polished chrome of the fenders. The car could only be a year old at the most, and someone had clearly been looking after it, even in her aunt's absence. The top was up and Peregrine wasted no time in folding it back: if you were driving a convertible, she reasoned, you should feel the wind in your hair. She settled into the royal blue leather of the driver's seat and caressed the steering wheel.

'Well, hello, beautiful!' she crooned.

Peregrine opened the glovebox and pulled out a pair of large, round sunglasses, settling them on her face. Somehow she'd known they'd be there.

The engine turned over on the first try, and she took a moment to enjoy its throaty growl before releasing the hand-brake and rolling down the drive. She was itching to stamp her foot on the accelerator, but the leafy suburban streets were not the right place; instead, Peregrine contented herself with getting to know her new toy, deciding to stick to main roads until she found a police station. Cruising along beside the river, she snapped the radio on, unsurprised to find it was tuned to a station playing the top forty. She turned up the volume, changed down to a lower gear, and for the next few minutes forgot about the past and the future. There was only her, the music, and her gleaming new car.

Seven

Peregrine swung the Austin-Healey into a space marked *Police Cars Only*, made a halfhearted attempt to tidy her windblown hair, then grabbed the journal and strode into the police station.

The front desk was unmanned, and she tapped her foot impatiently. From where she stood, Peregrine could see through into a communal office, crowded with grey metal desks and filing cabinets. Men sat at a number of the desks, some in suits, others with jackets off, shirtsleeves rolled up, and gun holsters on full display. Only one or two actually appeared to be working. She watched as a young female constable, blonde hair pulled back in a tight bun, crossed the room with an armful of files, weaving between desks, dropping off documents as required and effortlessly dodging a hand that reached to slap her backside as she passed by. Peregrine had thought the woman's tightly buttoned uniform looked uncomfortable and a bit dowdy, but seeing the young constable doing her job so calmly, she decided the heavy blue wool was actually a suit of armour. The policewoman ended her run at the desk closest to the counter where Peregrine stood. It was occupied by a youngish, rather good-looking man in a blue suit. He was busy flipping backwards and forwards through the pages of a notebook, occasionally jotting something on a foolscap pad to his right. The constable collected a stack of folders from his out-tray and moved around to a nearby bank of filing cabinets, where she began to sort and file the papers.

'Beats me why men don't know their ABCs,' the police-woman said.

Peregrine smiled, but the detective looked up with a frown.

'Keep your thoughts to yourself, Constable,' he said.

'Sorry, Detective Steed.' She pressed her lips together and bent her head to the task.

Tired of waiting and more than a little bit annoyed by what she'd just witnessed, Peregrine raised the flap in the front counter and marched through into the detectives' room. She flashed a smile at the policewoman as she steamed by, coming to a stop in front of the desk where the blue-suited detective sat, regarding her with some consternation.

'I've come to report a theft. Can you please help me?' Peregrine said, dropping the red journal down in front of him.

Detective Steed tilted his body sideways to look past her. 'Have you seen the front desk?'

'I've not only seen it, we've spent time together and got acquainted. It's very nice. If you like standing around.' Peregrine folded her arms, aware that the policewoman had abandoned her work and was now watching with avid interest and a broad smile. 'A man broke into my house and took one of my books. Well, I say "my books" but they were really my aunt's. They're mine now, though, and I don't like people coming into my house and steal-ing my stuff. It looked just like this'—Peregrine slid the leather-bound journal closer to Steed—'but it was number twenty.'

Detective Steed picked up the red book, opened it at random

and looked at the handwriting. His eyes grew wide and he flicked through the pages, stopping here and there to read a sentence or two. Finally he closed the cover and looked up at Peregrine, taking in her tousled hair, her frosted pink nail polish and the imperious arch of her eyebrows.

'You're Phryne Fisher's niece? Really?'

Peregrine met his gaze. 'Peregrine Fisher. Were you listening to what I said? There was a man in my house and he took one of these books! I'll never forget his nasty smirk. He was a horrible little man in a greasy hat and bad suit. No manners and a—' Peregrine broke off, realising Detective Steed was no longer listening but staring past her. She turned to see what had caught his attention.

'Sir?' Detective Steed sprang to his feet, the chair scraping across already-worn linoleum.

The man in the greasy hat, hands deep in the pockets of his crumpled coat, took two slow steps into the room. 'Is this young lady causing a disturbance, Detective?'

Peregrine's mouth opened in shock and she looked back and forth between Detective Steed and the new arrival. 'Not yet,' she snapped, 'but I'm about to!'

Steed hurried around his desk. 'Chief Inspector Sparrow, this is Peregrine Fisher.'

'Fisher?' The inspector's eyes widened.

'Phryne Fisher's niece,' Steed replied.

'Is that right?'

'Yes, it is.' Peregrine stepped into the inspector's space and looked him in the eye. 'You were trespassing on private property *and* you took something of mine, which I would like back.'

Sparrow smiled, a tight smile that didn't reach his eyes. 'Well, this is all very convenient. I'm glad you dropped by because we obviously got off on the wrong foot. Now you're here, we can get a few things straight.'

The inspector tipped his head, inviting Peregrine to accompany him away from the detectives' room. She hesitated for a moment then squared her shoulders and followed him into a side hallway. Sparrow pulled the door shut behind them, but instead of ushering her to an office, he immediately rounded on Peregrine, forcing her to back up until she was against the wall, his face inches from her own.

'Just so we're perfectly clear,' he said through gritted teeth, 'it's my job to make sure things run smoothly in this town, which means I can go wherever I want. Anywhere. Anytime. So don't ever get in my way. End of discussion.'

'Perhaps next time you could wait for an invitation, or at least phone ahead. Or didn't your mother teach you manners?' Peregrine raised her chin, refusing to let the inspector intimidate her.

Sparrow took a step back, but only so he could point a finger in Peregrine's face. 'Your aunt was a thorn in my side. The day I heard she'd crashed in the jungle was a happy, happy day. But you...' His lip curled, and he ran his eyes over her, from her toes to the crown of her head. 'Little Miss Fisher,' he said, 'you're just a tiny fish in a very big, deep, dangerous sea. Don't annoy me, Little Fish. Because if you start to annoy me...'

Sparrow put his hands on his hips, emphasising his paunch and a shirtfront stained with the remnants of lunch. And the gun holstered under his right arm. Then he leaned in again. 'If you annoy me, I'll come after you. And do you know what I do when I catch little fish? I batter them. And cook them. Then I chew them up and spit out their bones.'

His breath was hot and sour in Peregrine's face, and she was just contemplating the wisdom of a well-placed knee when the roar of a motorcycle attracted the inspector's attention. With a smirk on his face, he strolled off down the hallway, opened an exterior door and was gone.

Peregrine leaned against the wall, breathing heavily and swallowing down her anger and humiliation. Straightening up, she dusted herself off and headed back towards the detectives' room. Her hand was on the doorknob, but she didn't turn it. Instead, she spun around and hurried in the inspector's wake. Easing open the exterior door, she saw Sparrow standing in the car park. To Peregrine's surprise, he was talking to Birdie from the Adventuresses' Club. Helmet under her arm and wearing a grey leather jacket, she was standing next to a gleaming BSA motorcycle, Florence Astor by her side. Peregrine slipped out the door and stood quietly, curious to see what was going on.

'Birnside!' Inspector Sparrow greeted her cheerily. 'Dreadfully sorry to hear you've gone and lost your henchwoman in the jungle. Very careless! Still, it was bound to happen sooner or later. Guess it's all up to you now.'

'Chief Inspector Sparrow,' Birdie said tightly, 'Miss Astor is here for her interview.'

'I can't tell you how delighted I am. I'm sure you're keen for the whole thing to go...smoothly.'

Florence opened her mouth to speak, but Birdie held up a hand to stop her.

Sparrow pulled Phryne Fisher's red-bound book from his pocket and waved it in Birdie's direction. 'You know what I want. Every dirty little accusation that Fisher woman made against the police. Hand over the proof. All of it.'

Peregrine gasped then clamped a hand over her mouth; fortunately none of the group had heard her.

Birdie made a grab for the book, but Inspector Sparrow pulled back his hand and returned the volume to his pocket.

'Those were Phryne Fisher's private notebooks,' Birdie said angrily. 'I have no idea what's in them and no idea what you're talking about. You may as well be speaking Swahili.'

'Of course, Birdie *does* actually speak Swahili, and a number of other languages as well,' said Florence, lowering her sunglasses to peer at the inspector over the top of the rims. 'But it's been a while since she had to converse with someone whose native language is oafish.'

'Florence, go inside and wait for me,' Birdie said to her friend, gesturing towards the door where Peregrine stood, her gaze fixed on the inspector. 'Go on!'

Florence backed away, her attention still on Birdie and Inspector Sparrow; it wasn't until she spun around that she noticed Peregrine standing right in front of her.

'Oh! It's the heiress presumptive.' She removed her sunglasses and smiled at Peregrine. 'Well, this is a surprise.'

'Hello, Florence.'

The two women were silent as they watched the scene playing out in the car park. The inspector was now prowling around Birdie's motorbike. He came to a stop in front of the bike and shook his head. 'Oh dear, Birnside. That's not roadworthy! How long have you had that busted headlight?'

Birdie frowned at him, clearly puzzled. 'My headlight's not—'

Before she could finish the sentence, Inspector Sparrow pulled his gun free of its holster and slammed it butt-first into the headlight of Birdie's BSA.

She clenched her fists, but said nothing.

'Better get that seen to,' Sparrow said. 'I'll look the other way this time, but we don't want you getting a ticket now, do we?'

He smiled at Birdie, touched the brim of his hat, and turned away.

'You must've had a very bad war, Inspector,' Birdie called after his retreating figure.

Sparrow froze and his head came up slightly. He seemed to be about to say something or to swing around and confront Birdie again, but after a tense moment he resumed his walk back towards the police station.

Peregrine decided they'd seen enough; she didn't want the inspector to notice he had an audience. 'Come on, Florence.' She put an arm around the other woman's shoulder and ushered her through the door. 'I know a nice detective.'

Back inside the police station, Peregrine settled Florence into the visitor's chair on the far side of Detective Steed's desk.

'Miss Astor is here to make a statement about the murder of Barbie Jones,' she said, collecting a second chair for herself and sitting next to Florence.

Steed spread his hands in apology. 'The chief inspector has to be here for this.'

'Oh, I'm sorry.' Peregrine tilted her head and picked up the nameplate prominently positioned on the front of the desk. 'It says here that you're a detective. Detective James Steed. This is you, right? Or have you stolen someone's desk?'

Steed snatched the nameplate from her and put it out of Peregrine's reach. 'Chief Inspector Sparrow is in charge.'

'Of what? Intimidation and harassment? Or is that just his hobby? Come on, Detective Steed, now's your chance to do some detecting!' Peregrine raised her eyebrows and sat back in her chair.

The detective was saved from answering by the arrival of the blonde policewoman.

'Your tea and biscuits, Detective Steed,' she said, placing

the cup and saucer at his elbow. 'It's those digestives you really like—I've just opened a fresh packet.'

'Thank you, Constable,' Steed replied.

'Constable...?' Peregrine smiled encouragingly at the young officer.

'Connor, ma'am. Fleur Connor.' She ducked her head and hurried off.

'Now that we've clarified you *are* a detective'—Peregrine stared pointedly as Steed bit into a biscuit—'was that a police-woman or a tea lady? Because she looked like a policewoman to me.'

Steed choked slightly on his biscuit and took a swig of tea, managing to burn his mouth in the process. 'Constable Connor is a junior officer,' he managed to splutter.

Peregrine pushed forward on her chair, ready to start an argument, but Florence cut her off.

'For goodness' sake! Can we just get on with this? I've already told you I have no idea who might have wanted to hurt Barbie Jones. The only other thing you need to know—the only thing I can tell you—is that I didn't kill her. Barbie and I were friends.' She folded her arms impatiently.

'And, besides,' Peregrine added, 'why would Florence sabotage her own show with a dead body? It makes absolutely no sense.'

Steed opened his mouth to speak, but Peregrine wasn't finished.

'None. No sense, no motive, no murder weapon, and no evidence against Florence. It's probably a good thing poor Barbie was left in plain sight or you might not even have a body.'

The detective paused, waiting to see if Peregrine's speech was over, then leaned across the desk. 'People often do things that don't make sense. And your friend here'—he nodded at Florence—'had a very public argument with the deceased yesterday. People said

Miss Jones was constantly running late. Was the argument about that? A boyfriend, perhaps? Too many late nights?'

Peregrine nodded approvingly. 'See? Now you're starting to sound like a detective.' Then she angled her body close to Florence. 'The fight with Barbie isn't a good look,' she murmured.

Florence flapped a hand at them as though brushing away the problem. 'As far as I know Barbie didn't have a boyfriend. She was just perpetually late. And as for the argument, it was nothing. A silly tiff about one of the dresses. Barbie claimed it was too tight and was refusing to wear it, but I knew she was just being a prima donna; she hated the bias cut and all the flounces.'

'She hated the...what?' Steed's brow furrowed and his pen hovered uncertainly over his notebook.

'The bias cut and the flounces!' Peregrine sighed impatiently and tapped the desk.

'I have no idea what that is, so if you could just—' He broke off, held out a hand palm down, and patted the air in front of him. 'Tone it down.'

'Why? Because you don't know what a bias cut is? Do you think Inspector Turkey has a clue?' Peregrine's voice rose.

Steed winced and closed his eyes, just as Inspector Sparrow, accompanied by a white-faced and miserable Birdie, stepped into Peregrine's line of sight.

Sparrow pointed at Peregrine. 'You! Get out!'

Peregrine was ready to argue, but seeing the look on Sparrow's face, she bit back her smart remark. Now was not the time. She stood, snatched up the red notebook she'd brought and gave Florence a reassuring pat on the shoulder.

'Detective Steed.' She nodded at him then turned to leave.

Sparrow blocked her path. Seconds ticked by, the moment stretching, and it seemed the entire group held its breath. Then, with an exaggerated show of good manners Sparrow moved aside, allowing Peregrine just enough room to pass.

She stalked off without looking back.

Eight

When Detective James Steed arrived at Blair's Emporium the following morning, he found Peregrine Fisher's convertible, with its top down, parked directly in front of the store. Peregrine herself was leaning back with her elbows on the car's bonnet, face tilted to the sky, enjoying the sunshine.

'I was starting to wonder if you'd ever show up,' she said, eyes invisible behind dark sunglasses.

Steed ignored the jibe, staring at the baby-blue Austin-Healey in disbelief. 'Don't tell me you got the house too?' he asked, surprise and just a hint of envy in his voice.

'As a matter of fact I did! So you'll always know exactly where to find me, Detective.' Peregrine stood up and pulled off her sunglasses. 'Now I just have to convince Birdie and the rest of the Adventuresses that I can do my aunt's old job. I mean, it's not really that hard, is it? You start with the dead body, figure out when and how they were murdered, make a list of suspects, ask some questions, and find out as much as you can from the cops. The nice, helpful cops.' She put her hands behind her back and smiled sweetly at Steed, but he just shook his head.

'I've got real work to do.' He started walking towards the main entrance of Blair's Emporium, but after a few seconds, he stopped and turned.

Peregrine had been following right behind, and she was so close Steed was forced to take a step back.

'You can't just decide on a whim that you're going to be a detective!' he exclaimed. 'It doesn't work like that. I've been through the police academy, done three years of special training—'

'And I'm sure you learned a lot,' Peregrine said politely.

Steed forged on. 'I've spent countless hours—'

'Sitting in a police station having someone else bring you cups of tea?' Peregrine arched an eyebrow. 'Well, while you've been learning from the likes of Inspector Sparrow, I've been studying at the school of hard knocks.'

'The school of… When did you actually leave school?'

'I was fifteen. But I can pipe pink icing onto one hundred finger buns in five minutes, tease three beehives in an hour, compound enough nerve pills in an afternoon to knock out a mothers' club, and rebuild a Holden from the wheels up in three days with only four spanners. Among other things.'

'So you have some life skills. That's great. But unless the killer is a beauty queen who drove to a mothers' club bake sale with a carload of finger buns laced with nerve pills, you're still not a detective.' Steed turned, slapped his palm against the door to the emporium and pushed hard, intending to make a grand exit, but the door remained firmly closed.

'Here's another trick I learned in the real world.' Peregrine pulled the adjoining door open and sailed past Detective Steed.

He hurried to grab the door as it swung back and followed

her into Blair's Emporium, catching up as she paused to admire a grouping of mannequins dressed in tennis clothes.

'Do you know when Barbie died?' Peregrine asked.

Steed struggled with himself for a moment then sighed. 'Sometime early yesterday morning.'

'That's a bit vague and not particularly helpful. Can you tell me why she was killed then?'

The detective pulled back and looked at her in disbelief. 'No. Of course I can't. I've only just started my investigation.'

'I thought you said it was Sparrow's investigation,' Peregrine said innocently, lifting a price tag attached to a tennis skirt as she spoke.

'Why am I telling you anything anyway?' Steed stalked off across the black-and-white terrazzo shop floor. 'I have an appointment.'

'And I have so much shopping to do! I wonder what fashionable detectives are wearing this season?' Peregrine stepped onto a nearby escalator and turned to wave at Steed as she ascended to the lofty heights of Blair's ladieswear department.

Despite himself, the detective watched her until she reached the top and disappeared.

Steed then took the elevator to Terence Blair's top-floor office, trying—and largely failing—to order his thoughts. When the doors slid open, Joyce Hirsch, Blair's secretary, was waiting for him.

'Good morning, Detective. Mr. Blair isn't here.'

'He's not... Good morning, Mrs. Hirsch.' Steed's good manners won out over his annoyance.

'He asked that you meet him on the first floor. He likes to be seen by staff and customers. Especially at a time like this.' She leaned forward conspiratorially. 'He has to put up with such a lot.'

Steed decided not to rise to the bait and backed into the still-waiting elevator car. 'Thank you.' He touched the brim of his hat as the doors closed.

—

On the first floor, Peregrine hovered only a few feet from two men she assumed were Mr. Blair and his son; the younger one was, after all, wearing a badge that proclaimed him *Colin Blair, Assistant Manager*. James Steed was easy to spot as he hurried towards them, a lone man in a sea of femininity. His stride faltered slightly when he noticed her, idly stroking the fabric of a gown, and she waggled her fingers at him in a wave that was both discreet and deliberately annoying.

'Mr. Blair,' the detective said, while studiously ignoring Peregrine. 'Thank you for meeting with me again. Is there somewhere we can talk in private?'

There was a round of handshakes and comments on the terrible business of Barbie's murder, then Terence Blair began to lead the men away. Peregrine caught Detective Steed's eye as they walked past, and he flashed her a triumphant grin. She started to follow, expecting a long trek through the store, but had to suppress a laugh when they stopped only a dozen feet away at a department manager's table, tucked into a corner of the shop floor. Steed commandeered the manager's chair, leaving the Blairs to settle themselves in the seats usually reserved for customers.

Peregrine picked up a dress and carried it over to a mirror directly behind where Terence Blair and his son were sitting. She held the dress in front of her and stood before the mirror, pretending to assess the style. In the reflection, she met Steed's eye and quirked an eyebrow. He glowered at her then looked away.

'So...' Detective Steed leafed through his notebook. 'Just a few follow-up questions. How long had Miss Jones been working for Blair's as a house model?'

'About six months.' Terence Blair crossed one leg over the other, displaying a yellow argyle sock. 'She approached Colin initially.'

'It was just a standard job interview—until she started to get emotional,' Colin added.

'And that's all it takes for Colin. As soon as a woman gets a bit weepy, he's putty in her hands.' Terence gave a long-suffering sigh and shook his head, oblivious to the wounded expression on his son's face.

In the mirror, Peregrine gave Steed a wide-eyed look then swapped the dress she was holding for another one, pulling the pink fabric across her abdomen. Steed shot her a dirty look.

'Why did she get emotional?' he asked.

'Miss Jones told me she had to leave White's,' Colin explained.

Steed pulled his attention back from Peregrine. 'You mean H. R. White's? The department store across the road?'

'That's right,' Colin confirmed.

'Did she tell you why?'

'No. I was going to ask, but she was so upset. And the crying increased every time White's was mentioned.'

'It's always tricky taking on staff from White's,' Terence said, uncrossing his legs and leaning forward. 'We try to respect each other—well, from an operations point of view at least. You know, maintain a bit of distance and keep things cordial. They're our biggest competitor, but no one wants a full-on war. That just means lower profit margins all round.'

Peregrine decided she'd heard enough for now: she wasn't going to solve Barbie's murder by listening to the Blairs pontificate about business or by provoking James Steed, although it was fun watching him tie himself in knots. She dumped the dress she'd been holding on the nearest rack and plunged deeper into the store, looking for a way to get into the stockrooms.

Peregrine spotted a saleswoman carrying a teetering stack of shoeboxes and followed her to an unmarked door. The boxes wobbled alarmingly as the woman attempted to reach for the doorhandle, and Peregrine rushed forward.

'Here, let me,' she said opening the door and holding it wide.

'Why, thank you,' came the startled reply. Blair's clientele were not usually so considerate of the staff who pandered to them. The saleswoman squeezed past, her attention focused on not dropping anything and returning to the shop floor as quickly as possible. She failed to notice Peregrine following her through and scurrying off in the other direction, the tap of her own shoes on the linoleum masking the sound of Peregrine's footsteps.

Peregrine tried a few doors before finding one that was unlocked. Easing it open as quietly as possible, she peered around the frame. Stairs, scuffed and utilitarian. She headed down, past one door marked with a G and arrived at the basement level. Another door, slightly ajar, was directly in front of her. She stepped forward and applied one eye to the gap. The vast room was dimly lit and cluttered, but looked like it was unoccupied. Peregrine slipped through the door, closing it behind her. She seemed to be in a part of the storeroom reserved for display material. Discarded signage, backdrops for window displays, a partition papered in floral damask to resemble a wall, shelves and shelves of miscellaneous props and accessories and, off to one side, a giant wedding cake. Peregrine was running her hand over the wallpaper and wondering how she could examine the top of the wedding cake when suddenly she had the feeling she was no longer alone. The hairs on the back of her neck rose, and she slowly moved around the end of the faux wall.

A face, inches from her own.

'Oh!' Peregrine jumped back, colliding with something. Fingers clawed at her shoulder and she shrieked and spun around, hands out, ready to karate chop her attacker. Then her arms dropped to her sides and she sucked in a breath. 'Well, that's embarrassing,' she muttered.

Concealed behind the wallpapered partition were at least a dozen shop mannequins, some waving or pointing, standing normally or with legs in unnaturally twisted poses, some dressed, a few with moulded hair, a few that were bald and a number wearing wigs. And all of them were staring unblinkingly at Peregrine. She found herself checking each face, just to be sure there wasn't a real person hiding in their midst. When her heart rate had slowed, Peregrine moved past the crowd of dummies and continued to nose about, but there was nothing suspicious, just the detritus of a large store. Towards the back of the room she came across a pile of fashion magazines and noticed Barbie Jones on the cover of the topmost edition. Picking it up, Peregrine began to flick through the pages, but then, from the corner of her eye, she noticed another door in a dim corner of the room. Peregrine made her way over, skirting around a couple of beach chairs and a small carousel horse. The door was marked *Alterations* and stood slightly open. She pushed it wide. Overhead, a fluorescent light buzzed and faltered, but the tiny room contained only an empty clothes rack, a worktable, chair, dressmaker's form, and a sewing machine.

'Can I help you?'

The voice came from behind her and Peregrine spun around.

A man in a dustcoat and flat cap stood there, a female mannequin under each arm. The flickering light was reflected in his
spectacles, hiding his expression from Peregrine.

'Sorry! Gosh. I was just looking for the powder room. Must
have taken a wrong turn.' Peregrine gave him a quick smile.

'Miss!' A second voice came from the other side of the basement, and Detective Steed stepped into the light. 'You can't be
in here, miss. This area of the store is out of bounds to the general public. If you'd like to come with me…' He nodded to the
storeman. 'Mr. Knox.'

Peregrine hurried over and positioned herself just behind
Steed's shoulder, but Knox had already lost interest. He peered
earnestly at the detective.

'The other cop said I could still use the storeroom for my
ladies,' Knox said, hefting the mannequins under his arms for
emphasis. 'They don't like to be abandoned in strange places.'

'Yes, of course, Mr. Knox.' Steed nodded at him.

Peregrine couldn't repress a shudder as she and Detective
Steed watched the storeman carry his mannequins away. When
Knox had disappeared from view, Peregrine turned her attention to the detective and noticed he was holding a thick folder
of papers under one arm.

'What's in there?' she asked, pointing to the file.

Steed twisted his shoulder back, putting the folder out of her
reach. 'Confidential police documents, just rushed over from
the station,' he said.

She stared at him for a moment. 'Fine, don't tell me. I, however, have something I'd like to share with you.' She pulled Steed
over to the pile of magazines.

'Look! Last summer's edition.' Peregrine flipped through
until she found the double-paged editorial featuring Barbie

Jones in a variety of swimwear. She held it up for Steed to see. 'The article says Barbie Jones was one of Australia's top models and, quote, "the elegant face of H. R. White's Department Store".'

'Yes, but she left White's six months ago.' Steed took the magazine and slowly began to turn the pages, tilting his head occasionally as he did so.

'She must have been a huge catch for Blair's,' mused Peregrine. 'If I was Mr. White and someone had poached my star model, I might want revenge. And murdering Barbie Jones in Blair's Emporium in public wouldn't be a bad way to do it.'

'Barbie wasn't poached. It was her decision: she left.' Steed turned the magazine sideways.

'No, actually she said she *had* to leave.' Peregrine snatched the magazine from his hands.

'That was a private conversation.'

'In the middle of the ladieswear department!' Peregrine rolled her eyes. 'And what about that weird storeman who was just here? Don't you think he might be up to something?'

Steed took her arm and tucked it through his own. 'I'm escorting you from the premises, Miss Fisher.'

When they emerged onto the shop floor, Steed attempted to disengage his arm but couldn't. Peregrine wouldn't let go. Instead, she pulled him closer, rested her head on Steed's broad shoulder, and slowed her pace to a dawdle. Then she sighed. 'Isn't this lovely?' She smiled up at him.

'Miss Fisher...' Detective Steed gave his arm an experimental tug, but Peregrine clamped it tight with her own.

'Isn't this lovely, darling?' she said loudly. 'Would you mind waiting while I try a few things on, or should we go and choose the china for our wedding registry first?'

'Miss Fisher!' He blushed, looking around to see if anyone had noticed.

A matronly woman in a floral-print dress met his eye and smiled indulgently.

Peregrine continued to tease Steed until they were almost back at the main entrance to Blair's Emporium. She took her head from his shoulder but kept her arm hooked through his.

'Detective Steed…' she began.

He looked down at her face, so close, but didn't answer.

'How well did you know my aunt?' Peregrine asked.

Steed smiled wryly. 'Well enough to get me into trouble with my boss. It seems like you two may have that in common.'

Peregrine let go of Steed's arm, spinning so she was in front of him, walking backwards. She scrutinised his face.

'You helped her, didn't you? With investigations?' She pushed the door open with her back, smiling at Steed with incredulous delight.

'If Inspector Sparrow finds out you've been interfering with *my* investigation, we're both in serious trouble,' Steed said.

'That sounds like a yes to me!' Peregrine said.

'You—'

'Relax! I'm leaving. But I think you should consider the possibility that Barbie was killed because she left White's.'

The detective turned to stare at White's Department Store, assessing Peregrine's theory. 'But,' he wondered aloud, 'how would anyone from White's get into the rival store before opening hours?'

At that moment, Peregrine caught sight of the corner of a photograph protruding from the file Steed was still carrying. Deftly, she plucked it free and tucked it inside her cardigan, folding her arms and fixing a bland expression on her face.

'It wouldn't be that difficult,' she said. 'Someone on the inside.'

Steed turned back to her. 'Goodbye, Miss Fisher,' he said firmly.

Peregrine swung gracefully behind the steering wheel of her car and slipped on her sunglasses. 'Come and see me when you get stuck, Detective.'

As she watched Steed walk back through the doors of Blair's Emporium, Peregrine considered her next move. If she was going to solve Barbie Jones's murder, she had to figure out how to get back inside the store. Her aunt would probably have known what to do—but then, her aunt had the support of the Adventuresses' Club. She reached under her cardigan and pulled out the photograph she'd purloined from Steed; it was a close-up of Barbie Jones on the wedding cake. For a moment, Peregrine closed her eyes and turned away, then she made herself look, moving the photograph back and forth so the sun hit it from different angles. Something jarred on her senses and she stopped, staring, trying to work out what it was. She brought the picture close to her eyes and studied Barbie's legs.

Peregrine's lips curved in a triumphant smile. A clue. Now she really had to get back inside Blair's—and perhaps once she'd done that, the door to the Adventuresses' Club would open naturally.

Firing up the Austin-Healey, Peregrine pulled away from the kerb with a screech of tyres. She had to find a way in—to both organisations.

Nine

It was late in the afternoon by the time Peregrine accelerated up the driveway of her new home and brought the convertible to a smooth stop in the undercroft. She'd barely stepped out of the car when Florence Astor appeared, walking in from the street.

'Florence! What are you doing here?'

'Hello, Peregrine. I've come to collect my things: some rolls of wallpaper and fabric samples,' Florence explained as she crossed the last few feet of the drive. 'Phryne gave me carte blanche to redecorate her spare room. We were just about to start when she left.' She smiled sadly.

'Come in! I haven't had any guests yet,' Peregrine said, then paused. 'Well, no one I've invited and who I actually want in the house, anyway.'

She was just about to unlock the door when there was a loud crash.

Florence jumped. 'What was that?'

'Shh.' Peregrine put a finger to her lips. 'It came from in there.' She pointed to a door set deep under the house—a door she'd assumed led to a storage area. Motioning for Florence to keep back, Peregrine reached into her bag and pulled out what looked like a lipstick. Removing the lid, she twisted the base, but instead of a column of Shimmering Rose or Luminous Pink, a short but wicked-looking stiletto blade clicked into place.

Florence's eyes widened. 'Where did you get that?' she whispered.

Peregrine nodded towards the car. 'Glovebox.'

The women crept closer, Florence a step behind Peregrine, who held the lipstick dagger out in front of her. The door was open a couple of inches and they could hear someone moving about and, by the sound of it, rummaging through things.

Peregrine was still annoyed with herself for letting Sparrow walk away yesterday; there was no way today's intruder was going to get off so lightly. Without warning she kicked the door open and burst into the room, blade pointed and ready for action.

'Yaaaaaah!' she shouted as loudly as she could.

'Aaaaah!' the panicked intruder yelled.

Then everything stopped.

'Samuel?' Peregrine lowered her weapon in confusion.

Samuel, keeping a careful eye on Peregrine, put the box he'd been carrying on the workbench that dominated the small room.

'I just came to clean out my workshop,' he said.

'Workshop?' Peregrine looked around at the bench and shelves, which contained a vast array of miscellaneous tools, electrical items, spare parts such as cogs, springs, glass lenses, and cabling, and, disturbingly, something marked with a radiation hazard sign.

'Your aunt said I could use this space for my workshop while she was away—as long as I didn't use chemicals.'

Florence stepped forward. 'Samuel had a bit of trouble at the Adventuresses' Club.'

'A minor explosion in the kitchen. Barely a pop, really,' Samuel said heartily.

Florence cleared her throat and looked at Peregrine meaningfully. 'Boom!' she mouthed, demonstrating by splaying her fingers and expanding her hands away from each other. Then she looked at Samuel. 'It was actually three not-so-minor explosions.'

'Anyway, you don't have to worry,' Samuel told Peregrine, 'because I'm concentrating on my electronics work for now. Although I'm not plugging anything I make into the mains; for some reason your aunt was quite adamant about that. I've also been tinkering with gadgets, inventing things...like that!' He pointed to the lipstick stiletto in Peregrine's hand.

'You made this?' Peregrine looked from the blade to Samuel. He nodded.

'Very useful. I like it!' she said, impressed. 'So where are you setting up the new workshop?'

'I, ah, I haven't quite worked that out yet.' Samuel reached up and fiddled with the arm of his glasses, realigning them although they were already perfectly straight.

'So, why are you packing up then? That's silly! You may as well stay here until you find somewhere.' Peregrine smiled.

'Really?' Samuel seemed to grow a little taller. 'Thank you! And you've no cause for concern—I figured out what was causing the explosions.'

'That's...good?' Peregrine's smile faded. 'But maybe let's keep my aunt's no-chemicals and no-plugging-in rules for now, shall we?'

Florence turned her back to Samuel, who was happily

removing things from the box and returning them to the shelves. 'I'd still keep a fire extinguisher or two handy,' she whispered to Peregrine. Then, more loudly, 'I think this calls for a drink!'

'Excellent idea!' said Peregrine. 'Samuel? Come on.'

'Samuel is actually a bit of a genius with a cocktail shaker,' Florence said. 'Although if you're not careful, your head is likely to experience a different sort of explosion!'

Samuel locked the workshop and they made their way upstairs, where Peregrine waved him to the cocktail cabinet.

'It's all yours,' she said.

Florence dropped onto the white sofa with a sigh.

'Could you get some ice and three champagne glasses?' Samuel asked as he rolled up his sleeves.

Peregrine, who'd been about to join Florence, instead made her way to the kitchen.

'Champagne glasses?' she called.

'The chilled ones—in the freezer,' came the reply.

Peregrine returned to the lounge with the items Samuel had requested, plus some crackers and a jar of olives she'd found and tipped into a bowl. Seeing Samuel rummaging in the cocktail cabinet, she was aware of how at home both he and Florence were in the house, and although that was nothing to do with her, it made Peregrine feel a little bit less alone, a little bit more as though she belonged somewhere.

'Here you go.' She put the ice bucket and glasses down and backed away: far enough to give Samuel room, but close enough to watch him work and see what was going into the concoction she was about to drink. Peregrine had already explored her aunt's alcohol selection and had not been surprised to find there were at least half-a-dozen liqueurs and mixers she'd never heard of.

Samuel's awkwardness dropped away as he measured, sliced,

swirled, and strained, finally presenting Peregrine and Florence each with a deep red drink, garnished with lemon twists.

'Behold La Tour Eiffel!' he announced, taking the third glass for himself.

'Pimm's would have been a lot easier.' Peregrine sipped cautiously and her eyes widened. She sipped again.

'But not nearly as delicious!' Florence raised her glass. 'We should toast to your new abode, Peregrine! In fact, when are you going to have a housewarming party?'

Peregrine shrugged and lowered her eyes as she moved to the sofa and sat down. 'Who would I invite? I don't know anyone in this city.'

Florence flapped a dismissive hand at her. 'That's what parties are for! Your aunt knew everyone—it's such a pity you never had the chance to meet. I can imagine the party she would have thrown to introduce you to her friends! Phryne would have adored you—especially your cheek.'

'Cheek isn't going to get me very far with Birdie,' Peregrine said. She looked at Samuel. 'I still think she doesn't like me.'

He shook his head. 'You're wrong. The thing is, ever since your aunt disappeared, Birdie has been optimistic; she never stopped believing her best friend would turn up sooner or later. But handing things on to Phryne's heir—you—feels like the end of hope. Not only that. Birdie has always had impossibly high expectations—of herself and everyone else—and most people never measure up.'

Peregrine put her near-empty glass on the coffee table and reached for her bag. 'I'm sorry for Birdie, and I know I'm not my aunt, but I won't give up. I've tried hard all my life to be someone or belong somewhere, but not every woman has the chance to go to university or climb Kilimanjaro. That doesn't mean

I'm not Adventuress material, and I've been working on Barbie Jones's murder: look at this.'

She pulled out the photograph of Barbie and dropped it in the middle of the table.

Florence gasped.

'Sorry, Florence, I should have warned you.' Peregrine moved the bowl of olives to cover the upper half of Barbie's body. 'Don't look at her face; just focus on her legs.'

Florence and Samuel leaned in and stared at the picture. Seconds ticked past.

'Wait...' Samuel adjusted his glasses, looked again, then reached into his pocket and pulled out a silver compact. Opening it, he flipped the mirror, revealing a hidden magnifying glass.

'Clearly designed for my aunt, but that is very, very cool.' Peregrine nodded her head in appreciation as Samuel used the magnifying glass to examine the photograph.

'I see what caught your eye, but I'm not sure what...'

'Here.' Peregrine put out her hand for the compact then held it so Florence could see a magnified version of Barbie's legs. 'Look at her stockings,' Peregrine said.

Florence squinted. 'She should be wearing pantyhose with that short dress.'

'Forget about that. Look at the weave and texture of the stockings.'

'They're different. One's a heavier texture, a much denser weave. The other has an open, diamond pattern.' Florence sat back.

'But I don't understand.' Samuel looked at the photograph again. 'Her stockings don't match, but so what? Does that mean something?'

'Well, for starters it proves there's no way Florence had anything to do with Barbie's murder,' Peregrine said.

'I'd never make a fashion faux pas like that—you'd have to kill me first!' Florence exclaimed, then blushed, clearly horrified by what she'd just said.

'But we already knew Florence was innocent.' Peregrine patted the other woman's knee. 'Mismatched stockings are important because it suggests there's one stocking missing from the original pair.'

Samuel's eyes widened as the implication dawned on him. 'And you're thinking...'

'I'm thinking,' Peregrine confirmed, 'that a stocking is just the sort of thing you'd use to strangle someone.'

'So what are you going to do?' Samuel asked.

'I'm not sure,' Peregrine replied. 'I mean, I'm determined to find out who murdered Barbie Jones, but I haven't quite figured out how I'm going to do it. Yet. Plus, there's another mystery I have to solve. Why did that creep Sparrow break in here and steal one of my aunt's notebooks? What was so important about that particular volume?'

She jumped up from the sofa and hurried into the adjoining room, then reappeared in the doorway, brandishing one of the red books.

'Oh, those,' said Samuel. 'Each one represents a separate investigation.'

Peregrine nodded. 'I worked that out when I read them last night, but why did Sparrow want to get his hands on number twenty? Number nineteen was an investigation into a corrupt politician, and number twenty-one dealt with a nurse pressuring unwed mothers and running a baby-stealing racket, but I have no idea what my aunt might have written about in number twenty.'

Peregrine went to replace the book.

'You could always check the microfilm copy,' Samuel called after her retreating figure.

She walked slowly back into the room, book still in her hand, and stared at him open-mouthed. 'What did you say?'

'I said you could check the microfilm copy. Your aunt was keen to have duplicate copies of everything, and I guess we know why now. I transferred the contents of all the books to microfilm a while ago when I was testing my new camera and machine. I have the full set.'

Peregrine hurried over and hugged Samuel, causing him to blush furiously. 'Of course you have the full set!'

'Your aunt used to make Samuel blush just like that,' said Florence approvingly. She got up and crossed to the stereo, where she flipped through the record rack, checking the sleeves of several 45s until she found the one she was looking for.

'Maybe solving one mystery will help to convince Birdie I'm not so bad. Come on, Samuel, where's this machine of yours?' Peregrine tugged at his sleeve impatiently.

Before he could answer, Florence dropped the needle into the groove, and Johnny O'Keefe's 'Move Baby Move' blasted from the speakers. She danced her way over to Samuel and grabbed his hand. 'Plenty of time, Peregrine! Right now Sammy has to dance with me!'

'Not again,' Samuel groaned, but he allowed Florence to pull him forward into an open space.

'I need cheering up, and you know I love this song. Besides, you poured the drinks; you knew what would happen. Dance!' Florence swivelled her hips like she was dancing on *Bandstand* while Samuel hopped about awkwardly.

'Next time I'll cut back on the absinthe,' he shouted, as trumpets blared between verses.

Florence's response was to add an exaggerated backstroke move to her dancing, while Peregrine smiled indulgently and went to make a large pot of coffee.

By the time Peregrine returned, Samuel had set up his microfilm machine and Florence had disappeared.

'She's gone to bed in the spare room,' Samuel explained. 'Your aunt...'

Peregrine waved away his explanation. She was happy to have Florence use the spare bed—and, besides, the glowing screen of the microfilm reader was beckoning.

'I've loaded the film and it's really easy to operate, but I could help if you'd like,' Samuel offered.

'Thank you,' Peregrine said as she sat down and poured herself a cup of coffee. 'You're welcome to stay and have coffee, but I can do this.'

Samuel hesitated a moment, tucking his hands into the pockets of his jacket. 'In that case, I'll leave you to it.'

Peregrine smiled distractedly, already intent on the pages scrolling past on the screen. 'Goodnight, and thanks again.'

'If you don't mind me saying, you're a bit of a natural at this.'

'Hmm?' Peregrine looked at him properly.

'Detecting. You're a fast learner.'

'I haven't solved anything yet! But when I do...' She arched her eyebrows at him. 'Birdie can keep on being as cool as a Frigidaire, but at least she'll have to respect me.'

'I think you'll manage to defrost her heart. Goodnight, Peregrine.'

Samuel started down the stairs, but Peregrine didn't register the sound of the front door opening and closing. She was already engrossed in the microfilm copy of volume twenty of her aunt's investigative notebook. After a moment of scanning through the flowing script, Peregrine pulled a notepad in front of her and began to transcribe:

Our midnight visit to Madame Lyon's establishment in Collins Street turned up a few surprises and caused quite a bit of consternation, especially for the Chief Commissioner of Police and some senior officers...

—

Morning light filtered through the curtains, not yet bright enough to disturb Peregrine, who was sprawled facedown on the sofa, covered by a throw rug and with her head buried under a cushion. Pages of notes littered every surface around her. At some point after 1 a.m. she'd changed into pyjamas, intending to go to bed, but the pull of the notebook had been too strong, and she'd ended up working through most of the night.

'Rise and shine!'

Peregrine groaned and one of her arms fell off the edge of the sofa. Florence bustled in from the kitchen, dressed in yesterday's clothes and carrying a tray with fresh coffee and dry toast.

'Your aunt wasn't much of a morning person either,' Florence said, stepping over Peregrine's discarded shoes and carefully pushing pages aside to set the tray down on the coffee table. 'How much of the notebook did you copy out?'

Peregrine hauled herself into a sitting position, the hair on one side of her head sticking out at a crazy angle. She rubbed her knuckles, hard, into her eyes. 'All of it.'

Florence passed her a cup of coffee and Peregrine held it with both hands, inhaling the rich aroma.

'Do you remember some sort of raid on Madame Lyon's?' Peregrine asked.

Florence nodded, sipping from her own cup. 'Vividly! That police raid was front-page news. Something went wrong, apparently, and the commissioner was shot.'

'Not according to my aunt.'

Florence frowned. 'But he was taken away in an ambulance and nearly died. There was a huge fuss, but they never found the culprit.'

'First of all, according to my aunt's notebook, it wasn't the police raiding the joint, it was her! But there were several senior police officers already there in—shall we say—an unofficial capacity, and the commissioner was one of them. No one shot anybody, but the commissioner had a heart attack...in Madame Lyon's arms, mind you! My aunt said the madam was like a goddess guarding secrets the way she protected and cared for him. Anyway, the whole thing was clearly covered up, but in the notebook Aunt Phryne wrote that she had proof not only of the relationship between the commissioner and the madam, but also of some other stuff to do with police and the brothel.'

'That must be how she kept Sparrow at bay!'

'And that must have been what he was after when he broke in,' Peregrine said. 'Except that the proof wasn't recorded in the notebook he stole. Maybe Sparrow is hoping that now Aunt Phryne is gone, the evidence is lost as well. He might think he's safe, but he'd better not get too comfortable; I'm going to find out what my aunt had on him and then...' She picked up a triangle of toast and bit into it with a determined crunch.

'You need to get dressed before you can bring down the police force.' Florence tipped her head towards the other end of the house. 'Come on.'

Peregrine cast aside the throw rug, picked up her coffee and grabbed another piece of toast before following Florence through the house to the main bedroom. She found her in the adjoining dressing room, the doors of the wardrobes flung wide to reveal a collection of clothes so stylish, Peregrine felt as though she'd stepped into the pages of a fashion magazine.

'Oh. My. God. I haven't looked in here! What size was my aunt?' She wanted to finger some of the rich fabrics, but was afraid of spilling coffee or dropping crumbs.

Florence sized Peregrine up: the pink shortie pyjamas she was wearing left most of her tall, slender frame on display. 'About your size. And virtually all her clothes are still here. The only thing missing is the little black dress she was wearing when she took off for New Guinea. Well, that and a swimsuit.'

Peregrine looked at her disbelievingly. 'She went to New Guinea in a little black dress?'

'The language of style is universal. You can never go wrong in a little black dress. Here.' Florence reached in and pulled out a bright orange day dress.

Peregrine put down her cup, but before she could take the dress from Florence's hand they were interrupted by the ringing of the doorbell. She looked at Florence and shrugged, then grabbed the first coat that came to hand—which happened to be an André Courrèges original—and slipped it on before going to see who was on her doorstep first thing in the morning.

As Peregrine bounced down the stairs, she could see Detective Steed peering through the glass next to the front door. She twisted the latch.

'This is a lovely surprise,' she said. 'Come on in!'

Peregrine led the way back up to the lounge, giving Steed a good view of her long, bare legs in the process.

He pulled off his hat as he mounted the last steps, a frown creating a deep line between his eyebrows.

'Going somewhere?' He stared pointedly at Peregrine's coat.

'Places you can only dream about! Coffee?' She poured herself a fresh cup.

'No, I don't want coffee. I just want my photograph back.'

'Photograph?' Peregrine sipped her coffee, eyeing Steed over the cup's rim.

'Miss Fisher…' He pointed his hat at her.

Peregrine put a hand on her hip, causing the coat to gape open, revealing her pyjamas. 'Okay, okay, I only borrowed it. You really should keep a closer eye on things, Detective.'

She collected the photograph from the coffee table and handed it to him before curling up on the sofa with her coffee.

'It was very helpful,' she said. 'I think I've worked out what the murder weapon was.'

Detective Steed looked at the photo then back at Peregrine. 'From this photo?' he said disbelievingly.

She nodded, smiling serenely. 'It's actually quite obvious.'

Steed studied her face then inhaled sharply. 'You're really going to make me work for this, aren't you? But how can you expect me to take you seriously when you're sitting there, hardly wearing any…dressed in those pyjamas.'

Peregrine wrapped the Courrèges coat more tightly around herself. 'Look at Barbie's legs. Closely.'

Steed stared at the photograph for a minute then shrugged.

'Her stockings don't match—I think she was strangled with a stocking,' Peregrine said triumphantly.

Steed studied the photograph again and nodded slowly. Then he glanced over at Peregrine. 'I checked our records last night to see if Harvey White had any sort of police record,' he said in a low voice, as if he feared being overheard.

'And?' Peregrine leaned forward.

Steed crossed the last few feet of carpet separating him from Peregrine and sat down beside her.

'It seems Barbie Jones had him charged with assault.'

'See? I told you there was more to the story of Barbie leaving White's. Was he found guilty?'

Steed shook his head. 'The charges were dropped. Very quickly.'

'Why? Who made that decision?'

Steed stood and put his hat on. 'I can't tell you that.'

'Because you don't know or because you won't say? Covering for someone, perhaps?'

'It's more than my job's worth.'

Peregrine thumped back in the sofa, not bothering to see James Steed out. 'Sparrow,' she muttered.

Ten

After the visit from Detective Steed, Peregrine had returned to her bedroom to find that Florence had been busy. She'd not only selected a lovely blue-and-white shift for Peregrine to wear, she'd come up with a plan to get the young Miss Fisher admitted as an Adventuress.

Now it was early afternoon, and Peregrine was back in the rarefied atmosphere of the Adventuresses' Club. She stood in the hallway outside the Camelot Room, her ear pressed to the wood as she tried to eavesdrop on the meeting in progress. Florence had called the Adventuresses together without mentioning Peregrine's name, which meant it had been hard to convince Birdie to let her stay in the building, let alone wait in the hall. As Peregrine listened, she heard the scrape of a chair and then Florence began to speak.

'Adventuresses,' she said sombrely, 'now that Phryne Fisher isn't here to buffer us from what passes for a police force in this town, I believe the Adventuresses' Club is at great risk.'

'We're staring down the barrel of a one-way trip to purgatory, you mean.' Birdie's voice sounded bitter.

'That's putting it very bluntly, President Birnside, but you're right. We're in trouble and I know we all wish Phryne was here to keep us safe, but wishing won't make it so. We need a plan.'

There was a pause, and Peregrine, from her post in the hallway, pictured Florence meeting the gaze of each woman seated at the table.

'These are desperate times and we need to protect ourselves with whatever resources we have—and it seems to me that one of the greatest resources at our disposal is Phryne Fisher's legacy: her niece, Peregrine.'

'We're not that desperate!' Birdie retorted. 'Besides, if I were you I'd be more concerned about Sparrow painting a big bullseye on my back than wasting my time with—'

Florence cut her off. 'Sparrow gunning for me means he's coming for all of us. If I'm arrested on trumped-up charges, don't you think he'll use that to discredit every woman sitting at this table? We need to be ready to fight.'

'And you think we should let a failed hairdresser lead the offensive?' Birdie sneered.

'Peregrine Fisher is far more than that! And I think it's fair to say that most of us here—despite our achievements—might also struggle to excel if a curling wand and a jar of Dippity-do hair gel were the only tools in our arsenal.'

There were positive-sounding murmurs.

'Whatever you want to call it, Birdie,' Florence continued, forgetting formalities in the heat of the moment, 'a curious mind or something in the blood, I think Peregrine has it!'

'She worked out Barbie Jones was strangled with a stocking and why Inspector Sparrow stole that notebook!' Samuel's voice drifted through the door.

Peregrine had forgotten that, unlike her, he'd been allowed to remain in the Camelot Room while the meeting was held.

Despite being a man—and therefore not having a seat at the table—Samuel still had some status in the club. Ordinarily, Peregrine would be miffed by something like that, except now he was clearly on her side.

'And she needs us. Her mother is dead, she has no family…' It took Peregrine a moment to identify the soft voice as belonging to Violetta Fellini. 'She never got to meet her wonderful aunt—how sad for both of them! And you've seen her. She's not Phryne, but at the same time there is something… It almost feels like a little bit of Phryne is still with us.'

'What do you think Phryne would say, Birdie? Would she want us to welcome her niece, to at least give Peregrine Fisher a chance?' Florence's question was so quiet Peregrine had to press her ear harder against the door.

'Oh, good grief! Well played, Florence, well played,' said Birdie begrudgingly.

'In that case, as secretary of the Adventuresses' Club of the Antipodes, I'd like to formally move that we allow Peregrine Fisher to follow in her esteemed aunt's footsteps and become a fully-fledged Adventuress, specialising in investigation.' Florence delivered the motion in a rush.

There was a murmur of approval. Out in the hall, Peregrine clenched her fists and did a little victory dance. Then she heard Birdie's voice rise above the hubbub and pressed her ear against the door's mahogany panels once more.

'Not so fast! Before she can become an Adventuress, there are certain tests Peregrine will have to pass,' said Birdie. 'We'll have to arrange a day—'

'Nonsense! I'm sure Violetta and I can get everything set up straight away. You always say there's no time like the present, Birdie. Peregrine!'

The door opened abruptly and Peregrine half fell into the room.

'Yes! I'm great at tests! Are we doing it now? I'm ready!' Peregrine cracked her knuckles and beamed at the assembled women.

'Fine then, since Florence has so kindly offered to prepare the tests, we may as well get this over with.' Birdie's smile was overly wide. 'But…' She paused, and her eyes narrowed shrewdly. 'I propose Samuel as second candidate for the position of club investigator!'

There was a shocked silence. The Adventuresses glanced at each other, clearly surprised by Birdie's suggestion. Samuel looked like he wanted to say something but was too mortified to open his mouth.

'But he's a man!' Peregrine exclaimed.

Several women nodded and the tension in the room dropped a notch: someone had voiced what they were all thinking.

'Which means he's not eligible for full membership,' Birdie conceded. 'However, he's discreet, he knows this town inside out and his surveillance skills are first-rate. At a time like this, we need the best person for the job to protect our interests. Plus, I trust him implicitly.' She nodded her head once for emphasis.

Ignoring the implied slight, Peregrine summed up the situation. 'So you're saying it's him or me?'

'Whichever one of you succeeds… Let me rephrase that. Whichever one of you most closely meets the exacting standards of the club will be declared our official investigator.'

'Don't you all need to vote on this?' Peregrine asked. 'Second the motion? Something like that?'

'Let's not waste any more time on formalities.' Birdie stood.

'Meeting adjourned. Florence, Violetta, shall we get started? I'll outline the necessary tests.'

Birdie sailed out of the room and, after a moment, Violetta, followed by Florence, hurried after her.

—

Less than two hours later, they reconvened in a large shed at the rear of the property. Peregrine was surprised to find a small shooting range was already set up, the targets placed in front of a thick bank of straw bales. While most of the Adventuresses hung back, Birdie laid out two guns on a table and gestured for Peregrine and Samuel to approach.

'Choose a weapon,' Birdie instructed. 'Three shots each, the distance is twenty-seven yards.'

Peregrine gestured for Samuel to go first and, from the corner of her eye, saw Birdie smile with satisfaction.

Samuel took his time, picking up each gun and weighing it in his hand before finally making a choice. He squared up in front of his target, took up a double-handed stance, and fired off three careful shots. All hit the target well within the inner circles, although none actually made the bullseye.

'Well done, Samuel!' crowed Birdie.

Peregrine picked up the remaining gun in one hand, sighted along the barrel and pulled the trigger four times in rapid succession.

There was a moment's stunned silence. The centre of the target had been obliterated: all four shots had hit the bullseye.

Florence and Violetta smiled broadly, and Violetta clapped silently. Birdie, however, gaped at Peregrine in astonishment.

Peregrine shrugged nonchalantly as she engaged the safety catch and put the gun down. 'Rabbit shooting,' she said.

'I said three shots. You need to follow directives,' said Birdie irritably.

They moved down to the other end of the shed, where two sets of sturdy wooden drawers stood side by side. Violetta stepped forward with a tray on which a number of small, strange tools were arranged. Each had the same flat handle, but the tips varied from single points curved at different angles to wavy lines and tight squiggles.

Peregrine stared at them in confusion. 'What's the test? Do we have to perform some sort of weird medical procedure?' She looked at Birdie.

'They're lock picks. Your next test is to pick the lock on the top drawer. It's a race, but there are also points for finesse. Any scratches or damage will be penalised. After all, a good investigator should leave no trace.' Birdie pulled out a stopwatch.

'Ladies first,' said Samuel, gesturing towards the tray.

'Oh, I...' Peregrine reached into her hair, pulled out a bobby pin and twisted it back and forth until she was happy with the shape. She held it up. 'I've got my own, thanks.'

Birdie snorted and muttered something that sounded like: '*A hairdresser!*'

Peregrine ignored her and tested all the drawers on both pieces of furniture, just to make sure they were really locked; she wouldn't put it past Birdie to pull some sort of trick. Satisfied everything was secure, she knelt in front of one set of drawers, bobby pin at the ready.

Violetta held the tray out to Samuel. He looked into her eyes and paused, then collected himself and refocused on the array of picks, his hand hovering for a moment before selecting one.

'I think a raking pick will best suit the job,' he said. 'Thank you, Violetta.'

'You're welcome, Samuel.' She smiled.

'Are we doing this?' Peregrine called from her place by the drawers.

Samuel crouched next to her as the Adventuresses clustered around.

Birdie held up the stopwatch. 'Ready? And...go!' Her thumb clamped down on the start button.

Peregrine and Samuel both bent to the task, the only sound the ticking of Birdie's timer. Less than thirty seconds later, Peregrine pulled open the drawer and held both hands in the air.

'Done!' she yelled.

Everyone looked at Samuel.

'Nearly, nearly,' he muttered. Finally, after what felt like an eternity but was, in reality, only another forty-two seconds, he opened the drawer.

'Well done,' he said to Peregrine, sitting back on his heels.

'Just a moment.' Birdie edged between them. 'I need to inspect the locks for damage.'

Peregrine rolled her eyes as she moved aside.

There was silence as Birdie checked first one lock then the other, spending far longer examining Peregrine's handiwork. 'Well done both of you,' she said at last. 'Next test!'

Violetta led the contenders to a table that held nothing but two identical cocktail glasses, each filled to the brim with a golden yellow liquid.

'One of these is a normal cocktail,' Birdie explained, 'the other is a mickey finn.'

'Are you kidding?' Peregrine stared open-mouthed at Birdie.

'Nothing deadly,' said Violetta. 'Just a little chloral hydrate. You might fall briefly unconscious.'

'Your task is to identify the drink containing knockout drops—however, once you touch a glass, you must drink it!' Birdie clapped her hands. 'Begin!'

Samuel and Peregrine circled the table, bending down to gaze at the fluids, leaning in to sniff, trying to see something that would identify the spiked drink.

'Ha!' Suddenly, Peregrine let out a yell of triumph and dove across the table towards a glass. Her fingers stretched for the stem but Samuel got there first, snatching it from beneath her hand. Peregrine smiled.

Birdie groaned.

'Oh, Samuel!' Violetta put a hand to her mouth.

'Nicely done, Ms. Fisher,' said Birdie through gritted teeth. 'But how did you know which drink?'

Peregrine shrugged. 'I didn't. But if it's a toss-up between losing one challenge and swallowing a spiked drink, I'd rather lose. Smart women always know what's in their glass.'

Samuel stared with horror at the glass in his hand. 'Did she just trick me into…?'

'Yep!' Peregrine was delighted.

'But it might be…'

'And you touched it, so now you have to drink it!'

Samuel stared into the glass.

'No time for that now,' said Birdie briskly. 'We still have the final challenge!'

'But you said…' Peregrine gestured at the drinks.

'Flexibility, Ms. Fisher! An Adventuress needs to adapt! Outside, everyone!'

'This is rigged,' muttered Peregrine.

Florence patted her back consolingly. 'You're doing well. One more, that's all.'

'What's the point? Even if I win, Birdie will look me in the eye and tell me I lost.'

Rather than answering, Florence hooked her arm through Peregrine's and pulled her towards the final test.

—

On the first floor of the Adventuresses' Club, a narrow plank of wood had been positioned so it extended from the ledge of an open window across a corner to the balustrade of the adjacent balcony. One storey directly below stood a large clump of lavender. Unfortunately, it wasn't large enough to break a fall or even to provide false reassurance to an aspiring acrobat. Birdie had positioned herself in the garden—well out of the way—with a group of Adventuresses. On the balcony, Violetta and Florence waited, while in the room, leaning out of the open window, were Peregrine and Samuel. Samuel glanced down then abruptly pulled himself back inside, his face white. Peregrine turned and studied him; she could see he was trembling. She leaned out the window again and looked at Birdie.

'Look, do we really need to do this? I've passed your tests. You know deep down I'm the one! I really want this, and now you've seen I'm up for the job... Can't you just admit it?'

Birdie dismissed Peregrine's appeal with an impatient gesture. 'Physical ability and nerve are essential criteria so, yes, we need to do this. It's the final test. Who's first?'

'I-I'll go.' Samuel came and stood next to Peregrine, sweat beading on his forehead.

'You don't have to!' Peregrine grabbed his arm, but he shook her off.

'It's the final test,' he said, teeth clenched.

Samuel clambered onto the windowsill. Slowly he began to straighten up and put one foot on the plank, causing it to wobble in time with his trembling.

On the balcony opposite, Violetta bit her lip and turned her head away.

'Stop!' Peregrine shouted, pulling Samuel back into the room. 'Sorry, but this is just crazy. I really want to be an Adventuress—to be one of you.' She gestured at Birdie. 'But I can't do this. It's too dangerous. Someone could be killed!' She looked at Samuel, who was clutching the windowsill with one hand and mopping his brow with the other.

'Are you saying you give up? You're quitting?' Birdie called up.

'No! I'm not quitting.' Peregrine took a deep breath, aware that on the opposite balcony and in the grounds below, every Adventuress was focused on her. She patted Samuel's hand. 'I'm stepping aside. Samuel can have the job.'

There was a collective sigh from the assembled women.

Violetta clapped her hands. 'Peregrine! You did it! You passed!'

Samuel sagged with relief. 'Thank God! I thought you'd be scraping me off the front path. Even *I* was starting to believe you were serious about the whole test thing, Birdie.'

Peregrine's head swivelled as she looked from Birdie to Samuel to Violetta to Florence and back again. 'Wait. This whole thing was fake? The shooting, drinks, locks…everything was a setup? You people are all mad!' She stared at Birdie accusingly.

'Well, an investigator needs certain skills which we now know you possess,' Birdie began.

Peregrine snorted. 'Puh-lease.'

'But, no, it wasn't a setup. We had to test how far you'd go— what you'd sacrifice—to achieve your goal. Because ultimately, that shows us whether you will uphold our club motto: *Gloria in Conspectus Hominum.*'

'It means *Humanity Before Glory*, and that's what you chose, Peregrine,' Violetta explained. 'So you pass! Congratulations!'

'So I'm an Adventuress?' Peregrine asked.

Heads nodded and a number of voices murmured their approval and good wishes.

'And just to be clear, there are times when a bit of glory is a good thing?'

'Of course,' said Birdie. 'No woman should hide her potential or her achievements!'

'In that case, let's achieve a bit of glory!'

Shouldering Samuel out of the way, Peregrine nimbly sprang up onto the plank.

'Peregrine!' shouted Birdie.

Peregrine smiled and waved down at her then walked lightly to the middle, took a small bow, then continued across to the other side, jumping down to join Violetta and Florence.

'Peregrine Fisher!' Birdie yelled, her voice trembling.

Peregrine leaned over the balustrade and the smile disappeared from her face. She could see Birdie was genuinely upset.

'Peregrine Fisher, life is precious! Don't you ever, *ever*, risk yours unnecessarily again!' Birdie turned away abruptly.

'Sorry,' Peregrine called. Suddenly she truly realised not only how deeply her aunt's disappearance had affected the other woman, but also that maybe, just maybe, Birdie didn't hate her after all.

'We'll convene in the Camelot Room to discuss your first job.' Birdie walked inside.

Peregrine turned away from the edge of the balcony and was enveloped in a hug by Florence and Violetta.

'You were brilliant, Peregrine,' Florence whispered. 'I'm so proud of you.'

'Come on, Adventuress Fisher!' Violetta gave Peregrine an extra squeeze then hurried her inside.

—

Peregrine and Birdie stood side by side in the Camelot Room as Birdie spoke. A couple of Adventuresses had already left— shaking Peregrine's hand warmly then disappearing back to their own work and research—but most remained. Samuel had taken up his usual position, leaning against the wall by the door, and Florence and Violetta were seated side by side on one of the sofas, smiling whenever Peregrine looked their way.

'Peregrine's first job as our official investigator is to find out the truth about the murder of Barbie Jones, thus exonerating Florence. To achieve this—and at her own suggestion— she's going to go undercover and join the workforce at Blair's Emporium,' Birdie announced.

'I'll need a good disguise,' said Peregrine. 'People have seen me there already.'

'And Sparrow will be after you!' Florence added.

Birdie turned to her brother and smiled. 'Samuel? I think this is where you come in.'

Samuel rubbed his hands together in anticipation. 'Don't worry, I'll make her unrecognisable!'

Peregrine held up a warning hand. 'You're not dying my hair blonde.'

'Oh. Are you sure?' He sighed. 'Well, there are other options. Plus there are a few pieces of equipment I've been working on that might come in handy!'

'That magnifier compact was great!' Peregrine's enthusiasm matched Samuel's.

'I also have a wonderful tape recorder that will fit in your handbag, and a camera disguised as a cigarette case.'

'And I've already got the lipstick knife, although it would be hard to reach in an emergency. Perhaps you could put a switch-blade in something like a bangle or a hair clip?'

'Yes!' Samuel pointed an emphatic finger at her. 'Excellent idea! Although I won't have it ready for you in time for this job.'

Peregrine shrugged. 'It's only a department store.'

'But you're chasing a murderer, Peregrine,' Birdie reminded her. 'Department store or not, this is a dangerous mission and you can't afford to be complacent.'

'I won't let you down.' Peregrine held Birdie's gaze until the older woman looked away.

'Everyone...' The word came out with a fine crack. Birdie cleared her throat and tried again. 'Everyone, please officially welcome Adventuress Fisher!' She swallowed hard as the room erupted in applause.

As the remaining Adventuresses dispersed and Samuel rushed off to put together a disguise, Birdie held Peregrine back until, finally, they were alone.

'There's just one more thing...' Birdie began.

'I thought I'd passed all your tests,' sighed Peregrine.

'You did. More convincingly than I could ever have imagined. It made me think, well...' Birdie held up a finger, signalling to Peregrine to wait, and went to the bureau. She pulled something from the top section and Peregrine saw a shudder pass through her stiff shoulders. Then Birdie turned back to face Peregrine and extended her hand. Sitting on her open palm, the pearl handle turned towards Peregrine, was a golden revolver.

'It was your aunt's,' Birdie said quietly. 'It's no good to the rest of us—and Phryne would want you to have it.'

Stunned, Peregrine looked from the gun to Birdie's face, where a sad smile wavered before it was fixed firmly in place. Birdie moved her hand forward and Peregrine reached for the pearl grip, covering Birdie's hand with her own.

'Peregrine! Are you coming? We've got a lot to do!' Samuel called from somewhere deep in the house.

Peregrine took the gun then stepped in close, kissed Birdie swiftly on the cheek, and hurried from the room.

Eleven

Peregrine smoothed the front of her brown knee-length skirt as she sat down opposite Colin Blair in the vast office he shared with his father. She'd been hugely impressed when Florence Astor had managed to arrange an almost-immediate job interview for her, until the designer explained it was a dogsbody position with a high turnover of girls: each one arrived at Blair's bubbling with excitement and left within months, her shoulders slumped. But Peregrine was no stranger to soul-destroying jobs. Besides, not only was this all a ruse, dogsbody was the ideal undercover job—she would be sent everywhere and overlooked by everyone.

Peregrine had arrived twenty minutes early for her appointment and spent the time in the outer office, buttering up the secretary. From Mrs. Hirsch ('I'm not married, but Mrs. is so much more suitable for a woman of a certain age, dear') Peregrine had managed to discover who had keys to the inner office, what time Mrs. Hirsch arrived each morning and left in the afternoon, that Mrs. Blair was 'delicate,' and that the department store business was very lucrative. And that Joyce Hirsch had a cat named

Simpkins. All in all, it had been twenty minutes well spent. Now, seated in the inner sanctum, Peregrine gushed and giggled like the aspiring shopgirl she was supposed to be as her eyes wandered around the wood-panelled room, taking in every detail. If either of the Blairs had anything to hide, where would they put it?

'I'm so excited to have an interview for this job,' she said, adjusting her round-framed glasses. 'I've always loved Blair's Emporium, so working here would be an absolute dream come true for me!' Peregrine raised her voice a fraction and Terence Blair, signing papers at his own desk across the room, glanced up with a brief smile.

Peregrine ran a hand along the edge of the desk, admiring its polished surface, then leaned towards Colin eagerly. 'Can I ask—and I hope you don't think I'm forward, because I'm really not *that* kind of girl, it's just that I have a nose for perfumes and that sort of thing—what's that scent you're wearing? It's sort of mossy and lemony and spicy all at the same time! *So* masculine!'

Disconcerted, Colin stared at her for a moment, but there was nothing to see in Peregrine's face but eagerness.

'It's called Pour Monsieur. It's French.' He dropped his eyes back to the papers in front of him.

'French! Well, no wonder it's so nice. I'd love to go to France! That's where some of the best fashion comes from, isn't it? I've always been interested in fashion—that's a handsome suit you're wearing, by the way; you can tell a lot about a man by the way he dresses—and my late mother and I used to love shopping at Blair's. It was always an occasion when we'd travel into town, step through that big front door and...'

Peregrine continued to prattle on enthusiastically as Colin Blair scanned her job application and hastily concocted résumé.

'Well,' Colin said loudly, cutting through Peregrine's

monologue, 'Miss Astor certainly gives you a glowing reference: punctual, reliable, always well-groomed, shows initiative.'

He looked across at her, mouth pursed and eyes narrowed slightly in consideration.

'I try my best.' Peregrine smoothed a hand across her pigtailed hair. Behind the round lenses, her lashes fluttered.

'Thank you for coming in. I have a number of other candidates to interview, but we'll let you know.' Colin's tone was cool.

'Time is money. Stop wasting it!' The edict came from the other side of the room.

Peregrine and Colin both looked across at Terence Blair. He was staring at his son, while the pen in his right hand tapped impatiently on the desk blotter.

'Pardon, Father?' Colin's businesslike tone was gone, replaced by something Peregrine couldn't quite identify. Fear? Frustration? She filed the thought away.

'Sounds like you don't need to interview anyone else, Colin.' Terence Blair bent his head to his paperwork, ending the conversation.

Colin stared at his father for a moment longer, then glanced down at the application in front of him. He straightened his already-straight tie.

'You're aware that this is an entry-level position? Just running errands and such?'

'Oh, yes! I love Blair's, and I'm hoping this is just the first step. I really want to work my way up to the very top—a sales position on the cosmetics counter—and I'm willing to do *anything*!' Peregrine gave him her most winning smile.

'In that case, the job is yours. Only a one-month trial to begin with, but if that proves satisfactory, we'll consider making the position permanent. Five days a week, nine to five, half an hour for lunch. And we frown very much on gossip and talking to the press. There's been a bit of interest from the newspapers since…recently, so your discretion is imperative.'

'I understand completely. I'm known for my discretion.' Peregrine nodded solemnly.

'Welcome to Blair's.' Colin reached across the desk and shook her hand.

'When do I start?'

'As soon as you like.'

'Today? Right now?' Peregrine asked eagerly, widening her eyes in a show of excitement.

Across the room, Terence Blair chuckled. 'She's keen! With that attitude you'll go far, young lady. Maybe even head of cosmetics one day!'

'Do you think so, Mr. Blair?' Peregrine gasped.

'Yes, well, one step at a time.' Colin was all business again. 'If you go along to the personnel department, there's some paperwork to complete, then someone will get you a uniform, show you around and get you started on a few basic tasks. Give them this.' He scribbled something on a piece of paper and slid it across the desk.

'Thank you, Mr. Blair! You won't be disappointed!' Peregrine stood and gathered up the note and her handbag, beaming at Terence Blair.

The older man returned her smile. 'Nice to meet you, Miss…?'

'Foster. Penny Foster.'

'Nice to meet you, Miss Foster.' Terence Blair winked at her, and Peregrine responded with a waggly-fingered wave as she left the office.

She was in.

~

After a lightning tour that largely consisted of showing Peregrine where the time clock was and which areas were staff only, she was sent to take an urgent delivery of Vis a Vis to the fragrance counter. Ten minutes later, job done, she was lurking in ladieswear, hoping to find some of the house models who had been part of the murderous bridal fashion parade. From experience, Peregrine knew that the best way to avoid being noticed and told off by a more senior employee was to always look like you were in the middle of something. Moving quickly meant you were on an urgent errand, but when lingering was necessary, a slow and meticulous task was called for. Peregrine positioned herself next to a tabletop display of scarves and, looking around to be sure no one was watching, quickly reduced the entire lot to a jumbled mess. Then she began to carefully refold each one and stack them according to colour and price. She expected to be there for an hour at least, but not long after she'd started, Detective Steed stepped purposefully from one of the elevators. Peregrine angled her body slightly, hoping he wouldn't recognise her. Not yet, anyway.

'Detective Steed?' someone called from across the shop floor.

Peregrine looked in the direction of the voice. A large florid-faced man in a too-small suit was bearing down on the elevator bank.

'Harvey White of H. R. White's, the premier department store in town—and the safest. Ha!'

Detective Steed only had time to nod in acknowledgment before the elevator to his right pinged and the doors opened, disgorging Terence and Colin Blair.

'White!' hissed the elder Blair. 'Why are you in my store?'

'Just doing my civic duty,' said White with a smirk. 'The good detective requested my presence, so being the fine, upstanding citizen that I am, I complied.' He spread his arms wide and dipped his head in a mock bow.

Steed stepped between them. 'Thank you for coming, Mr. White. We've arranged for an interview room to be set up over here. If you'll come with me...' He tried to usher Harvey White away, but the other man had spotted Colin Blair standing a step behind his father.

'This must be the pup! Still trailing after Daddy.'

Terence took a menacing step forward, shoulders bunched, fists clenched.

'Father, customers,' Colin said quietly.

Immediately, Terence Blair deflated and his mouth, which had been in the process of curling into a snarl, reshaped itself into a stiff smile.

'You're right, Colin,' said Blair senior. 'We have customers. You remember what those look like, don't you, White?' Terence Blair smoothed down his tie and strolled away, hands behind his back, his son by his side.

Harvey White laughed and cupped a hand to the side of his mouth, ready to call after the retreating figures.

'Mr. White!' Steed used his cut-it-out voice, honed during several years as a uniformed officer. 'This way.' He ushered Mr. White through a staff-only door and along to an employee's tearoom that had been temporarily made over for police business. The detective only realised someone had followed them in when he heard the door close.

'Tea, gentlemen?' Peregrine asked, walking behind Harvey White to where a large urn steamed.

Steed frowned. It took him a moment to link Peregrine

Fisher's voice with the glasses, pigtails, and black-and-white Blair's pinafore of the woman in front of him—then his eyes widened in shock.

'Yeah, with plenty of sugar, love.' Harvey White leered at her.

'Detective?' She smiled sweetly at Steed.

'No. Thank you.' He turned to White, looked back at Peregrine, then forced himself to focus on the man in front of him. 'Barbie Jones. I understand she left your employ about six months ago. Is that correct?' Steed flipped open his notebook and waited.

'Left is putting it nicely. I gave her the boot.'

'You fired her?' Steed's eyes flicked involuntarily to Peregrine, but her back was turned as she fussed with cups and saucers. 'I was given to understand that she was the face of White's.' He looked past White again.

Peregrine half turned, glancing over her shoulder at him, eyebrows raised.

'What happened?' Steed persisted doggedly. 'Were you unhappy with Miss Jones's work for some reason?'

'She wasn't the right image for White's anymore. We're a family store, and I found out she no longer shared the same values. Barbie Jones was having a bit too much fun.'

Behind Harvey White's back, Peregrine had stopped making tea and turned around to give Detective Steed a meaningful look.

'Sorry, what?' Steed's confusion took in Peregrine and White, but it was White who answered.

'Come on, Detective! There are the good girls—the sort you take home to mother—and there are good-time girls: the sort your mother warned you about. I found out Barbie was trying to get that new pill: the one for single girls who like to...you know. That told me straight away exactly what kind of girl she was. I'm a Catholic—church every Sunday—and I have a lot of customers who were raised the same way. If it got out that the face of White's had the morals of an alley cat...'

Peregrine slammed a cupboard closed. 'Sorry.'

'So you fired Miss Jones for wanting the contraceptive pill?' The detective tried not to look at Peregrine, focusing on his notes.

'I'm not a heartless bastard! I offered to make an honest woman of her.'

'You...proposed?' Steed asked, incredulous. 'We have a police report claiming you tried to force yourself on her.'

Harvey White shrugged expansively. 'Women! You try to do the right thing, and they take it the wrong way. Never know what's good for them.'

Peregrine had stepped forward to deliver a cup of tea and was leaning over when White patted her backside. She yelped and splashed the liquid into his lap.

'Jeez, watch it!' he yelled.

'So sorry, sir.' Peregrine dropped a dishcloth in front of him.

'Like I was saying...' White jerked his head in Peregrine's direction. 'Anyway, it was a pity about Barbie Jones: she brought in customers. Good little earner, that redhead.' He looked down at his lap. 'Are we done? I've got to get cleaned up.'

'Yes, thank you, Mr. White. I'll be in touch if there's anything else.' Steed stood and shook hands, then escorted Harvey White out.

When he returned, Peregrine was sitting in the chair he'd just vacated, legs stretched out in front of her, drinking a cup of tea.

'Please tell me you think that old lech is guilty,' she said without bothering to look at Steed.

'It doesn't look as though Mr. White is particularly upset about losing his model to Blair's.'

'Yes, but Barbie turned him down, then tried to have him charged with assault. What would that do for his good Catholic image?' She pushed a teacup across the table to him.

'Except the charges went away.' He picked up the cup, sipped, and winced.

'Right.' Peregrine nodded, then noticed Steed's expression. 'Too sweet? Anyway, even if it wasn't Mr. White, we've got another suspect now.'

'We do? Who?' Steed forced himself to take another mouthful of tea.

'The boyfriend.'

'Miss Astor said Barbie didn't have a boyfriend.'

'Detective, if Barbie Jones was planning on taking the pill, she had a boyfriend.'

Steed looked at her, and Peregrine saw realisation dawn in his eyes.

'Anyway,' she said, 'I need to get back to work. You can fill me in on anything you find out later.'

James Steed opened his mouth, ready with a sharp retort, but Peregrine had already gone.

—

Peregrine checked her watch as she hurried through the ladieswear department, her sensible shoes soundless on the black-and-white floor. She needed to find Barbie's boyfriend and, from everything Florence had told her, the person most likely to know about that was Pansy Wing. The two models may not have been close, but in Peregrine's experience rivals knew just as many intimate details about each other as friends, sometimes more. The difference lay in how they got their information and what they did with it.

At this time of day, the house models would be in the corner of ladieswear devoted to couture. Here, the wealthiest customers—whose size and measurements were kept discreetly on file—could watch the models parade in the designs of their choice, observing the quality, fit, and movement of the clothing from every angle, without having to remove so much as a glove.

Peregrine rounded the corner and came to an abrupt halt. Pansy was walking towards her in a sapphire-blue silk cocktail dress. As she watched, the model stopped, turned, put a hand on her hip, and turned again.

'Too fast! Turn again, and this time pause. Give me a chance to see the back! I shouldn't have to tell you how to do your job. Barbie knew how to model properly.'

Until she'd started complaining, Peregrine hadn't noticed the woman sitting immediately to her right: Florence had described Maggie Blair to a T.

'Again, slowly,' Mrs. Blair said, then sighed. 'I don't know what we're going to do without Barbie. I suppose you think you'll be the star of the show from now on, but...' She sighed again as she looked Pansy up and down. 'I'm not sure how our customers will relate to a woman with your...exotic look.'

Pansy spun back, all her poise gone. 'This particular dress also comes in cherry red, Mrs. Blair,' she said in a tight voice.

'Red is for harlots! I'll take it in the blue. Terence has always loved me in blue. Next!' She waved a dismissive hand.

Peregrine followed as Pansy stalked off to change into another outfit, catching up with her in the dressing room. The model's hands were contorted behind her back as she struggled with a zipper, and Peregrine dashed forward to help.

'Old cow!' fumed Pansy, stepping out of the dress and kicking it into a corner. 'I've worked here for ten years and she's never once called me by my name. Probably doesn't even know what it is!' She wrenched another dress from its hanger.

'I know who you are.' Peregrine picked up the crumpled blue dress and shook it out. 'You're Pansy Wing, and you're one of the most famous models in this country.'

Pansy, wriggling into a new dress, paused with the fabric bunched around her hips. 'Do I know you?'

'No, I've only just started working here. I'm Penny Foster, and I'm a huge fan of yours! Your photographs and modelling work are always so beautiful. I just love your elegant style!'

Pansy tilted her chin and stared at the wall, her face freezing into a mask. 'Elegance is all about pretending you're somewhere else. Focus on the distance, think pleasant thoughts, and pretend you're made of plastic.' She broke her pose and yanked the dress the rest of the way up.

'Your work is so much more than that! It's almost art! And I suppose you're going to be Blair's top model now that Barbie Jones has…gone?' Peregrine widened her eyes behind the round-rimmed glasses.

'It was going to happen anyway. I hate to badmouth someone who's dead, but everyone knows Barbie's work had been slipping badly.'

'Slipping? How? Was she caught up with a new boyfriend or something?' Peregrine asked breathlessly, hoping gossip would get her what interrogation would not.

Pansy didn't disappoint. 'I don't think Barbie was seeing anyone; she would have been crowing about it if she was! No, she was just being even more of a pain than usual. Wouldn't come out drinking and partying with everyone, she was late in the mornings, *so* moody, wasn't eating properly... I mean, we all take care of our figures, but she was living on dry crackers and soda water!'

'*Was she?*' Peregrine realised she might have sounded too interested and softened her response. 'I mean, that sounds really difficult for you to have to deal with.'

She pulled up the zipper on Pansy's new dress and gave the hem a tug. Pansy turned to face her, hands on hips. The dress, a cream and gold brocade sheath, hugged her in all the right places.

'Will Maggie Blair be able to cope or does it emphasise my exotic looks?' Pansy asked, pulling a face.

'The only thing old Mrs. Blair needs to cope with is the fact that no matter what she thinks of your appearance, every dress she wears will always look better on you.' Peregrine smiled and was rewarded when the corner of Pansy's mouth curled up in a matching grin. Hopefully, Peregrine thought, she'd made an ally, or at least opened up a source of information. She gestured towards the shop floor. 'I should get back.'

'Yeah, and I should get this over with. Nice to meet you, Penny Foster.' Pansy plastered a beatific smile on her face and sailed out of the dressing room.

As she made her way back to the tearoom-cum-interview room, Peregrine saw Constable Connor walking swiftly through the lingerie department. The policewoman did a double take when she recognised Peregrine, then nodded in approval.

'Constable Connor,' said Peregrine. 'What are you doing here?'

'Just delivering the postmortem report to Detective Steed.'

'Do they let you drive a patrol car?' Peregrine asked enthusiastically.

'Hardly. I'm lucky if they reimburse me for the tram fare.' Fleur Connor grimaced. 'Speaking of which...' She raised a hand in farewell, and Peregrine continued on to the tearoom, where Detective Steed was standing, holding an open manila folder and leafing through its contents.

'Nice to see you let Constable Connor deliver other things besides cups of tea!'

Steed snapped the folder shut and moved to the other side of the table, causing Peregrine to smile.

'Relax! I'm not going to steal your postmortem report,' she said.

Steed raised his eyebrows, sat down, and put the file on the table in front of him, folding his hands over the top. 'Forgive me if I don't take your word for it.'

Peregrine shrugged and leaned a shoulder against the door-frame. 'So Barbie Jones was pregnant?'

'How did you...?' Steed's jaw dropped and he glanced involuntarily at the folder clamped beneath his hands.

'I just spoke to Pansy Wing, and she told me how Barbie had been acting recently. The soda and crackers diet was the clincher. Pity Pansy hadn't heard anything about a boyfriend. Have you had any luck there?'

Despite himself, Steed shook his head.

'Well, you know what that means!' Peregrine pushed herself off the doorframe and began pacing back and forth.

Steed watched her for a few seconds, a frown creasing his brow. 'Her boyfriend was shy?'

Peregrine stopped and gave him a pitying look. 'Not shy. It means he was taken.'

Steed still looked blank.

'Taken! Married, engaged, off the market, already had a

girlfriend!' She stopped pacing and put both hands on the table, leaning towards Steed. 'The sort of boyfriend who might be even more unhappy than usual to find out Barbie Jones was pregnant.'

Steed's eyes widened.

Peregrine tapped her fingers on the table. 'I'll see you later, Detective Steed. I've only got a few hours to go before my shift ends, and there are quite a few people I need to see.'

'You have to stop interfering in police business, Miss Fisher!'

But he was speaking to an empty room.

—

James Steed sat there in silence for a quarter of an hour or so. Outwardly, he didn't seem to be doing anything, but on the inside his mind was racing, occupied with the details of Barbie Jones's murder. Unfortunately, it didn't lead him anywhere.

'Good, you're still here.' Peregrine was in the doorway again. 'Detecting.'

'Miss Fisher.' Steed sighed. 'What do you want now? Because whatever it is, the answer is no.'

Peregrine made a show of lowering her glasses and peering at him over the top of the frames. 'Well, I was sent by Mr. Blair's secretary to tell you there was a phone call for you and to escort you to an extension, but I can just as easily relay your message to Inspector Sparrow and tell *him* the answer is no.' She turned and disappeared.

'No! I mean wait!' Steed jumped to his feet and hurried around the table. Hurtling through the door, he almost crashed into Peregrine, who was waiting just one step away.

'This way, Detective.' She grinned.

Peregrine took him out onto the shop floor and across to a deserted cashier's desk. 'Press that button for the switchboard operator and tell her who you are,' she instructed.

Steed picked up the receiver then stared at her pointedly. 'Don't you have somewhere you need to be?'

'Hmm? Oh, sorry,' Peregrine said and started to walk away.

Detective Steed pressed the button she'd indicated, and Peregrine immediately reversed direction and came to stand next to him.

He turned his back and hunched his shoulders. Peregrine leaned in.

'Inspector Sparrow?' Steed said, and immediately pulled the receiver away from his ear. There was no need for Peregrine to get close: she could hear every word clearly.

'Steed! I've got the chief commissioner breathing down my neck, damn it! I've just assured him everything is under control, but then I go looking for your report and there doesn't appear to be one. Where is it?'

'Sir—'

'It's bloody nonexistent, isn't it? Because instead of locking up the crazy cow who had the dress show, you're *still* down there wasting time on... What *are* you wasting time on?'

'The details—'

'Do. Not. Matter. Arrest that woman!' Sparrow spluttered, his voice made tinny by the phone line.

'Florence Astor? I don't believe we have enough evidence against her yet, sir.' Steed tried to sound firm but reasonable.

Peregrine leaned into the detective's line of sight and gave him a thumbs-up. He turned his back again.

'What more evidence do you bloody well need? She was there, she and Barbie doll had an all-in catfight the day before—'

'It wasn't quite—'

'*And,*' Sparrow went on, 'Astor's one of those mad witches who—'

Peregrine gasped and there was silence.

'Is someone there with you, Steed?' Sparrow's voice was suddenly quiet; it was far more intimidating than the full-volume tirade.

Steed widened his eyes at Peregrine and made a cutting motion across his throat. She nodded and pretended to button her lips. 'No, sir,' said Steed. 'There must be some static on the line.'

'I don't need any more bloody static from you or the phone company.' Sparrow was back at normal volume. 'So stop pissing around, show a bit of guts, and lock that woman up!' There was a loud click—actually more of a crash—and the connection was broken.

'You know Florence had nothing to do with it, right?' Peregrine said softly.

Steed sighed. 'Miss Fisher, I...' He shook his head in frustration. 'I have to go.'

'You can't arrest her just because he says so.'

'And I can't not arrest her because *you* say so,' he replied, settling his hat firmly on his head. 'Besides, Inspector Sparrow has Miss Astor in his sights. Trust me. It will be much better if I find her first.'

Peregrine rummaged in the pocket of her pinafore, pulling out a folded piece of paper which she passed to Detective Steed. 'You might need this then.'

'What is it?' he asked, unfolding it and reading Peregrine's loopy writing.

'I was going to go there after work. It's the address of Florence's dress salon.'

He refolded the paper and tapped it in the palm of his hand. 'Thank you, Miss Fisher.'

'Will you come to my place later? Tell me what you find?'

Steed hesitated, but Peregrine's concern was obvious.

'No promises,' he said gruffly.

'Thank you, Detective Steed.' She smiled.

Steed nodded in return, then Peregrine watched as he made his way across Blair's polished floor towards the elevators and was lost to sight behind a display of gleaming whitegoods.

—

It didn't take long for James Steed to walk from Blair's Emporium to the enclave of chic boutiques that was home to Florence Astor's salon, but on arrival he was frustrated to find the door firmly shut. There was no calligraphed sign to indicate the establishment was *Closed for lunch 1–2,* or the designer would be *Back in five minutes,* and knocking failed to produce a response. Steed cupped his hands against the glass and peered in, trying to see beyond the mannequins and the four-panel French room divider that made up the window display. He changed position, moving his head from side to side until he found the right angle.

The shop interior was completely empty. Not just empty of people, but devoid of everything: stock, fixtures, furnishings… Even the carpet was gone, exposing the bare wood of the floor. In fact, the only thing he could see was a haphazard pile of letters, spilled across the floorboards just behind the door. Clearly Florence Astor hadn't been here for some days.

Steed moved back to the door and assessed the situation. There was a small gap at the bottom—an obliging postman must have been stuffing the mail through that way—but rattling the knob only showed him that everything was tightly locked. A passerby stared curiously and Steed backed away, keen to avoid drawing attention. It was then he noticed the rubbish bin tucked just around the corner in the adjoining laneway. Sitting on top of the assorted detritus was a twisted wire coathanger. Steed grabbed it and wrestled with the wire until he was satisfied. Then, after checking for more curious pedestrians, he crouched down, pushed his makeshift hook under the door and slowly dragged Florence Astor's post out into the open. It took him several attempts, but within a few minutes he'd retrieved most of it. Discarding the coathanger, James Steed shuffled quickly through the pile before tucking everything into his pocket.

Now he really needed to find Florence Astor.

—

Peregrine opened the door almost as soon as Steed rang the bell. She'd changed out of her Blair's uniform and was now dressed in capri pants and a short-sleeved shirt in shades of pink and aqua.

'Did you find Florence? Is she okay?' Peregrine asked, bare feet slapping on the wooden stairs as she raced ahead of her guest and turned down the volume on the record player. 'Sorry, I was just doing my nails.' She held up a bottle of frosted pink polish and wiggled her toes for emphasis.

Steed was momentarily distracted, but then he pulled the bunch of envelopes from the pocket of his overcoat.

'To answer your questions, no, I didn't find her, and I don't know how she is. I was actually hoping she might be here.'

'Well, no,' Peregrine said, spreading her arms wide. 'You mean she wasn't at her salon?'

'Not only was she not at her salon, I'd say she hasn't been there for a week or more. The place was deserted, locked, and stripped of all furnishings. And there was all this'—he brandished the mail—'piled up behind her door.'

Steed passed the post to Peregrine and, as he had done earlier, she thumbed through the thick stack.

Peregrine frowned. 'I don't understand. Florence told me she was run off her feet finishing the collection for New York.'

'When you see Miss Astor, give her that lot and tell her I really do need to speak with her as soon as possible. There's something going on, and she clearly hasn't been straight with you.'

Peregrine nodded, subdued. 'Of course I'll tell her.'

Detective Steed studied her for a moment and seemed about to say something else, but he settled for a sombre nod. 'I'll let myself out,' he said.

But Peregrine wasn't listening. She was staring at the pile of envelopes in her hand, trying to understand what it meant, and wondering if she really was cut out to be a detective after all. She liked Florence, and all the other Adventuresses liked and respected her too. Was it possible they were all wrong? Peregrine hated the doubt that had crept into her mind, but she couldn't ignore what Steed had said: Florence was hiding something.

Peregrine threw herself down on the sofa and dropped the envelopes on the seat next to her. She picked up one, turned it over and hesitated. Then quickly, before she could change her mind, Peregrine stuck her thumb under the flap, ripped the envelope open, and drew out a single sheet of paper. It was a bill, and stamped across it in angry red letters were the words *Final Notice*.

She cast it aside and opened the next, and the next. Bill after bill, some long overdue, some with additional threats and demands, all for large amounts of money. It seemed Florence owed everyone, from the fabric supplier and the button maker to the electricity company and the Board of Works. And her landlord. In fact, as Peregrine discovered, Florence owed the landlord so much money that she had been served with an eviction notice.

'That explains the empty salon,' Peregrine murmured.

She worked her way through the pile, growing more and more concerned but also more confused: Florence hadn't said a word about any financial problems—but, even so, how could Florence's lack of money have anything to do with Barbie Jones's murder? Peregrine knew from years of experience that the first thing you did when you owed money was pack up and get out of town. At least, that's what she and her mother had always done.

She tore open the last envelope, expecting to find another letter from an irate creditor, but as she pulled it out Peregrine realised this was heavy paper, not the thin carbon triplicate of an invoice. She unfolded it and read. And felt her stomach drop.

'Oh, Florence,' she groaned.

Peregrine read the terse message again, but it was exactly the same the second time around. She was holding a letter of demand, but this was written by a lawyer on behalf of Miss Barbara Jones.

Florence owed Barbie Jones money, a lot of money, and Barbie Jones had wanted it back. Immediately.

Peregrine carefully folded the letter and tucked it back into the envelope. She needed to talk to Florence, and if the designer wasn't at the Adventuresses' Club, surely Birdie would know where to find her. Unless Florence had found somewhere else to work? Peregrine thought back to her first foray into the basement rooms of Blair's Emporium, and the door marked *Alterations* tucked in a dim corner. Florence deserved a chance to explain before Peregrine told anyone else about her money troubles, so if there was a chance she was holed up and working late at Blair's...

Besides, it wouldn't hurt for Peregrine to have another look at the scene of the crime.

Twelve

Peregrine was not surprised to find her aunt's wardrobe included a variety of outfits suitable for covert night-time excursions: they were not only darkly coloured; they were also cut for ease of movement, enabling the wearer to run, jump, or engage in any number of athletic pursuits without so much as straining a seam. Needless to say, they all came equipped with numerous pockets and were stylish enough to pass unremarked in all but the most formal of situations. She selected fitted pants, a black turtleneck, and an almost space-age jacket with a hood large enough to shadow her face if necessary. The shoe cupboard yielded the perfect pair of black plimsolls—exactly the sort of thing for scaling walls and walking on roofs, Peregrine thought ruefully—and she was ready to go.

Cruising slowly past Blair's Emporium in the Austin-Healey, Peregrine was on high alert for any sign of police or security guards, but everything seemed still: no uniformed officers on the street, no moving shadows within. She drove a few blocks farther uptown, parked the convertible in a quiet side street, and made her way back to the store on foot. Although it was close to 11 p.m., there were still a few people out on the city streets, and from somewhere Peregrine could hear a jazz quartet playing, experimenting with time signatures as they rolled the music from piano to saxophone to bass to drums before all diving into the finale. Realisation hit her as she listened to the music, and she glanced down at her outfit. Perfect. She had inadvertently come disguised as a beatnik.

The facade of Blair's Emporium was ablaze with lights, but Peregrine had no intention of breaking in through the main door. Instead, she loitered in front of the windows, waiting until there was no passing traffic before slipping down a narrow lane along the side of the building and around to the trade entrance. The lane was dark, lit only by a single light suspended over the back door to Blair's. Peregrine pulled a bobby pin from her hair and began to twist it, keeping to the deeper pockets of night as she covered the final few feet. She was reaching for the lock when suddenly the handle turned and the door began to open. Peregrine leaped back then darted behind an assortment of rubbish bins and old wooden crates, where she crouched, waiting to see who would come out. Cautiously, she raised her head until her eyes were just above the level of the pile of crates. A security guard was standing in front of the doorway, soft light spilling from the store's interior. He looked up and down the lane, inhaled deeply, then fumbled in his shirt pocket, pulled out a packet of cigarettes, and lit up.

Peregrine eyed the tantalisingly open door then lowered her head and eased herself backwards. There wasn't enough light to see anything much here so, carefully, she ran her hands over the ground in slowly-widening sweeps. On the third pass with her left hand her questing fingers brushed against something and she stopped, reversed the movement, and prodded the object:

cold and smooth. A bottle. Perfect. She hefted it in one hand then inched to the edge of her hiding place.

The guard was still there, rocking backwards and forwards on the balls of his feet as he smoked, staring up at the night sky. Peregrine waited until he shifted his weight, turning ever so slightly away from her. Then she lobbed the bottle into the air, watching as it arced over the guard's head to crash down in the darkness somewhere on the other side of the door.

'Who's there?' the guard called, flicking his cigarette to the ground. 'Who's there?' He fumbled at his belt for a moment, then a powerful torch beam lit up the brick wall on the opposite side of the lane. Peregrine ducked back out of sight, keeping one eye on the guard.

He shone his torch in the direction the noise had come from, then stepped away from the door, turned his back to Peregrine's hiding spot and slowly began to walk, moving his torch left and right as he probed every dark nook and shadowy angle.

Peregrine counted to three then stood and raced for the entrance, her rubber soles barely a whisper on the cobblestones. She sprang through the open door and kept going, just in case the guard decided to return, and only slowed when she'd put a few corners and a good length of passageway between them.

Everything looked different at night. In the glow of the dim, sulphurous security lights, it took Peregrine a moment to get her bearings, but then she made her way directly to the stairs and down to the basement storage area. The crowd of mannequins was even creepier in the half-dark, but Peregrine ignored them, drawn across the room by a soft whirring sound emanating from behind the closed door marked *Alterations*. Carefully, she eased the door open and peered around it to see Florence, head bent over a sewing machine, all her attention focused on the black fabric she was slowly feeding beneath the needle. Peregrine let out a sigh of relief and stepped into the room.

Florence jumped, her foot slipping from the sewing machine's power pedal. 'Good God!' she yelped. 'Oh, it's you, Peregrine. What are you doing here at this hour, and why on earth are you sneaking up on me?' She put a hand to her chest.

'Sorry. I didn't mean to startle you.' Peregrine looked around the tiny room, taking in the bolts of fabric, the single rack of clothes—some finished, some little more than tacked-together shapes—and the professional-looking Bernina sewing machine. The last time she'd been in this room, it had looked as though it was hardly used, but now it seemed Florence had taken over the space. Peregrine inhaled. The faint smell of machine oil hung in the air, a sign that Florence had been here for hours, running the machine until its motor grew hot.

'What *are* you doing here?' Florence asked again.

'Looking for you.' Peregrine gestured to the rack of clothes. 'Florence, what's going on?'

'Oh, I just had a few last-minute things I needed to finish off. These are for Blair's, so it's easier to do them here than take them back to the salon.' She smiled broadly at Peregrine.

'Florence…' Peregrine paused, wanting to be gentle. 'I know about the salon. Is this where you're doing all your work?'

Florence's shoulders sagged and tears welled in her eyes. 'The landlord put up the rent. I had to get out.'

'Come on, Florence—I said I knew. It's not just the rent.' Peregrine pulled the bunch of envelopes from the pocket of her jacket and put them down in front of the other woman.

Picking one up, Florence fingered the open flap, swallowed, and met Peregrine's worried eyes. 'I'm in quite a bit of debt, actually.'

Peregrine perched on the end of the worktable. 'But I

thought you were doing really well! Your clothes are in all the magazines, you've got the wallpaper and interior design range, and Samuel said a department store in New York was going to stock your label.'

A lone tear traced its way down Florence's cheek. 'The American deal fell through, but I'd already borrowed heavily for fabrics and notions… I wanted it to be the most eye-popping collection I'd ever put together! I had to let all my cutters and seamstresses go, and they've all been with me for years. I thought the bridal show might be enough to keep things afloat but then…'

Peregrine put her hand over Florence's and gave it a gentle squeeze. 'Why didn't you say something to Birdie? Or anyone?'

'I thought I could fix it. And I was so ashamed and embarrassed. How could I have let this happen? I didn't want Birdie to know. She'd try to offer me money, and the club doesn't have any. Bad enough for Birdie and the Adventuresses to think I'm a failure without ruining them too.'

'No one would ever think of you as a failure, Florence.' Peregrine paused then nodded at the pile of letters. 'There's one in there from a lawyer. Barbie Jones's lawyer. You owed her money too, and she wanted it.'

Florence squeezed her eyes closed. 'I hadn't paid her for her catwalk work for a while—well, not with money. I'd been making her one-of-a-kind dresses instead. But even before that, before everything fell apart, I convinced Barbie to invest her own money in the Florence Astor label. Promised her she'd not only make a profit, I'd make sure she modelled in New York. It would've launched her career in America.'

'How did she find out things had come undone?'

Florence shook her head vigorously, as though she didn't

want to even think about it. 'I don't know. Gossip? Friends somewhere? She confronted me. Demanded to know what was going on, then demanded her money. I begged her for time, but...' She flicked a finger at the pile of letters, causing them to spill across the table.

'When? When did she confront you?'

Florence looked at Peregrine. Her face was bleak. 'The day before the bridal show.'

'Did you know she was pregnant?'

'What? No!'

'Maybe she didn't know your business was in trouble. Maybe she just realised that being pregnant meant she couldn't have a career in New York, and she'd need her money back to plan for the future.'

'It doesn't matter, does it? Poor Barbie's dead now, and if people weren't talking about me last week, they soon will be.'

'People talking isn't important. What is important is that you owed Barbie money and argued about it. It's just a matter of time before the police find out—if they haven't already. You need to go and talk to Detective Steed, Florence, and tell him everything.'

'He'll think I killed her.'

'I'm afraid Sparrow's already trying to pin Barbie's murder on you. There's no sense in giving him the satisfaction of dragging you down to the police station; much better if you talk to Steed. I'll come with you.'

Florence gave Peregrine a weak smile. 'Thank you, but I don't know if I can do it. Besides'—she smoothed the black fabric that was suspended halfway through the sewing machine—'I need to finish this dress. I *have* to finish it.'

Peregrine studied Florence. She could see how much it

meant to the designer to complete the dress she was working on. It was something Peregrine understood: to have some sense of accomplishment, however small, when everything in your life seemed to be in tatters.

'I'll wait,' she said.

'No, I'm going to be a while.'

'I don't mind. You shouldn't be here alone.'

'I'll be fine. It won't be the first time I've sat in this room until the early hours. Go.' Florence tipped her head towards the door.

'If you're sure...' Peregrine hesitated.

'Yes! Go!'

'And in the morning, I'll come with you to the police station.'

Florence drew in a deep, shuddering breath and nodded. Then she grabbed Peregrine's hand and squeezed, hard. 'You're so like your aunt. Thank you, Peregrine.'

Peregrine lingered in the doorway, watching as Florence adjusted the needle and began to sew again. Then she left, pulling the door closed behind her. The sound of the sewing machine drifted after her through the basement, into the stair-well, and seemed to follow her up and through the silent store until finally Peregrine found a door she could unlock. She let herself out into the night.

—

Back at what she was starting to think of as her home, Peregrine changed into a silk robe and stood in front of the wall of glass, looking out at the night-time city. She had gone to Blair's intending to search for clues, but after hearing Florence's story and seeing her despair, it would have been awkward to hang around and rifle through the storeroom; almost as though she didn't believe Florence's version of events and was looking for something to corroborate the story. And if there was one thing Peregrine knew for sure it was that, whatever was going on with money, Florence Astor had not killed Barbie Jones. She didn't know how or why she was so certain, but she was, and nothing mattered more than clearing Florence of any allegations Inspector Sparrow could throw at her. Tomorrow they would go to the police and then, when Peregrine was back at Blair's, Penny Foster would find an excuse to visit the storeroom.

Peregrine climbed into the pink bed, nestling deep into the mound of pillows, but it was a long time before she finally drifted off to sleep.

~

When she staggered out in the morning, Peregrine half expected to find Florence in the kitchen, but there was no welcoming aroma of coffee, and the stove was cold. She stood still for a moment, feeling the house around her, and knew she was alone.

Peregrine realised she had no idea where Florence lived, but a call to the Adventuresses' Club would quickly solve that. First, though, she needed a shower and coffee, although not necessarily in that order. In the end, she took her coffee into the bathroom, where she gazed longingly at the deep bathtub before settling for a hot shower, her coffee cup in easy reach. It wasn't the most leisurely start to the day, but it certainly woke her up.

Back in her aunt's silk robe, Peregrine settled on the sofa, tucked her legs up and picked up the blue Ericofon telephone. Her first call was to the club. Samuel answered, but when

Peregrine told him why she was calling, he quickly passed the phone to Birdie.

'Are you sure about Florence's salon?'

'Good morning to you too, Birdie,' said Peregrine. 'Yes. She told me everything last night.'

'And you left her working at Blair's.' It was a statement, not a question.

'Florence wanted to finish the dress she was working on, and then I was going to take her to see Detective Steed this morning so she can clear everything up. I just assumed she'd come here when she was done.' Peregrine sipped from her second cup of coffee.

'Well, she's not here either.'

'I didn't think she was. I just wanted her address or phone number.'

Birdie was silent, although Peregrine was sure she could hear the sound of Birdie's finger tapping, fast and anxious, on the polished wood of the table in the hall of the Adventuresses' Club.

'I'll go to Florence's apartment and take her to the police station. I've dealt with Sparrow before when he's tried this sort of thing, and I know what to expect. And I'll call Adventuress Bevan. She's a lawyer—actually likely to be appointed a Justice of the Supreme Court soon, if the boys' club doesn't close ranks—and I'll have her meet us there. You go to Blair's as usual. It's possible Florence simply worked through the night and is exactly where you left her. If not, it's more important than ever that you find Barbie Jones's killer.'

Peregrine imagined Birdie standing in the vast hallway, coloured by morning light filtering through the stained-glass panels that flanked the club's front door. She could picture the

Adventuress with a straight back and determined expression, fully dressed in her jodhpurs and sweater, motorcycle boots firmly buckled. Somehow—even in her mind—Peregrine couldn't see Birdie in a dressing gown and slippers. It just seemed so…unprepared.

'Peregrine? Are you still there?' Birdie barked down the line.

'Yes. I was just thinking we need to prepare for anything, and that sounds like a plan covering all the possibilities. Although I'd really like to tackle Sparrow myself.'

'Don't worry. I'm sure you'll have plenty of opportunities for that in the future,' said Birdie grimly.

'In that case, I'd better get to Blair's. If I find Florence, I'll get her to call you; if not, I'll come to Greenwood Place after work.'

—

As far as Peregrine was concerned, the role of Penny Foster, Girl Friday, didn't extend to catching a tram to work like most other employees in the city. Unfortunately, that meant parking the Austin-Healey several blocks away, where no one from the store would see it, then walking back to Blair's. Under the circumstances, it was a hardship she was quite prepared to live with.

Driving in that morning, shifting gears as she accelerated and wove through traffic, Peregrine found herself thinking about Eric and how much he'd love her new car. Then she realised with a start that she'd been too busy to miss him, and felt a pang of regret. The note she'd left had only said she was coming to Melbourne: perhaps she should write again, send Eric her address? Or maybe not. They'd had fun, but he was so much a part of her old life… She shook her head, chasing away the thoughts. Right now, finding Florence was all that mattered. She could sort out her feelings for Eric later. Peregrine spun the wheel, sending the Austin-Healey powering around the final corner.

Several men stared with open envy as the convertible swung smoothly to the kerb, but covetousness turned to confusion when Peregrine stepped from the car dressed in her black-and-white pinafore and sensible shoes, with Penny Foster's glasses and hair rounding out the outfit. Two young men who had moved closer to inspect the car now turned their eyes on her.

'Can't be hers,' said one, loudly enough for Peregrine to hear. 'Too much car for a girl like that.'

The second one laughed. 'Yer not wrong there.'

Peregrine pulled off her glasses and walked straight up to them, watching their eyes widen with shock. She stood toe to toe with the first one. 'I'd offer you a spin—one hundred and fifteen miles per hour—but you know what? I think it would be way too much car for a couple of little boys like you.'

Then without another word she strolled away, leaving them standing on the footpath, mouths hanging open in astonishment.

Ten minutes later Peregrine joined the stream of men and women making their way through the employees' entrance of Blair's Emporium. As soon as she was inside, she knew something was wrong. The air crackled with tension and the buzz of voices. Everywhere she looked, members of staff were huddled together, talking in low tones, anxious eyes sliding left and right. And no one seemed to be heading out to the shop floor.

'What's going on?' Peregrine asked the nearest person, an immaculately made-up young woman whom she vaguely recognised from one of the accessories counters.

The girl leaned in and whispered, 'The police are here again and they're not letting any of us in!' Her voice was breathless with excitement. 'Some of the girls are saying Mrs. Blair's finally lost her marbles and cut all the frocks to ribbons, but the lads think there's been a holdup!'

Peregrine felt her stomach clench and pushed past the girl. If the police were here, she didn't think it was because Mrs. Blair had damaged the stock.

'Hey!' the girl huffed.

But Peregrine wasn't listening. She excused her way through the milling crowd until she reached the front, where a police constable suddenly stepped into her path, barring her from going any further.

'Sorry, miss, can't let anyone through,' he said, sounding officious and not at all sorry.

'I'm looking for Detective James Steed,' Peregrine replied.

'Detective Steed? He's rather busy, miss.'

'I have something important to tell him.'

The officer looked at her determined face, then over his shoulder. 'I can see that he gets a message…' he began, but Peregrine had already ducked past him and was hurrying directly to the elevators, where a knot of people were gathered. Even from thirty yards away she could see Steed, his lean frame towering a few inches above the others. A flashbulb popped, and as he turned to avoid the glare, he saw her approaching and strode forward to intercept her.

'Miss Fisher!'

'What is it?' She tried to dodge around him, but Steed stepped with her, blocking the way.

Then he put a restraining hand on her arm and pulled her in close, lowering his head and speaking softly. 'Miss Fisher.'

The tone of his voice sent a shiver through her. She looked up at him.

He studied her face for a moment. 'It's Florence Astor.'

On some level Peregrine knew what he was trying to tell her, but she still asked, 'Is she okay?'

James Steed shook his head very slightly. 'I'm afraid she's dead.'

Peregrine pulled off her glasses so she could look at him properly. 'I don't understand,' she said. 'I came to talk to her last night, down in the alterations room. We were going to come and see you today.'

She shook off his hand and ran the final few steps. Steed caught up with her just as she reached the open doors of the elevator, this time grabbing her arm tightly and pulling her to a stop.

There was no elevator.

But from the ground floor where they stood, it was possible to look down the shaft and see the roof of the elevator car where it sat, parked in the basement level. And on the roof of the car lay Florence, oddly crumpled, one shoe missing, and a pool of blood around her head.

An anguished groan escaped from Peregrine and she whirled to face Steed. 'What? How?'

He put an arm around her, easing her back from the void. 'The doors on the third floor are wedged open with a chair,' he said gently. 'We need to make a formal identification, and the coroner will have to carry out a…give his report.'

'No.'

'I'm very sorry, Miss Fisher.'

'I thought she'd be fine. She was a bit upset but…I should never have left her alone.' Peregrine stifled a sob. 'Some detective if I can't even…'

Steed led her gently to an armchair, one of a number dotted throughout the store for the benefit of weary shoppers and bored husbands. 'This is not your fault,' he said firmly.

'What, are you encouraging me to be a detective now?' Peregrine asked bitterly. 'I don't know what I was thinking, why I thought I could... But that's it. I'm done.'

'You're not going to give up, are you?'

Peregrine stared at him, her face bleak and streaked with tears. 'You and Birdie think I only started this detective work for a bit of fun, but that's not true. I did it because Florence Astor asked for my help, and I know from my own experience how bad things have to be before you do that. That's why I said I'd investigate: because someone I'd only just met was desperate. And then, when I got to know her, Florence was so lovely and kind! She became one of the only friends I have in this city, and I didn't just let her down, I—' Peregrine's voice cracked as she roughly swiped her hands beneath her eyes. 'Who would do something like that to Florence?'

Steed frowned then crouched down next to her, hands on the arm of the chair. 'You think somebody...?'

'What else? Florence told me she'd be fine, and like an idiot I let her convince me, and I left her in that basement all alone.'

'Miss Fisher, Inspector Sparrow believes it's a case of suicide. He's already saying Miss Astor murdered Barbie Jones and was then so consumed by guilt that she killed herself.'

'Suicide?' Peregrine exclaimed loudly, making Steed wince. 'No,' she said fiercely. 'Florence Astor did not kill Barbie Jones, and she did not kill herself. I don't believe it.' She looked at him. 'And you don't either, do you? Regardless of what Sparrow says!'

'It adds up,' Steed said, but there was no conviction in his voice.

'Oh, no! And if you and your boss think you're going to pin Barbie's death on Florence and sweep a second murder under the carpet, you'd better think again!'

Peregrine pushed herself out of the chair and straightened her pinafore, then started towards the staff-only access to the basement stairs, her footsteps quick and decisive.

'Miss Fisher!' Steed called. He glanced at the police and other assorted officials, some of whom were staring back with undisguised curiosity. 'Damn it,' he muttered, and set off in pursuit.

By the time Detective Steed caught up with her, Peregrine was standing outside the door to the alterations room, holding the doorknob but unable to bring herself to turn it.

'This is where I left her last night,' Peregrine said as Steed came to stand next to her. She didn't look at him, instead staring at her hand on the knob.

Steed edged her out of the way. 'I should go in first. Miss Astor might have left a note.'

Now Peregrine rounded on him and her eyes flashed angrily. 'Florence did not kill herself. You could at least keep an open mind! Aren't detectives supposed to get evidence first and then work out what happened, rather than deciding what happened and then trying to make the facts fit?'

'The facts...' Steed shook his head. 'Let's see what's in here, shall we?' He pushed open the door and, after a quick glance, allowed Peregrine to precede him into the room.

It was all perfectly ordinary.

The sewing machine was draped in a cover, the bolts of fabric were propped tidily in a corner, and a dozen or so dresses in various states of completion hung on the rolling rack that sat against one wall. On the end of the rack was a garment bag, while a large Hermès tote, presumably belonging to Florence, sat on the floor near the door.

'Does anything stand out?' asked Steed.

'Well, for starters there's no note,' said Peregrine briskly.

Steed opened his mouth, but she held up a hand, cutting off whatever he was about to say.

'When I left she was still working on a black dress and that'—she pointed to the garment bag—'wasn't there. I don't remember seeing her tote next to the door either. It looks like she'd packed up and was about to leave.'

Steed crossed to the garment bag and used the end of his pen to push the zip down, just enough to see that it contained a black dress. He returned to Florence's bag, crouching next to it on the floor. It was open, some of the contents clearly visible. He peered more closely, looked at Peregrine hovering nearby, then reached in with his pen and—being careful not to touch anything with his hand—fished around for a moment. When he pulled the pen out again, there was a single stocking suspended from its tip: a stocking with an open diamond pattern.

Detective Steed held the stocking in the air between them. There was moment's silence, then Peregrine threw up her hands in exasperation.

'Great!' she exclaimed. 'You've found the stocking that was used to strangle Barbie Jones! Do you really think if Florence was the killer she'd be carrying it around with her? Anyone could have put that there, and you know it.' She marched out of the room.

'You've got to admit it makes sense, though,' Steed called to her retreating figure. 'Inspector Sparrow might be right!'

But Peregrine wasn't listening. She disappeared behind a row of shelves. Seconds passed.

'Detective!' Peregrine called. Her voice carried a note of urgency, and Steed dropped the stocking back into the bag. As he straightened up she reappeared, one arm extended in front of her. Dangling from the end of her fingers by its sling-back strap was a lady's black shoe, its spiked heel bent but still attached to the sole.

'Recognise this?' she asked him.

'It looks like the one found with Miss Astor.'

'And?'

'The heel is broken.'

Peregrine twisted the shoe around so he could see the front, holding it close to the detective's face. 'Now look at the toe.'

'It's badly scuffed,' Steed said.

'Exactly!' Peregrine said triumphantly.

Steed rubbed a hand across his jaw and his brow furrowed.

'Don't you see what this means?'

'Florence broke her shoe so left it behind?'

Peregrine frowned. 'Are you *trying* to annoy me?'

'I'd never do that.' Steed held up his hands in surrender. 'Besides, I thought you were giving up on being a detective.'

'How can I when your boss is trying to frame Florence and you clearly don't understand fashion?'

'I admit my sartorial education was not extensive, but that's all I'll admit.'

Peregrine's eyebrows rose. 'First of all, no woman—let alone a designer like Florence—would go out in shoes scuffed so badly. Second, this is an expensive shoe, and heels don't just break on a flat floor. And third...' She looked at him.

'Go on,' said Steed.

'Third, are you seriously going to tell me Florence limped up to the third floor in one shoe before throwing herself down the elevator shaft?'

'I see your point.'

'Someone attacked Florence here and her shoe was damaged and lost in the scuffle.'

'Then the killer tried to make it look like suicide by throwing her down the shaft,' Steed said, his eyes alight as the pieces fell into place.

'Welcome to the murder investigation, Detective. I told you Florence wouldn't kill herself.'

Suddenly Peregrine went white and the shoe fell from her hand, clattering to the concrete floor. 'Oh,' she groaned. 'You don't think Florence was still alive when—' She put a hand to her mouth.

Without thinking, Steed put an arm around her, drawing her in close. 'Don't think about it. The coroner will be able to tell us, but you can't dwell on that sort of thing or you'll be no good to anyone.'

Peregrine allowed herself to be held, and for a brief spell she relaxed. Then she gathered herself together and straightened up. 'Florence must have known something about Barbie's death.'

'Or seen someone or something...' Steed trailed off, his eyes darting around the basement. Then he looked at Peregrine again. 'Go home, Miss Fisher, just for today.'

'But I should—'

'You've had an awful shock. Whatever you should do can wait one day. Leave the investigation to me: it is my job, after all. Besides, I think right now Miss Birnside might need you more than Blair's Emporium needs a Girl Friday.'

Peregrine nodded. 'Birdie will be crushed. I should be the one to tell her.'

With his arm still resting lightly around her, Steed began to guide Peregrine towards the exit.

Just then, a loud crash came from the other side of the basement, causing them both to jump. The storeman emerged from the shadows. Once again, he had a shop dummy under each arm.

'Mr. Knox,' Steed said, in a way that was both question and acknowledgment.

'Oh. Detective. Miss.' Knox looked first at Steed then at Peregrine, light glinting off his glasses. 'Not in your way, am I? I was told I could just get on with things.'

'By...?' Steed let the question hang in the air.

Knox licked his lips anxiously. 'One of the other policemen.' He hefted the mannequins under his arms. 'It's just that I have to look after my ladies. If I'm not careful, the salespeople move them around, and they get hurt—damaged. One of the girls even went missing!'

'A missing girl?' Steed asked, suddenly tense.

The storeman jerked his head to the left. 'Audrey here,' he said, indicating the mannequin under his arm. Peregrine and Steed dutifully looked at the blank-faced plaster figure, currently dressed in a green mini.

Steed's shoulders dropped, and he let out a heavy breath.

'Don't you worry, Detective—I knew she'd be about somewhere so I hunted her down!'

Peregrine winced, but Knox didn't seem to notice.

'She was here all along, just stuck in a corner over there. Only she's missing an arm. How someone managed to lose her arm, I'll never know. But I'll find it or get her a new one. Either way, she'll soon be back to her lovely self and ready for the shop floor!'

'Fine, Mr. Knox.' Steed inclined his head, inviting the other man to pass. 'Just stay out of the alterations room until further notice, all right?'

'Of course.' Knox's face was unreadable behind his thick glasses as he effortlessly carried the two dummies past them, into the section of the basement set aside for an assortment of male and female mannequins and torsos. Peregrine and Steed watched as he carefully stood each figure upright, gently dusted them off, and pulled a wig—long and black—from the pocket of his coat. Reverently Knox stroked Audrey's bald head before placing the wig on the other mannequin and adjusting the angle of its fringe, murmuring to both inert forms as he did so.

'Is it just because I'm a woman that I think the way he's acting is really creepy?' Peregrine whispered.

'No. He is genuinely weird,' Steed whispered back, then raised his voice. 'We'll let you get on with your work, Mr. Knox!'

'Hmm? Oh, right you are!' Knox began whistling a tune to himself.

As she and Detective Steed walked out of Blair's Emporium and into the morning sunshine, Peregrine still had the melody stuck in her head. It wasn't until she'd walked all the way back to the Austin-Healey and was sitting behind the wheel that she remembered the name of the tune.

The storeman had been whistling a song called 'Endless Sleep.'

Thirteen

The rest of the day was a blur. There was no need for Peregrine to break the news to the members of the Adventuresses' Club: when Birdie had gone to look for Florence, the police were already at her apartment. Peregrine arrived to find the mansion on Greenwood Place strangely silent, its normal undercurrent of activity and enterprise replaced by a heaviness that seemed to squeeze the air out of every room.

Birdie spent the afternoon with a glass of whisky at her elbow, seesawing between sorrow and anger, her rage directed at Sparrow, police, men in general and herself, for not being there when Florence needed her.

'It seems to be something I'm good at,' she told Peregrine in an unguarded moment. 'Not being there when it matters most.'

'If anyone's to blame, it's me,' Peregrine responded. She was sitting sideways in a large wingback chair, her legs dangling over one of the arms.

Dirty coffee cups and crystal tumblers were scattered about the room, and a plate of sandwiches, their edges dry and curling, lay untouched on the table. Violetta and Samuel were seated together on an overstuffed sofa, but the other Adventuresses had retreated to different parts of the house, unwilling to intrude on their president's raw grief.

'Neither of you is to blame,' Violetta said, quietly but firmly.

Peregrine and Birdie both turned to her in surprise; Violetta had been largely silent since hearing the news and they had all but forgotten she was in the room.

'We *know* Florence didn't do anything, either to herself or to Barbie Jones, therefore there was nothing for either of you to see in her demeanour to provoke a reaction. The only person to blame is the person who murdered her.' Violetta nodded once for emphasis.

'Violetta's right.' Samuel leaned forward. 'And this is getting us nowhere. Peregrine, you need to get back to Blair's.'

Peregrine nodded. 'I think so too, although I thought I might stay here tonight.' She inclined her head very slightly in Birdie's direction.

'Yes.' Samuel's voice was full of relief. 'I think that's a very good idea.'

'Not on my account,' said Birdie, suddenly defensive.

'No, no,' Peregrine replied. 'Just until we have a better idea of what's going on.'

Now Birdie sat up and rested her forearms on her thighs. 'But that's exactly the problem, isn't it? We have no idea what's going on! If Florence was killed because she knew something about Barbie's death, why didn't she tell someone?'

'Maybe she didn't think it was important.' Peregrine swivelled around and put her feet on the floor.

'Or it was something she only found out last night?' said Samuel.

The energy in the room had changed.

'Could it be that Barbie and Florence were killed for the same reason?' asked Violetta. 'I mean, not because of something Florence discovered about Barbie's murder, but something that had happened in the past, to both of them?'

Everyone stared at her for a moment, then Samuel's eyes widened and he pointed an emphatic finger at her. 'You mean like Barbie owed someone else money—which is why she tried to get it back from Florence—and because *Barbie* didn't have it, she was killed, and then the same person came after Florence?'

Violetta nodded enthusiastically but Peregrine wrinkled her nose.

'I suppose it's possible, but it sounds very confusing,' she said.

'Peregrine's right,' Birdie said. 'You're making it too complicated.'

Violetta shrugged. 'It's just a hypothesis. It's what scientists do: look for different explanations and ways to refute the idea that something occurred by chance.'

'We already know that Florence's murder is connected to Barbie's,' Peregrine objected. 'She wasn't just a random victim.'

'Ah, you know it, but you have to prove it. Science and investigation—both rely on solid evidence!'

'At the moment, all I know is that Barbie Jones was pregnant and no one seems to have any idea who her boyfriend was.' Peregrine stood up as she spoke and idly picked up a sandwich, then just as quickly put it down again.

'So...' said Birdie.

'So that's where I'll start. Tomorrow.'

Peregrine and Birdie looked at each other. Nothing was said, but something passed between them: a resolve, an agreement not to rest until the person who had killed Barbie and Florence was caught.

—

The next morning Peregrine was back at Blair's Emporium in her Penny Foster guise. She had come armed with her own black clipboard and a range of excuses as to what she was actually doing, from checking stock levels to monitoring customer interest in displays and sales. It worked very well, enabling her to move about the store with ease, but by late morning it had brought her no closer to learning anything about Barbie Jones. She'd eavesdropped, gossiped, and even asked a couple of pointed questions, but no one admitted to knowing about a boyfriend. Peregrine had also ventured into the menswear and appliances departments in the hope that Barbie's mystery man might be one of the salesmen, and either the urge for a bit of locker-room bragging or shifty avoidance would point her in the right direction. A couple of young men had in fact eagerly confessed to a relationship with the stunningly beautiful model, but the first one was howled down by his mates, and the second one blanched and began to stammer and backtrack when Peregrine hinted at the possibility of a pregnancy. She left convinced that whoever Barbie's boyfriend had been, he wasn't one of the salesmen on Blair's shop floor.

Peregrine had just decided to try her luck with Pansy Wing and the other house models when she rounded a corner and almost crashed into Maggie Blair, a pile of shopping bags and hat boxes at her feet.

'Mrs. Blair!'

'Ah, Miss Foster! Excellent timing!' Colin Blair appeared from behind his mother.

'Hello, Mr. Blair.' Peregrine brandished the clipboard. 'I was just...'

He shook his head then waved a hand towards the pile of shopping. 'Whatever you're doing can wait. Mother has been rather extravagant this morning. Would you take all this up to the office and leave it with Mrs. Hirsch?'

'Of course, Mr. Blair.' Peregrine smiled at the older woman, whose attention seemed to be entirely taken with a display of gloves. 'That's a lovely necklace you're wearing, Mrs. Blair. Most unusual.'

'Hmm?' Mrs. Blair looked down at her décolletage and lifted the necklace, holding it out for Peregrine to admire. The long gold chain was interspersed with ruby-red beads and at the very end hung a large gold disc, decorated with an intricate cloisonné pattern in shades of red and blue.

'I've never seen anything quite like it,' said Peregrine, bending in for a closer look.

'That's hardly surprising, dear. You won't find anything like it in this country! My husband bought it for me on one of his overseas trips. He's so thoughtful like that, always buying me gifts, and each time it's something special and unique.'

Colin Blair cleared his throat and glanced pointedly at his watch.

'Thank you for showing me, Mrs. Blair.' Peregrine began to gather up the boxes and bags. 'I'd best get your things up to Mrs. Hirsch now.'

'Oh.' Colin Blair reached into his pocket and handed Peregrine another small package, this one wrapped in plain brown paper. 'Give that to Mrs. Hirsch too, please, Miss Foster.'

Peregrine, her hands already laden with bags and boxes, looked at him helplessly for a moment then stuck out her chin. 'If you could just…'

Obligingly, Colin Blair tucked the final parcel into the crook of Peregrine's neck, and she clamped her chin down, holding it in place.

'Thank you,' she said.

—

Joyce Hirsch looked up from her desk as the elevator doors opened and Peregrine staggered out. 'Has Mrs. Blair been stripping the shelves again?' she asked.

'Hang on.' Peregrine still had the small parcel tucked under her chin. 'Could you…?' She leaned forward over the secretary's desk. Mrs. Hirsch held out her hands and Peregrine let the parcel drop.

'Phew! I wasn't sure I was going to make it!'

She moved to the side of the desk and, as carefully as possible, allowed the rest of the boxes and bags to fall from her hands.

Mrs. Hirsch eyed the heaped purchases. 'I honestly have no idea what Mrs. Blair does with it all! She'd have to wear something new every single day and she probably still wouldn't have touched half the things she owned.'

'One of the benefits of being married to the boss, I suppose.' Peregrine pushed some stray hair from her face.

'Benefits? I don't know about that.' Mrs. Hirsch was still holding the small, plain-wrapped parcel and now she shook it pointedly at Peregrine. 'This'll be Mrs. Blair's medication.'

'Medication? I didn't realise she was sick.' Peregrine tried to look politely concerned.

'Not *that* sort of sick.' Joyce Hirsch cast a cautious eye towards her boss's closed door then turned back to Peregrine and tapped her temple meaningfully. 'Here.'

Peregrine widened her eyes. 'I had no idea. The poor thing.'

'Yes, and she's been worse lately. Hopefully whatever's in here will do the trick.' She dropped the package into her desk drawer.

'Worse how?'

'Oh.' Joyce looked at the closed office door again. 'The bridal fashion parade set her off. She was a top model you know, back in the day. Beautiful woman! But she can't seem to come to terms with the fact that, even if you're stunning, beauty fades. She wanted to be in the parade, but Miss Astor put her foot down. And didn't that cause a ruckus! Why, Mrs. Blair was so upset she took off on the morning of the parade! Young Mr. Blair—poor man—had no idea where his mother had gone, and of course with the state she'd been in… He got the South Yarra police involved. Reported her missing and then sat in that police station for half the morning while they combed the streets! Apparently, they were talking about dragging the river when she turned up.'

'Gosh! Was she okay?'

'Dazed and a bit confused but none the worse for it, thank goodness. Colin even managed to get her here to see some of the fashion show, although in hindsight that probably wasn't the best idea.'

'Colin Blair seems very dedicated to his mother.'

'Oh, he is!' Joyce Hirsch leaned forward, her eyes bright. 'Always looking out for her.'

'What about Mr. Blair? I mean Colin's father?'

'Such a busy man! He indulges his wife'—Joyce gestured at

the mound of shopping—'but running this place means he has precious little free time. It's all he can do to squeeze in a game of squash two evenings a week!'

'Squash! My father plays squash! Perhaps he and Mr. Blair know each other. Where does Mr. Blair play?'

'Royal Southern, every Tuesday and Thursday night. He's been a member there for years.'

'Oh.' Peregrine let her face fall. 'Different club. Well, thank you, Mrs. Hirsch. I really should be...'

The elevator pinged. Peregrine glanced over her shoulder and was horrified to see Inspector Sparrow emerging. Quickly she turned her back and began fussing with Mrs. Blair's purchases, arranging the bags into a neat line while keeping her shoulders hunched and face carefully averted.

'Inspector!' Joyce Hirsch called, her tone suddenly brusque. 'I'll let him know you're here.'

'No need, Mrs. Hirsch. I'll tell him myself.'

From the corner of her eye Peregrine could see Mrs. Hirsch frantically pressing buttons on the intercom even as she heard the door to the inner office open.

'Sparrow!' Terence Blair's voice held annoyance, surprise and something else Peregrine couldn't identify. She risked a glance in the direction of the Blairs' office. Sparrow had left the door open and she had a clear view of the two men, although they were now talking too softly for more than the occasional word to reach her.

Inspector Sparrow and Terence Blair were standing in front of the large desk. Blair was clearly agitated, shaking his head, and moving his hands in sharp, tight gestures as he spoke. By contrast, Sparrow was completely at ease. He hadn't bothered to remove either his hat or coat, and he stood calmly as Blair talked, at one point replying with a huge yawn. Then, as

Peregrine watched, Sparrow snapped his fingers and stuck out a hand. In response, Terence Blair reached into the pocket of his sharply tailored chalk-stripe suit and pulled out a roll of money. Without counting it, he dropped the bills into Sparrow's outstretched palm then turned away.

Peregrine ducked her head again as Inspector Sparrow doffed his hat—a gesture of exaggerated sarcasm rather than polite farewell—and turned to leave. The office door slammed behind him.

'Always a pleasure, Mrs. Hirsch,' Sparrow said as he passed through the outer office.

Peregrine waited until she heard the elevator doors slide closed before she straightened up.

Joyce Hirsch's lips were pursed in distaste. 'Odious man,' she muttered.

—

Mrs. Hirsch sent Peregrine off to the accounts department with a stack of approved invoices and, after completing that task, Peregrine returned to the ground floor of the emporium. She was still determined to have a proper search through the basement storeroom, but that would have to wait; right now she needed to see Detective Steed, and she was hoping he'd stride through the main doors sooner or later. Peregrine managed to while away an hour straightening sales tables, tweaking floral arrangements and directing customers, and was just beginning to think he would never come when the distinctive silhouette of James Steed, artfully backlit by the morning sun, filled the doorway of Blair's Emporium.

She threw the lemon-coloured angora twinset she'd been

holding onto a nearby counter and hurried to intercept him before he reached the escalators.

'Good morning, Detective!' she called.

He stopped abruptly, shoulders immediately tense. 'Miss Fish—'

'Penny Foster! You remember!' Peregrine bustled to a stop in front of him.

'Miss Foster,' said Steed through gritted teeth. 'I'm rather busy this morning.'

'Just a quick word, Detective. It is important.' Peregrine widened her eyes and gave him a hard look.

'Five minutes.' Steed led her to a quiet recess beneath an escalator. Leaning against the wall, he folded his arms. 'Well?'

'Someone got out of bed on the wrong side this morning!'

Steed took a deep breath. 'I'm under a lot of pressure to finalise the investigation. The inspector wants to make a public announcement about Miss Astor's role in the death of Barbie Jones.'

'Oh. Oh, no! Well, maybe this will help you to find the real killer. Maggie Blair was desperate to be a catwalk model again, but Florence said no. Then on the morning of the bridal fashion show, Mrs. Blair went missing for several hours—no one knows where she was or what she was doing!'

Steed shook his head. 'That's not right. Maggie Blair was at home with her son, Colin. They were running late but arrived here in time for the end of the show. Colin Blair has given his statement.'

'Well, then he's lied to you. Mrs. Hirsch, the Blairs' secretary, told me Colin reported his mother missing to South Yarra police early that morning. He was at the police station while they were looking for her and then she just turned up—in a daze, supposedly, but well enough to make it to Florence's show. Check with South Yarra if you don't believe me. Or get Constable Connor to do it!'

Steed narrowed his eyes but let Peregrine's jab go. 'I'll call them myself right now, because if what you're telling me is true, I'd like to have another chat with Colin Blair.'

'What do you mean, if it's true?' Peregrine's voice rose.

Above them, a woman leaned over the edge of the escalator and peered down, her face alight with curiosity. Steed met her eye and touched his hat politely, waiting until the moving stairs had carried her away before returning his attention to Peregrine.

'Nothing,' he soothed. 'You said it yourself the other day: a detective checks the facts before making assumptions.'

Peregrine, hands on hips, rolled her eyes in exasperation. 'I said a detective gathers evidence rather than trying to make the facts fit a theory!'

Steed shrugged. 'It amounts to the same thing. Anyway, I need to go.'

'Before you do, speaking of evidence…I saw your boss take a bribe from Terence Blair this morning. How's that for evidence?'

'What? What did you actually see?'

'I was up in the secretary's office and Sparrow arrived—he didn't recognise me—and marched straight through to see Blair. The door was open and I saw Mr. Blair take a big roll of notes from his pocket and give it to Sparrow.'

Steed shrugged and jammed his hands into his pockets. 'Could have been a donation to the Police Widows and Orphans Fund,' he said, although his voice lacked conviction.

Peregrine snorted. 'Oh, come on, Detective! More like a donation to the Inspector Sparrow Retirement Fund. If it's not a bribe, then it must be a blackmail payout!'

'Miss Fisher!' Steed barked.

Peregrine, shocked, took a step backwards.

'Leave it alone! You don't know what you saw. I need you to stop meddling in this investigation and, above all, I need you to stay out of Inspector Sparrow's way! Now, if you'll excuse me, I have police business to attend to!' He yanked down the brim of his hat then pushed past her.

Stunned, Peregrine watched him stalk off and step onto the escalator. She could see his flushed face as he rose to the next floor, but Detective Steed didn't look at her, instead keeping his eyes rigidly focused on the back of the woman in front of him.

—

Steed expected Peregrine would try to follow him again. Of course he was going to do exactly what he'd told her: talk to his colleagues at South Yarra police station then confront Colin Blair. He knew the story Peregrine had passed on to him was probably true, and Maggie Blair did not have an alibi for the time of the murder, but he had no intention of letting Peregrine know that. Helping Phryne Fisher had almost cost him his job, and just when order seemed to have been restored, just when James Steed was starting to feel in control of his own cases, Peregrine Fisher had burst into his life.

He barely registered the garden furniture, barbecues, and beach umbrellas as he strode through Blair's outdoors department, his mind entirely focused on the investigation and following up on Peregrine's work. He realised he was being childish, and that he'd have to apologise to her later, but it *was* just a little bit galling to discover information this way.

Then there was Inspector Sparrow and the money.

Whatever was going on there could not be good, but Steed couldn't see himself broaching the subject with the boss: *Oh, by the way, sir, I understand you palmed a wad of cash from Terence Blair. Anything I should know about?* That would be career suicide, at the very least. Steed had known for a while that his boss could be a bit dodgy, acting in a way some coppers would describe politely as 'old school.' But in the interests of his own job—not to mention a somewhat grudging respect for the man he thought Sparrow had once been—Steed had kept his head down. Now, though, with the evidence right in front of him, Detective Steed was angered by his own inability to act, and for the first time he was ashamed of being part of the police force. He hadn't meant to take that out on Peregrine either, but perhaps his strong reaction would make her back off. Of course, if Peregrine Fisher was anything like her aunt, his outburst had probably made her more determined than ever to get to the bottom of things.

Passing through sporting goods, Steed approached the Blair's Tea Garden, an elegant, palm-filled café within the store. The smell of toast and something sweet wafted out to meet him, and his stomach rumbled in response. Unfortunately, there was no time for food. Steed's destination was actually the bank of four public phone booths located just outside the café. He let himself into the nearest one and the heavy glass door closed with a satisfying thump, instantly muting outside sound. If Peregrine was hovering around somewhere hoping to listen in, she was going to be disappointed.

His smugness was quickly tempered by the fact that it took less than five minutes to be connected to the desk sergeant at South Yarra and confirm that Peregrine was right. Colin Blair had reported his mother missing at 6.30 a.m. on the morning of the bridal show.

He told officers he had no idea how long she'd been gone from the house and she didn't turn up until almost half past nine.

Steed set the receiver down with a clunk and stood for a moment, then with a sigh left the booth to look for Colin Blair. He'd only taken a couple of steps when he saw someone disappear behind a display of croquet sets—someone tall and slender with dark brown pigtails and wearing a Blair's pinafore. Quick as a flash he raced after the vanishing figure, grabbed her arm, and spun her to face him.

'Really, Miss Fisher!' Steed said triumphantly.

Then stopped.

The girl whose arm he was holding was not Peregrine Fisher. Steed looked at the horrified expression on her face and felt himself blush.

'Sorry. I'm terribly sorry. I thought you were... Sorry,' he mumbled, releasing her arm and backing away.

Steed glanced around, half expecting to see Peregrine laughing at him from across the room, but he was alone. Chastened, he went to confront Colin Blair.

—

As it happened, Peregrine was nowhere near James Steed. Feeling offended, she'd left him to his bad mood and headed in the opposite direction. Now she was back in the basement storeroom. The night she'd broken into Blair's, Peregrine had hoped she might find the stocking used to strangle Barbie Jones. Instead, she had found Florence, and the missing murder weapon had turned up the following day, placed to cast suspicion on the designer. This time, Peregrine wasn't quite sure what she was looking for.

'What did you discover, Florence?' she whispered to herself. 'Why did someone want to kill you?'

The door to the alterations room was closed and taped off, but Peregrine knew there was nothing for her in that room except regret. She stood there and surveyed the storage area, hoping something would catch her eye, something that Florence might have noticed as she was leaving.

Nothing.

The props were all as she remembered them, and the crowd of dummies seemed unchanged. Peregrine shivered as she recognised one-armed Audrey in her green dress, although the mannequin's bald head had now been covered by a floppy, broad-brimmed hat. She moved across to the rows of shelves—the place where she had stumbled across Florence's lost shoe—to see if they held anything interesting. She found more props, but also an aisle full of shoes and accessories. Here the shelves were sectioned off and neatly labelled with the names of each of the house models. Shoes, gloves, hats, bags, and pieces of jewellery were all tidily arranged in each section. Peregrine found an empty space with Barbie Jones's name on it, while the shelf directly below was marked as Pansy Wing's spot. And sitting right at the front of Pansy's allocated space was a long gold necklace with red stones and a circular disc enamelled in blue and red.

Somewhere a door closed softly. Without thinking, Peregrine snatched up the necklace and stuffed it into the pocket of her uniform.

'Hello?' she called. 'Is someone there?'

Footsteps, moving slowly across the concrete floor, were her only answer. Peregrine glanced behind her, but the aisle of shelves ran right to the wall: she was trapped in a dead end. She patted her pockets, trying to find the lipstick knife, only to remember it was still in her handbag, locked securely in the employee's cloakroom. She swore silently, frantically scanning the shelves for something to defend herself with. As the footsteps drew closer, Peregrine spotted a pair of silver stiletto pumps on Pansy's shelf, grabbed one by the toe box, and gave it an experimental swing. It wasn't going to kill anybody, but if she could whack someone with the point of the heel, it might do enough to get her out of this tight spot.

A shadow appeared at the end of the row of shelves, growing more intense as the footsteps got louder. Peregrine raised the shoe over her head and held her breath. Then a man was standing there, blocking her escape.

'All right, miss?' It was the storeman, Knox, light glinting off his glasses.

'Oh!' Peregrine's hand fell to her side, although she didn't let go of the shoe. 'Mr. Knox! You startled me!'

'It's you, is it, Miss Foster? What are you doing down here all alone?' He was still blocking the end of the aisle.

'I was just...' Peregrine looked at the shoe in her hand. 'Miss Wing sent me to collect her silver shoes. She needs them to go with the outfit she's wearing. I think these are the right ones! It took me a while to find them—there's a lot of stuff down here!—but then I saw these shelves with all the models' names on them, so...' Peregrine's words tumbled over each other.

'You've only got one,' said Knox.

'Pardon?'

'One shoe. You'll need both.' He nodded at the shelf.

'Of course.' She picked up the other shoe and held them both up for him to see. 'It's great that you have this section all labelled for the models and such.'

Peregrine began to move slowly towards him and was relieved when he stepped aside, allowing her to pass.

'It's all the little extras the models need for their outfits—shoes and gloves in the right size, that sort of thing,' Knox explained.

'What about the jewellery? Do they share necklaces and brooches and things?'

'No, no, never jewellery! The models put dibs on the samples and floor stock. Anything that's been pulled for use in-house.'

'You know a lot about it!'

Knox suddenly looked shifty. He lowered his gaze and shrugged. 'I have to keep an eye on things, that's all. Anyway. Can't stand around and talk all day. Got a delivery run.' He turned his back on Peregrine and began hefting boxes onto a hand trolley.

'I'll...get these to Pansy then.' Peregrine started across the room, trying not to look as though she was hurrying. A small, still-panicking corner of her brain wondered if the exit to the stairwell would now be locked, but to her relief the handle yielded to pressure and she was able to heave the heavy door open. As soon as it thudded shut behind her, Peregrine exhaled, her tension dropping. Slowly she climbed the stairs to the ground floor, thinking about what she'd found. Emerging into the shabbiness of the staff-only area, Peregrine was still deep in thought, trying to work out where Pansy Wing would be at this time of day. It was vital that she talked to the model as soon as possible, and not about shoes.

'Hold it!' a man yelled from somewhere behind her.

She froze, her heart rate skyrocketing again, then cautiously turned. Peregrine was shocked to see the storeman approaching, struggling to keep control of the over-laden hand trolley.

'How did you get up here so quickly?' Peregrine's frayed nerves betrayed her, and the question ended with a high-pitched squeak.

He stared at her for a beat before answering. 'Freight elevator.'

'Oh. Of course.' Peregrine swallowed. She studied Knox, trying and failing to read his expression behind the thick glasses. The only thing that really stood out was the whiteness of his knuckles as he held the trolley in a death grip.

'Couldn't trouble you to get the outside door for me, could I?' he asked casually. 'Not allowed to prop it open. Not since...'

Peregrine hesitated, wondering if this was all some sort of elaborate trick. But, then again, she was supposed to be a detective, and while it might not be the best way to unmask a criminal, if he tried anything, she'd be ready. 'Sure.' She made the word sound cool and relaxed.

Peregrine trailed the storeman down the hall. When he stopped a few steps from the exit, she sidled past, her back to the wall, and flung open the door, letting the momentum carry her out into the open air.

Knox followed.

'Ta, miss,' he said, as he parked the trolley next to the open back doors of a white van.

Peregrine watched as he loaded the boxes into the van, chastising herself for being so jumpy. As Knox swung the van's doors closed, she saw they were discreetly adorned with the logo of Blair's Emporium, an interlocking *B* and *E*. She hadn't changed her mind about him—the man was definitely strange—but he was just doing his job.

'I have to get back,' she called.

Peregrine was still holding Pansy's silver stilettos, but as she made her way through the store to ladieswear, she reached one hand into her pocket, closing her fingers around the necklace.

―

Peregrine hid the shoes behind her back as she entered the models' dressing room, but she needn't have worried: Pansy Wing was touching up her make-up and was completely absorbed in the task.

'Miss Wing! I'm glad I found you,' said Peregrine.

'I'm about to leave. What is it?' Pansy leaned closer to the mirror and swept on a stroke of mascara.

'I found something that I think belongs to you.' Peregrine pulled the necklace from her pocket and held it up high enough that Pansy could see it over her reflected shoulder. Light glinted from the gold disc as it turned a lazy circle.

'Yeah, that's mine. Thanks. I don't want to lose it. Pop it in my purse, would you?' She stretched her lips wide and began applying coral-coloured lipstick.

'The thing is'—Peregrine lowered her voice conspiratorially—'you probably shouldn't wear it around here. Someone is bound to notice and then, well, you know how people like to gossip.'

In the mirror, Pansy frowned. 'What on earth are you talking about?'

'I don't mean to interfere. It's just that it's a fairly distinctive necklace, and Maggie Blair has one that's identical.'

'So?'

'So…she said her husband bought it for her—on an overseas trip.'

'What are you trying to say?'

Peregrine shook her head in exasperation. 'Look, men think they're smart when really they just lack imagination. Same gift, two women. One for the wife and one for the girlfriend!'

Pansy met Peregrine's gaze in the mirror, her eyes growing

wide as the meaning of Peregrine's words sunk in. She spun around.

'Oh, my God! You think Terence Blair and I—? Oh, my God, no! He's old!'

Peregrine looked at the model sceptically. 'It's okay. I won't tell anyone.'

'But I'm telling *you* that I'm not involved with him. I have a boyfriend! Terence Blair is...' She shuddered. 'Besides, that was Barbie's necklace. No one came to claim her things, so we—the models—split her stuff between us.'

Peregrine looked at the necklace in her hand. 'So this belonged to Barbie?'

Pansy nodded emphatically.

'Now things are starting to make sense!'

Pansy pulled the chain from Peregrine's grasp and was about to tuck it in her handbag when she stopped, her hand frozen in mid-air. 'Are you saying Barbie and Terence Blair were *having an affair?*'

'That's exactly what I'm saying. And I think I know when they were meeting, too! Do you mind if I...' Peregrine held out her hand for the necklace.

'Take it!' The model let go of the chain abruptly, as though it had burned her fingers, and Peregrine snatched it as it fell.

'Thank you, Pansy. You've been really helpful. Oh—here! These are yours!' Peregrine thrust the silver stilettos at Pansy and almost ran from the dressing room, desperate to get to sporting goods then make her escape from Blair's Emporium. She had other plans for the afternoon.

Fourteen

Peregrine stood in front of the reception desk at the Royal Southern Squash Club, twirling her new racquet. She'd chosen a Teddy Tinling tennis dress—white dacron and cotton squared off with a band of blue—which was now attracting the admiring glances of a number of expensively attired women. It was clear the Royal Southern was a rather exclusive club.

The man behind the desk had eyed Peregrine coolly the moment she walked through the door, gauging her appearance against some unwritten code. Apparently she'd passed the test, because he had immediately relaxed, his face breaking into a welcoming smile. Now he was searching through a reservations book, running his finger down a column of names.

'Blair, you said?' he asked.

'That's right, Mr. Terence Blair,' Peregrine replied, giving her high ponytail a toss. 'I was supposed to meet him here, and he was going to give me a lesson. Perhaps he's running late?'

'I'm afraid I don't have a court booked under that name.'

'Well, there must be a mistake. I'm sure it was today! He

told me he plays every Tuesday and Thursday evening, but he'd make a special time for us on Friday. And I was so looking forward to it.' Peregrine's lip quivered and she inhaled shakily.

'I'm not sure what else I can... Oh, now, please don't cry.' The man looked suddenly desperate. 'Let me just...' He leaned over the back of his chair and stuck his head into an inner office. 'Randy, there's a young lady here—'

Peregrine couldn't hear the rest of what he said, but he turned back with a relieved smile. Seconds later an athletic young man in tennis whites appeared. With thick blond hair, a deep tan, and broad shoulders, he looked like he'd stepped out of an advertisement for high-end watches or sports cars. He smiled at Peregrine, displaying his perfect and dazzlingly white teeth. Then he vaulted the small gate that separated the business side of things from the reception area.

'I'm Randolph, the club pro.' He stuck out his hand. 'I hear you came for a lesson, but'—his smile grew even wider—'some incredibly stupid guy stood you up.'

Peregrine accepted the proffered hand and they shook, but the pro didn't immediately release his grip.

'Come on. I'll look after you.' He gave her hand a gentle tug.

'No, really. Thank you, but that's not necessary. I must have got the day wrong. I was sure Terence Blair said our date was for Friday, but he definitely told me he played here every Tuesday and Thursday, so maybe I mixed things up. I can come back another time.' Peregrine pulled away, just enough to get her hand back without bruising Randolph's ego. She smiled coquettishly.

'You're here now. Shame to miss out. Besides, I haven't seen Terence Blair for months.' He flashed his teeth again.

'Months?'

'That's right. Now, I've got a free court, and I see you've got a racquet, so let me show you how to play the game.' He reached out again, this time hovering his hand behind Peregrine's shoulder.

'I'm sure you've got other things to do, Randolph,' Peregrine protested.

'Not for the next hour. And please, call me Randy.'

Peregrine smiled again and allowed herself to be ushered into the heart of the Royal Southern Squash Club.

The squeak of their shoes on the wooden floor echoed as Randy led her onto the squash court and closed the door behind them. He'd collected a racquet on the way, but now he set it down in the corner.

'Won't you be needing that?' Peregrine asked.

'Not yet. First we have to discuss grip and swing.' Randy flashed his broad, toothy smile.

'Actually, could we discuss Terence Blair first?'

'Blair?'

Peregrine nodded. 'You said you hadn't seen him for months.'

'Nope. Here, let me show you how to grip the racquet.' Randy stood close behind Peregrine and, reaching around, wrapped his right hand over hers and the handle of the squash racquet.

'Are you sure? Because he told me he was here every Tuesday and Thursday evening.' Peregrine tried to lean her body forward.

'I'm here most days and every evening, and he hasn't been in. Now, your back swing should be...' He moved Peregrine's right arm back, bringing her shoulders against his toned chest.

'Have you seen him at all in the last few months?' Peregrine tried to ease the left side of her body away.

Randy shook his head and she could feel his chin brushing her hair. 'A couple of Saturday mornings, but never during the week. Here, you need to square your body up.' He used his free hand to pull Peregrine's left shoulder back against him. 'Bend your knees a little...' Randy pushed his own knees into the back of Peregrine's legs. 'I've got a couple of balls, so if you're ready...?'

'Oh, I'm ready.' Peregrine sounded sweet but her teeth were gritted.

Randy kept hold of her racquet as he pulled a squash ball from the pocket of his shorts then reached forward with his left hand. 'Get ready to swing! On one, two...' He tossed the ball into the air. 'Three!'

Peregrine slammed her head backwards, catching him hard on the lower part of his face.

'Bloody hell!' Randy yelled, releasing his grip and pressing his hands over his mouth.

'I'm *so* sorry! I was trying to watch the ball as you threw it in the air. Oh, dear. Are you okay, Randy?'

'Are you nuts? I think I broke a tooth. Ow.'

'I think maybe I should go,' said Peregrine, already halfway out the door. 'Really sorry, Randy, but thanks for the game!'

—

Peregrine drove straight to the police station. She didn't want to go inside and risk running into Inspector Sparrow, so she parked where the Austin-Healey wasn't too obvious but still gave her a good view of the front door. Even though she hadn't quite forgiven Detective Steed for being so prickly, Peregrine needed him if she was going to exonerate Florence, which meant telling him what she'd uncovered.

Sitting in the dappled shade of a magnificent elm tree with the convertible's top down, Peregrine finally felt the knot between her shoulder blades begin to loosen. It had already been a long and rather difficult day, and she was looking forward to immersing herself in the hot scented water of her divinely deep bathtub, drink close at hand, and organising her jumbled thoughts. Until then, the balmy air was a welcome reviver.

She'd been sitting in the car for half an hour and was just wondering whether it would be easier to pass the information to Constable Connor instead when Detective Steed appeared, pushing his hat on as he came down the steps of the police station two at a time.

Peregrine got out of the car and waved. Steed saw her immediately. He stopped, slowly shook his head, then with a single backward glance at the police station, he put his hands in his pockets and strolled over to join her. They leaned side by side on the bonnet of her car.

'Busy afternoon?' he said, staring pointedly at Peregrine's squash attire.

'Yes, actually,' she replied coolly.

Steed swallowed and looked Peregrine in the eye. 'Listen, Miss Fisher. Before you say anything I want to apologise for the way I reacted earlier. You were right about Maggie Blair disappearing for several hours on the day of the bridal show, and Colin Blair did go to South Yarra police station.'

'See?' Peregrine tried to keep the triumph out of her voice. 'Did you talk to Colin?'

'Yes. I asked him why he'd said nothing, and he got very defensive—almost aggressive! He's very protective of his mother.'

'And?' Peregrine prompted.

'He told me it wasn't relevant to anything and therefore none of my business. I reminded him it was a murder investigation, which made everything my business.'

'Yes, but where was Mrs. Blair?' Peregrine was getting exasperated with the pace of the detective's storytelling.

Steed, however, was clearly enjoying himself and Peregrine's mounting frustration. He smiled and relented. 'Colin Blair claimed his mother's medications had been changed recently and they were putting her in a bit of a mental fog. Apparently she'd simply wandered off in a daze.' He held up a hand before Peregrine could ask the next question. 'And, yes, I confirmed the new medication with her doctor.'

'So Maggie Blair has no alibi for the time Barbie Jones was killed.' Peregrine frowned and bit her lip.

'Miss Fisher, didn't you hear what I just said? She was in a drug-induced state. Hardly capable of murder.'

Peregrine shook her head. 'You confirmed she was taking a new medication but not that it was causing her problems. You still only have Colin Blair's word for that—and, as you just said, he's very protective of his mother.'

'But why would Maggie Blair kill Barbie?'

'Because her husband was having an affair with Barbie Jones!'

'What?'

'He's the mystery boyfriend!'

'How did you find that out?'

'From a necklace—two, actually. Terence Blair gave his wife and girlfriend identical necklaces, and he was meeting Barbie every Tuesday and Thursday night when he was supposed to be playing squash.'

'Well, that explains your little dress.'

Peregrine pinched the sides of the short skirt and bobbed her head, miming an ironic curtsy. 'Just confirming the facts, Detective.'

'But you've seen Maggie Blair. Even if she wasn't in a daze, she's not strong. Certainly not strong enough to strangle a healthy young woman like Barbie then pose her on the cake like that.'

'Passion and anger can give you amazing power. Besides, who's to say these drugs you keep talking about didn't cause some sort of weird thoughts or give her super strength? I've heard that can happen.'

'I still don't see it, but I'll do some more digging,' said Steed begrudgingly.

'While you're at it, have another look at Terence Blair.'

Detective Steed pulled off his hat, ran a hand roughly through his hair and let out a frustrated sigh. 'But I thought you just said Maggie Blair—'

'Both of them had motive. Mrs. Blair's was jealousy, but think what it would mean for Terence Blair if the world found out he had a pregnant model mistress! Mr. Blair could have killed Barbie because she'd become a problem.'

'Fine! I'll go over the file again and see if anything stands out about either of them.' Steed closed his eyes and took a deep breath. 'Thank you for the information, Miss Fisher.' He inclined his head in Peregrine's direction.

'You're welcome, Detective Steed.' She smiled at him, then winced and ducked her head slightly. 'Just one other thing.'

'Out with it.'

'I know you don't want to hear it, but Sparrow took that money from Terence Blair. Your boss is covering up for something.'

Peregrine could see the muscles in Steed's jaw working, and it took a moment before he finally spoke.

'Just leave well enough alone, Miss Fisher, or you'll get us both in trouble.'

Steed moved over to the driver's door of the Austin-Healey and opened it. He jerked his head towards the car's interior.

Peregrine locked eyes with him for a moment before she calmly stepped past, sat sideways on the driver's seat, and gracefully swung both legs in.

'Thank you, Detective. I'll be seeing you.' She turned the key in the ignition and waited for him to close the door.

Steed stepped back. 'No doubt, Miss Fisher.'

Peregrine dropped the handbrake and accelerated away, leaving Detective Steed standing in the road.

—

After the Austin-Healey had disappeared from view, James Steed walked slowly back into the police station. It was late in the afternoon, and the detectives' room was largely empty: only two desks were occupied and the door to Inspector Sparrow's office was closed. There was a small chance the boss was still in the station, but it seemed unlikely; the atmosphere lacked a certain tension. Then Steed caught sight of Constable Fleur Connor standing by his desk, clearly loitering with intent. He didn't need any more drama, and it was almost enough to send him back out into the street, but before he could react she'd spotted him.

'Detective!' she called.

'Constable Connor. What is it?' He threw his hat at the coat rack as he passed and felt slightly better when it found its mark rather than falling to the floor.

Fleur Connor was looking decidedly cagey. She stood with her shoulders pressed against the bank of filing cabinets, keeping the entire room in view, and waited until he'd sat down before stepping forward. Pulling a hand from behind her back, she slid a file onto his desk blotter.

'Someone dropped this,' she said quietly, with a glance across at the other detectives.

James Steed stared down at the folder on his desk. It was damp and slightly water-stained, the corners singed and blackened. 'Dropped it where?' he asked loudly, looking from the file to Fleur and back again.

Fleur Connor grimaced and patted the air with her hand to shush him.

'Dropped it *where?*' Steed asked again, this time in an undertone.

'In the bin for destruction. I was emptying everything into the incinerator when I saw…when this one slipped off the top.'

Steed studied the constable's face, but Fleur had plenty of practice at hiding emotions, and her expression was a professional blank. He turned his attention back to the folder, opened the cover and looked at the topmost page. His eyes widened.

'This is the Barbie Jones file!' he hissed.

'Is it?' Fleur said blandly. 'I thought it looked important.'

Steed began turning pages, scanning the details, moving faster and faster. 'Everything is in here. This is still an active case!' His voice rose again and one of the other detectives looked up curiously. Steed met his eye and nodded in apology, waiting until the other man returned to his work before picking up the next page. He frowned.

'This can't be right,' he muttered.

Fleur Connor leaned in, glanced at the heading and stood up straight. 'I daresay you're correct, Detective. It's not right. It's not right at all.'

Steed glanced at her sharply. 'This is the autopsy report for Florence Astor. What's it even doing in this file?'

'I believe Inspector Sparrow had the file last, sir. Perhaps you could ask him?'

'Damn it.' Steed swore softly. Then he looked up at the policewoman. 'Thank you, Constable Connor.'

'My pleasure, sir. If there's nothing else...'

'No. Go home. And, Constable? I think it best we keep knowledge of this file'—he gestured to the damaged documents—'to ourselves for now.'

'What file, Detective? I just tip the bin into the incinerator; I have no idea what might be in there. Goodnight, sir.' She gave him a quick professional smile and walked briskly from the room.

James Steed remained in the office long after the last detective had left and the night shift had taken over at reception. He sat at his desk, illuminated only by the circle of light cast by a battered Planet lamp, and read through everything. Nothing had changed since he had last looked at all the interviews, reports, and photographs relating to the death of Barbie Jones, but this was the first time he had seen the pathologist's report on Florence Astor. As the significance of what he was reading sunk in, Steed realised a couple of things. The first was that Peregrine Fisher was right—again—and Florence Astor had not killed herself. The second was that Inspector Sparrow had a hidden and highly suspect agenda of his own and unless he, James Steed, did something, Florence Astor would be blamed and the real killer would go unpunished.

The problem was that any serious attempt by Steed to confront his boss over the case would result in his instant transfer to a one-man station somewhere in the back of beyond. He only had one choice. Steed slammed the file shut and snapped off the light, plunging the office into darkness.

Fifteen

Peregrine stood in the doorway wrapped in her aunt's silk robe, tendrils of hair escaping from her up-do and curling damply around her neck.

'As you can see, I wasn't expecting company.' She turned and started up the stairs, leaving the door open. 'And I certainly wasn't expecting you.' Her bare feet left damp footprints on each tread.

Detective Steed stepped across the threshold, closing the door behind him. He had one foot on the stairs when, in a sudden burst of caution, he went back and threw the deadbolt, locking the door securely.

Peregrine was standing in the middle of the lounge room when he got there. She'd put on a pair of fluffy mule slippers but otherwise had made no concession to his presence and the robe clung to her damp skin.

'Well, Detective?'

Steed hesitated. 'Look, Miss Fisher, I owe you another apology for my behaviour earlier.'

'Yes, you do.' Peregrine folded her arms.

'And I'm sorry. I really am. It's just a very difficult situation and I have to tread carefully. My boss—'

'Sparrow.'

'He was a good cop once, and he's still a good detective—he's taught me a lot—but something happened, years ago. I don't know what, I've only heard rumours, but he changed.'

'If you're trying to make me feel sorry for him…'

'I'm not. The thing is, in the force everyone, *including* Sparrow, has to answer to someone, and for the moment I have to answer to him. I don't always like it, but if doing my job—and continuing to do it as best I can—means putting up with Sparrow's occasional digressions, well…' Steed shrugged.

Peregrine sniffed, unimpressed. 'How you deal with Sparrow is entirely up to you. I just don't want Florence Astor's name and legacy ruined. Not to mention the fact that there's still a murderer on the loose.'

'I agree completely, which is why I'm here.' Steed reached inside his overcoat and pulled out the damaged file. He held it out to Peregrine. 'You didn't get this from me and you can't tell anyone you have it or mention the information you find in it. Well, anyone other than the Adventuresses, I should say, because I know you'll tell them anyway.'

Peregrine frowned. 'What…?' She took the file and leafed through the first few pages, then stared at him in astonishment. 'You're giving me a police file?'

'Officially that file no longer exists, and I'll deny ever being here. Unofficially…' Steed rubbed a hand across his jaw and from where she stood Peregrine could hear the faint scratch of his five o'clock shadow.

'Unofficially?' she echoed, raising an eyebrow.

'Unofficially, take a look at the postmortem report on Florence Astor.'

'What am I going to find?'

'The pathologist says quite plainly that not all of Miss Astor's injuries are consistent with a fall from a height.'

Peregrine closed her eyes and clutched the file to her chest. 'I knew Florence wouldn't kill herself.'

Steed nodded. 'I'm sorry, Miss Fisher.'

'And you're really not going to do anything about it? Two women are dead!'

Steed dropped his head, unable to meet Peregrine's fierce gaze. 'My hands are tied.'

'Rubbish! I know Sparrow's type. I've met plenty of men like him before and trust me: if you back off or keep quiet, they don't stop; they just keep grinding you down. The only way to deal with bullies is to defy them. Refuse to be a victim. So stand up to Sparrow and don't be so spineless!' Peregrine slammed the file down on the coffee table and, unable to contain her anger, began pacing the room.

'Don't you think I'd do that if I thought it would achieve anything?' Steed said.

Peregrine came to an abrupt stop in front of him, hands on hips.

'Don't you think I've been trying to think of a way to deal with this?' Steed sounded close to breaking point. 'A way that wouldn't end up with Sparrow taking it out on me, you, and probably the entire Adventuresses' Club? Because believe me, when Inspector Sparrow's unhappy, everybody's unhappy. And he has powerful allies.'

Peregrine's face softened and she reached out to place her hand on his arm. 'I'm sorry, Detective,' she said. 'I've had a small taste of what Sparrow can be like, but I guess I hadn't quite understood the position you're in.'

Steed nodded miserably. 'I'm sorry too, Peregrine…Miss Fisher. In the end, giving you this file was the only solution I could think of. But if you and the Adventuresses come up with any solid leads, the investigation will have to go further and there'll be nothing Inspector Sparrow or anyone else can do.'

Peregrine smiled. 'My goodness, Detective Steed! Does this mean you think I have the makings of an investigator after all?'

Steed returned her grin. 'Is that the time? I have to go.' He handed her a card. 'I've written my home number on the back, just in case.'

'Why, Detective!' She swatted his arm playfully then took a step back. 'Thank you,' she said quietly.

'Don't mention it. I mean, really, don't mention it—especially not to the inspector!' Steed moved to the top of the stairs then paused, serious once again. 'There is one thing I'll say, though. If crossing professional paths with your aunt taught me anything, it's never to underestimate a woman named Fisher.'

The top of Steed's hat was just disappearing when Peregrine called out, 'Detective! One more question! About my aunt!'

Steed came back up a couple of steps so he could look at her over the top of the planter box.

'I was going through her old case notes. In a copy of the notebook that the inspector took, there's a reference to Madame Lyon being like the goddess who guards secrets. Did Aunt Phryne ever say anything to you about a goddess or a hiding place? Anything like that?'

Steed shook his head. 'Your aunt and I were colleagues of sorts and I like to think we were also friends. But Phryne Fisher's secrets were always strictly her affair. The one time I asked her something along those lines she stared down her nose and said telling me would entirely defeat the purpose, because then it wouldn't be a secret anymore.'

Steed touched the brim of his fedora in farewell and vanished down the stairs.

—

Peregrine carried the file into the bedroom, climbed into her pink bed, and spread the pages out around her, except for the information about Florence. Steed had told her the most important thing—Florence had not committed suicide—but she wasn't quite ready to read a detailed account of her friend's injuries. There was no question in Peregrine's mind: Florence had been killed because she'd discovered something about Barbie's murder.

'So if I find Barbie's killer,' she murmured, picking up the first page, 'I'll know who killed Florence.'

The hours crept by as she shuffled back and forth between the papers, scribbling notes, looking for something that would point her to a solution. But as the darkness outside her window gradually faded into dawn, Peregrine realised the only thing she'd learned was that Barbie Jones had a landlady who was either very motherly or very concerned about her tenant's safety. According to the file, Detective Steed had spoken to Mrs. Dulcie Meadows, who confirmed Barbie was in her own apartment by 11 p.m. the night before the bridal show. Mrs. Meadows knew this because Barbie had flicked her lights on and off to signal she was safely home.

Peregrine looked at the notes she had made: the phrase

safely home was so heavily circled the pencil had broken through the paper.

'Why "safely home"? And why was Barbie signalling to her landlady in the first place? Was she afraid of something?' Peregrine mused, leaning back against a mound of pillows. She'd already gone over Dulcie Meadows's statement four or five times and there was nothing out of the ordinary except for those two little words. But if Mrs. Meadows was very close to Barbie, she might know more.

Peregrine made a note of the landlady's address then returned all the loose pages to the folder, being careful to keep everything in order. Despite staying up all night, she was wide awake and buzzing with energy, eager to get on with the job. However, 6 a.m. on a Saturday was what her mother would have called an ungodly hour and not a good time for social calls, let alone pumping a stranger for information. There was time for a quick nap before Peregrine paid a visit to Dulcie Meadows, and she snuggled down between the silk sheets and closed her eyes, trying to relax. Details of the case kept bouncing around in her brain, but just when Peregrine was about to give up on the idea of getting any sleep, she remembered one of Pansy Wing's tricks for looking serene: *think pleasant thoughts.*

'Pleasant thoughts,' she sighed. 'Pleasant thoughts.'

And just before drifting off, she remembered Detective Steed had called her Peregrine.

—

Peregrine found Mrs. Meadows's house and the lady herself; she was outside on the street, sweeping a path that already looked immaculate. The floral apron protecting her beige house dress was equally spotless, and her blue-rinsed hair was set in a style copied directly from the Queen Mother. The overall effect was of a woman who brooked no nonsense, and Peregrine could feel herself being sized up as she approached on foot. The Austin-Healey was parked around the corner, and Peregrine had dressed in a way she hoped was fashionably demure: stylish enough that she could pass herself off as one of Barbie Jones's friends, but prim enough to meet with an older woman's approval.

'Mrs. Meadows?' Peregrine moved her sunglasses to the top of her head.

The woman stopped sweeping. 'Yes, I'm Mrs. Meadows.' Her voice was cautious.

'My name is Peregrine Fisher. I'm—I was—a friend of Barbie's. From the store.' Peregrine hated telling a lie like that, but if it meant finding Barbie's killer, she was prepared to make an exception.

'Oh, pet!' Mrs. Meadows propped her broom against the fence, wiped her hands on her apron and bustled forward. For a moment Peregrine thought she was going to be hugged, but the older woman grabbed both her hands and squeezed tightly. 'Poor Barbie! Such a lovely girl! I can hardly bear to think about it.'

'She told me how kind you were: how you kept an eye on things and looked out for her signal when she got home.'

Dulcie Meadows turned to look up at the first floor of the block of apartments directly across the road. 'Well, I did worry—young thing all alone in the city—and I can see her balcony from the window of my lounge room, here.' She let go of Peregrine's hands to gesture to the triple-fronted cream-brick-veneer house behind them.

'So whenever she came in late, Barbie would turn the lights on and off a couple of times?'

'That's right. And sometimes I'd give a little wave.'

'Did she wave back on that last night?'

'No, but she didn't always wave back. That night she flicked the lights as usual but she didn't wave. I think she must have been worried about something, because she sat up for ever so long. I could see her up there in her little lime green dress...' Dulcie Meadows sighed and her chin gave a tiny wobble.

Peregrine felt her pulse quicken. 'Why would Barbie be worried? Was she having trouble with her boyfriend?' She watched to see how Mrs. Meadows would react, but the other woman simply shook her head.

'I don't think so. She certainly never said anything.'

'But you thought she was worried,' Peregrine persisted.

Mrs. Meadows patted her arm. 'There, dear, it's probably just me being all dramatic, what with everything. It was just that she didn't usually sit up so late—at least not when she had a big show the next day. And after the stalker...'

'Stalker!' Peregrine stared open-mouthed at the other woman.

'Well, not really. Barbie thought I was being quite fanciful when I pointed out the white van to her. It was parked in our street several nights a week these last few months—right in front of the apartments! She said it was nothing and I wasn't to worry. But I'm sure that's why she agreed to our little signal with the lights. Just to set a silly old woman's mind to rest. Funny—I haven't seen the van this past week.' Mrs. Meadows frowned and stared thoughtfully at a spot in the road currently occupied by a battered grey Morris Minor.

'Mrs. Meadows...' Peregrine began.

Dulcie snapped out of her reverie. 'Yes, dear?'

'I wonder...I don't suppose you could let me into Barbie's apartment, could you?' Peregrine crossed her fingers behind her back. 'It's just that she borrowed a favourite dress of mine. It's rather special—I had to pay it off bit by bit each week—otherwise I wouldn't bother you.'

Dulcie Meadows studied Peregrine for a moment then her own face broke into a smile. 'You young girls and your frocks! I'm not so old I don't remember what it was like to scrimp and save for pretty things or to swap clothes. I'll have to send you up by yourself, mind; my knees aren't what they used to be.' She rummaged in the voluminous pocket of her dress and pulled out a bunch of keys.

Peregrine could hardly believe her luck. 'Thank you, Mrs. Meadows. That's very understanding of you.'

'Nonsense, dear.' She sorted through the keys until she found the one she wanted, detaching it from the chain and handing it to Peregrine. 'The lock can be a bit sticky, but just give it a jiggle. Drop the key back when you're done.'

'I'll be as quick as I can.' Peregrine smiled as she palmed the key. This was much easier than sneaking in and picking locks.

She let herself in the front door of the apartment building as Dulcie Meadows retrieved her broom and resumed sweeping.

Minutes later, Peregrine stood in the doorway of Barbie's apartment and let her eyes roam around the lounge-dining area and kitchenette. It all looked tidy. Well, as tidy as she'd expect, anyway. There were some record albums spread across the top of the stereo and the throw pillows on the couch looked as if someone had pushed them aside, but otherwise everything seemed normal. As though Barbie had popped down to the corner shop and would be back at any moment. Peregrine crossed to the window and looked out. She could see Mrs. Meadows still sweeping, and she also had a clear view straight into the landlady's lounge room. Dulcie Meadows would definitely have been able to see Barbie. As if to confirm Peregrine's thoughts, the other woman suddenly looked up and waved. Peregrine waved back, then stepped away from the window. She was supposed to be collecting a dress; she didn't have much time.

Turning to the couch, Peregrine ran her hands between the frame and the seat cushions but came up empty-handed. Absently, she picked up one of the throw pillows and plumped it up. She was about to place it where she thought it should be— upright in the corner between the armrest and the backrest— when a faint smell reached her. She pounded the cushion again and inhaled. Aftershave, not perfume: a man had been here recently. Peregrine dropped the cushion and carefully examined the top of the couch. If Terence Blair had been sitting on this couch, there was a chance she might find some stray hairs. At first Peregrine couldn't see anything, but then she moved her head and the line of sight shifted; there was something there. Carefully she plucked at the couch's fabric then examined her find, holding it up to the light.

'What on earth…?'

Between her fingers were several strands of orange fibre. Peregrine frowned at them for a moment then pulled out a handkerchief, carefully wrapped it around the fibres, and stowed the small bundle in her pocket. She stood for a moment, frowning, thinking about Barbie Jones and Terence Blair. With a sigh, Peregrine turned and went to look in the bedroom.

Things weren't quite as tidy in here, but the bed was made and there were no clothes on the floor. Peregrine opened the wardrobe, wondering what she should take in case she had to show Mrs. Meadows 'her' dress. Flicking quickly through the hangers, she selected a heavily beaded, pink silk shantung shift and pulled it out. Then she hesitated. She couldn't bring herself to make off with Barbie's dress. If Mrs. Meadows asked, she'd say Barbie must have sent it to the dry cleaners. Peregrine replaced the beaded dress and was just about to close the wardrobe when she realised something. There was no green dress. Dulcie Meadows had said she'd seen Barbie on her last night wearing a lime green dress, but there was nothing like that here.

Peregrine went through the wardrobe again then got down on the floor and peered under the bed. Nothing. Dusting herself off, she went and checked the bathroom. No green dress. It made no sense, but Peregrine didn't have time to think about it now; Mrs. Meadows would be beginning to wonder what was keeping her.

As she hurried across the lounge room towards the door, her hip caught one of the records sitting on top of the stereo and sent it spinning to the floor. It was The Beatles' *Please Please Me*, and the fall caused the LP to partially slip from its cover. Peregrine stooped to pick it up and was about to let the vinyl drop back into the sleeve when she saw something else tucked in with the record. She pulled it free.

'Ha! Yes!' Peregrine was triumphant. In her hand was a photograph of Barbie Jones, but this was no modelling shot. Barbie was leaning back with her head against Terence Blair's chest, gazing up at him with adoring eyes, while Blair looked back at her with an expression Peregrine couldn't quite decipher— something between bemusement and desire. She tucked the photo up her sleeve, replaced the record and let herself out of Barbie Jones's apartment.

Peregrine returned the key to Mrs. Meadows and reported that she had not found her dress. She was keen to get to the Adventuresses' Club, but the sympathetic landlady was eager to help.

'Barbie was very careful with clothes, dear, and I'm sure she would have sent your dress to be cleaned before returning it,' Mrs. Meadows explained, and then proceeded to give detailed directions to the nearest dry-cleaning establishment.

Finally Peregrine made her excuses, gave Dulcie Meadows her phone number—'Just in case the dress turns up, dear'—and started back to the Austin-Healey. Once she was sitting comfortably in the driver's seat, she pulled the photograph of Barbie and Terence Blair from her sleeve, wanting to study it again. As she propped the picture up on the steering wheel, a cream-coloured Ford sedan turned into the far end of the street and cruised in her direction. It looked just like the unmarked cars she'd seen parked at the police station. Peregrine immediately tossed the photo into the passenger footwell and pulled out a compact, flipping it open and holding it up to shield her face. Hopefully she was wrong and it was just an ordinary car, nothing to do with her or Barbie Jones. The Ford slowed to a crawl as it passed Peregrine's convertible and she risked a glance at its driver.

Inspector Sparrow. He locked eyes with Peregrine and his face turned red.

'You!' he yelled.

'Inspector! What a charming coincidence! I'd love to stay and chat, but I have somewhere else to be.' Peregrine twisted the key in the ignition and the Austin-Healey roared to life.

Sparrow pointed a menacing finger at her. 'Stay right where you are!'

'What?' Peregrine cupped a hand behind her ear, then with a shake of her head she put the car in gear and peeled out from the kerb. She watched in the rear-view mirror as Sparrow executed a three-point turn and started after her, only to be thwarted when an oblivious local reversed out of his driveway.

'So long, Sparrow!' she cheered.

As horns blared behind her, Peregrine swung around the corner and pointed the convertible in the direction of Greenwood Place.

—

She burst through the door of the Adventuresses' Club and thrust the photograph at an astonished Samuel.

'Quick, hide this!'

Birdie appeared in the hallway. 'Peregrine? What's going on?'

'Sparrow's not far behind me.'

Birdie jerked her head at Samuel. 'Make it disappear.'

Just then the gate buzzer sounded.

Birdie hit the switch on an intercom. 'Yes? Can I help you?'

'Chief Inspector Sparrow!' His voice echoed around the hall. 'Open this bloody gate now or I'll—' The rest of what he said was lost in a burst of static.

Birdie sighed. 'You'd better go before he does whatever he thinks he's going to do,' she said to Samuel.

'What about this?' He held up the photograph.

'Give it to me.' It was Violetta, drawn from her laboratory by the commotion. She plucked the picture from his hand.

He nodded, tugged the sleeves of his cardigan up ever so slightly, and strode off to respond to the inspector's demand.

'Where will you put it?' Peregrine asked.

Violetta pulled up the front of her fitted sweater, tucked the photograph between the waist of her skirt and slip, then smoothed the sweater back into place. 'Where he would never dare to look.' She lifted her chin and fixed a look of icy disdain on her face.

'You are full of surprises!' said Peregrine admiringly.

Violetta winked then schooled her face again as the front door burst open and Inspector Sparrow stormed in, Samuel trailing in his wake.

Sparrow stomped up to Peregrine and leaned in so his face was less than an inch from her own. 'What were you doing at Barbie Jones's apartment?'

Over his shoulder, Peregrine saw Birdie start forward and she gestured with one hand, low and small, to stop her. 'I have no idea what you're talking about, Inspector,' she said coolly.

'Don't lie to me, Little Fish.' Sparrow's teeth were clenched. 'I know you were there, and I know you went in.'

Peregrine arched one eyebrow but said nothing.

'I have spies everywhere,' he hissed. 'Did you take something?'

'No, but I think you might need to take something for your blood pressure. Your face has gone awfully red.'

Sparrow straightened, breathing hard. Then he threw his arms wide. 'I know you took something. I could tear this place apart if I wanted to.'

Now Birdie stepped forward. 'You'd need a warrant for that.'

He whipped around to stare at her.

'I can call our legal adviser, if you like. She's in the building.' Samuel came and stood next to Birdie.

'Personally, I have far more important things to attend to,' said Violetta from the opposite side of the room. She waited until the inspector had spun around to face her before pointedly turning her back and walking away.

Sparrow looked from Peregrine to Birdie and back again, eyes bulging and the muscles in his jaw bunching. Suddenly he flung back his jacket, revealing the gun holstered under his right arm. Samuel gasped and took a small step forward, hands slightly raised, ready to make a grab. But Birdie curled her lip in disgust.

'Well, who would have thought a man would resort to violence?' she said.

Sparrow twitched his upper body, as though he was going to move towards Birdie, but she stood her ground.

'I don't need the gun, Birnside,' he said. 'I can make your life—all your lives—a complete misery and I'd barely have to lift a finger. You have no idea what I'm capable of. But for a start, I'll be announcing to the press that your little club is a communist front: a hotbed of sedition and a breeding ground for murderers, as evidenced by the death of Barbie Jones at the hands of Florence Astor!'

'You wouldn't dare!' Birdie sneered.

'Watch me!'

Birdie and the inspector glared at each other furiously until Peregrine stepped between them, forcing Sparrow to look at her instead. 'What will it take for you to leave us alone?' she asked.

Inspector Sparrow's eyes became calculating slits and he stared hard at Peregrine. Then a smile spread across his face. 'Well, aren't you a fast learner, Little Fish? Birnside should take lessons from you!' He looked at Birdie again. 'Because that's how this town works. Just give me what I want and then we can all go on our merry way.'

Peregrine's hands curled into fists, but she took a deep breath. 'And what is it you want?'

'Your aunt created lots of problems, Little Fish. She has an item that she shouldn't have, something that means a lot to someone very important. I promised I'd recover it for him.'

'What sort of item?'

'Film. Very personal film.'

'Is that what you were really after when you broke in? But you couldn't find it, could you? My aunt was way too smart for you.' Peregrine smiled faintly.

'Watch it, Little Fish. If you make me any angrier, we won't be able to do a deal.'

'But if I find this film and hand it over, you'll leave us alone?'

'You have my word.'

Birdie snorted.

Peregrine, Samuel, and Birdie stood, unmoving, as Inspector Sparrow slowly made his way out through the front door. He paused on the porch and looked back.

'Don't keep me waiting, Little Fish. I'm not a patient man.' He raised his greasy hat and started to walk away.

'Hey, Sparrow!' Peregrine called from the threshold.

Sparrow turned.

'I just realised: you're named after a small pecker!' She slammed the door.

Sixteen

There was silence in the Adventuresses' Club. Then Peregrine, her back pressed against the front door, exhaled heavily.

'That actually went better than I expected,' she said, checking to make sure the door was locked.

'His gun...' Samuel began.

Birdie clapped him on the shoulder. 'Sparrow was never going to use it. Besides, if he'd even so much as thought about it, there's always the umbrella stand.'

'The umbrella stand?' Peregrine asked as she came to join them.

Birdie reached behind her and pulled a long, double-edged blade from the porcelain receptacle.

'You keep a sword in the umbrella stand?' Peregrine said, touching a careful finger to the metal.

Birdie shrugged. 'For emergencies only.'

'Has he gone?' Violetta had approached while they were talking.

'For now.' Samuel smiled at her. 'What happened, Peregrine?'

'I was leaving Barbie Jones's apartment and Sparrow saw me. I wonder why he was there on a Saturday?'

'Maybe he was looking for this? I hope it was worth it.' Violetta handed the photograph to Peregrine.

'Definitely. It's proof that Barbie Jones's mystery man was Terence Blair. The necklace and the lack of squash games were good, but this picture confirms it.' Peregrine held the picture up so they could all see it.

'And you found it in Barbie's apartment?' Birdie said.

'Yes. It was well hidden, too! But I also found something else. And then there's the file.'

'What file?'

'The police file that's currently hidden in the Austin-Healey. I found that secret compartment in the boot.'

'Secret compartment?' Birdie's voice shot up an octave.

Peregrine looked from one incredulous face to another. 'Let's go and sit down,' she said, leading the way into the Camelot Room. 'I've got a lot to tell you.'

⁓

Samuel made coffee while Peregrine retrieved the file from the car. Once they were all seated around the oak table, Peregrine told them everything that had happened since she was last at the Adventuresses' Club, beginning with the identical necklaces and her squash lesson.

Then she slid the police file across the table to Violetta. 'I was hoping you could have a look at this and see if there was anything...'

Violetta read the label on the folder then gave Peregrine a nod, clearly impressed. 'Of course I will look, but where did you get it?'

Peregrine explained how she had come into possession

of the damaged file as calmly as she could, stressing that Detective Steed was on their side. But when she told them what it contained, Birdie exploded, grief and fury mingled in a multilingual, expletive-laden tirade against Inspector Sparrow. The others let her rage for several minutes, until finally Peregrine went and stood behind Birdie's chair, resting both hands on her shoulders.

'That's why we're here, Birdie,' she said. 'We're not going to let him do that to Florence. We're not going to let Sparrow win.'

'But you promised him the film,' Birdie groaned.

'For starters, I have no idea where my aunt might have hidden it, so I couldn't hand it over even if I wanted to. And besides, I may be young, but I'm not stupid. If I give him that, what's to stop him harassing us anyway?'

'Whatever is on that film must be how Phryne Fisher was keeping the inspector at bay!' Violetta exclaimed.

'Exactly. And that's an edge we can't afford to lose.'

Peregrine gave Birdie's shoulders a squeeze and, in return, Birdie reached up and patted her hand. 'Spoken like a true Adventuress,' she said, her voice low. Then she straightened her spine and got back to business. 'But, in that case, you'd better fill us in on the rest of it. We probably don't have a lot of time.'

Peregrine returned to her seat. 'Once I'd read about Barbie's night-time signal to her landlady, I wanted to know if there was a reason for it—that's why I went to talk to her. And I found out that Mrs. Meadows had often seen a white van parked in the street at night over the past months. She thought Barbie had a stalker, but Barbie denied it. Mrs. Meadows also told me she'd seen Barbie at her window on her last night alive wearing a lime green dress, but I couldn't find a green dress anywhere in the apartment.'

'Could she have worn it to the store the next day?' asked Samuel. 'It might still be there somewhere.'

Peregrine frowned. 'I doubt it. That would mean she'd worn the same dress two days in a row, and women—especially a woman whose business is based on the way she looks—wouldn't do that. But now you've reminded me of something...' She stared blankly at the opposite wall then shook her head. 'Nope. I don't know what it was.'

'It might come to you later.' Samuel leaned across and topped up her coffee. 'What else?'

'Wait a minute.' Violetta held up a hand, although her attention was on the police file.

Three pairs of eyes fixed on her. She flipped a page, read some more, then flipped it back and looked up.

'This doesn't make sense,' she said.

'Peregrine's already told us that Florence's injuries—' Birdie began, but Violetta cut her off with a brisk shake of the head.

'Not Florence. I mean, yes, it's clear her death was not the result of a fall. There was a certain shape to two of the head wounds consistent with being hit by a rounded object, not impact with a flat surface. Plus there were some plaster fragments in her hair, yet the elevator shaft is all concrete.'

Birdie winced and sucked in a breath. Violetta's eyes widened in shock at her own lack of sensitivity. 'I'm sorry, Birdie, I was caught up in the science. I didn't mean...'

Birdie shook her head. 'It's okay, I know. Keep going. What doesn't make sense?'

'The time of Barbie Jones's death.'

'In the early hours on the morning of the fashion show,' said Samuel.

Violetta shook her head. 'That is what it says here'—she

pulled a page from the report and set it to one side—'but when I look at the photographs of the body and read the pathologist's report, it isn't possible.'

Peregrine, Birdie, and Samuel looked at each other, then back at Violetta.

'You'd better explain,' said Peregrine.

Violetta selected several photographs from the file, some of Barbie's body at the crime scene and some taken at the morgue. She spun the images around so the others could see and then pointed with a pencil.

'When Miss Jones was found, she was already in full rigor. That is, the body—all her limbs, everything—was stiff, yes?'

The others nodded.

'And you see here, the bruising on her neck is well developed?' She pointed to a close-up of Barbie's neck.

'It's quite obvious,' agreed Birdie.

'Now look at this picture, this discolouration here and here.' Violetta's pencil tapped on two of the morgue photographs.

'It looks like heavy bruising,' said Samuel.

'Livor mortis, the pooling of blood in the body after death has occurred.' Violetta checked to make sure everyone understood her. 'All this'—she fanned her hand above the photographs—'means Miss Jones could not have died on the morning of the show. She must have been killed much earlier—probably around twelve hours before the stated time of death.'

'But that can't be right,' said Samuel. 'The landlady confirmed Barbie was home at 11 p.m. the night before the show.'

Violetta shrugged. 'The science doesn't lie.'

'What if...' Peregrine spoke slowly, considering her words. 'What if Dulcie Meadows only *thought* she saw Barbie at the window?'

'You think it might have been someone else—like the person from the white van?' Samuel leaned forward.

'If Violetta is right…' Peregrine began.

'Not me, the science.' Violetta tapped the file for emphasis.

'Right,' Peregrine amended. 'Violetta has proven scientifically that Barbie was already dead when the landlady saw a figure in a green dress at the window.'

'Which means the killer was someone who knew about the signal!' Samuel snapped his fingers.

'Exactly,' said Peregrine. 'Someone like Terence Blair, the boyfriend.'

'Or'—Birdie leaned forward—'whoever was watching Barbie's apartment from the white van.'

'And as I discovered today, not only does Blair's Emporium own white delivery vans; Lewis Knox, the storeman, has easy access to them.' Peregrine put her elbows on the table and dropped her head into her hands. 'I'm not sure who to suspect anymore!'

Violetta flipped through the police report again then closed it with a snap. 'The police only checked alibis for the morning of the fashion show, not the night before.'

Peregrine groaned.

'There's nothing else for it,' said Birdie briskly. 'We'll just have to question everyone ourselves. As soon as possible, and preferably without that excuse for a police inspector getting wind of it.'

Peregrine groaned again.

'Perhaps if we start with who might have been standing in the window of Barbie's apartment.' Samuel pulled off his glasses and polished them. 'Unless the landlady is particularly near-sighted, it had to be someone with roughly the same build. One of the other models—or even Mrs. Blair, perhaps?'

'Peregrine, was there nothing else in the apartment that might give us somewhere to start?' Birdie asked.

Peregrine tipped her head up so her chin was in her hands. 'It's probably nothing, but when I was looking at Barbie's couch, I found some weird orange fibres.'

'Did you say orange fibres?' Violetta asked, her voice urgent.

Peregrine sat up. 'Yes, here.' She pulled her handkerchief from her pocket and unfolded it, revealing the few short strands she'd collected.

Violetta's brow furrowed and she opened the report again, rapidly scanning documents until she found what she was searching for. She jabbed an emphatic finger on the page. 'Florence had orange fibres caught under her fingernails!'

'Does the report say what they were?' Birdie asked.

Violetta shook her head disdainfully. 'Only that they were synthetic.' She pulled the handkerchief towards her, picked up one of the strands and rubbed it between her fingers. Then she gave it a gentle tug. 'The tensile strength seems reasonable.' She held the fibres up to the light. 'I must run some tests, which will take time, but it is some sort of acrylic, I think.'

'Acrylic? They make wigs out of modacrylic, don't they?' Peregrine stared at the fibres in Violetta's hand.

'That would be logical: a synthetic copolymer of at least thirty-five per cent acrylonitrile. Violetta looked at Birdie and arched an eyebrow. 'But only someone with hairdressing experience would know they use modacrylic for wigs.'

'Touché.' Birdie inclined her head graciously. 'Would you care to outline your thoughts, Adventuress Fisher?'

Peregrine flashed Birdie a quick smile. 'Either someone is using a wig just to disguise their own appearance, or they used it specifically to mimic Barbie Jones's red hair. We know Florence was holding a wig just before she died. Maybe she saw someone carrying it or wearing it, put two and two together and then...'

Birdie shook her head. 'Why? Florence was in a department store surrounded by models and dummies and wigs! Why would she think one red wig was suspicious?'

Peregrine closed her eyes, trying to picture the scene. 'Perhaps there was more to it than just the wig. Or perhaps,' she said slowly, 'Florence *didn't* know there was anything odd about the red wig, but she said something or asked a question that made the murderer think she did.'

'Knowledge can be a dangerous thing,' said Violetta sombrely.

The room fell silent. Birdie closed her eyes and leaned back in her chair and, as Peregrine watched, the mask of control dropped from her face, leaving Birdie's emotions exposed. It was almost too much, and Peregrine quickly moved her attention across the table to Violetta and Samuel. They quietly slid pages of the file to each other, communicating with looks and gestures.

Out in the hall, the grandmother clock marked the half-hour. Time was running out.

Mentally, Peregrine ran back over everything she'd discovered at Barbie's apartment and her thoughts snagged on the white van. She gasped.

'What, Peregrine?' Violetta asked.

'Lewis Knox!'

'The storeman?' Samuel said. 'What about him?'

'Not only does he have access to Blair's white van...' Peregrine looked at the three faces staring back at her. 'But when Detective Steed and I saw him last, Knox was messing around with the mannequins. And one of them was wearing a green dress.'

They all stared at each other as Peregrine's words sunk in.

'I have two things to say,' said Birdie. 'For God's sake, Peregrine, promise me you'll carry your aunt's gun at all times.'

Peregrine nodded. 'I promise.'

'What's the second thing?' Samuel asked.

'I never thought I'd say this'—Birdie rubbed her eyes with the heels of her hands—'but I think Peregrine should call the police.'

—

James Steed was sitting in the back corner of the coffee shop when Peregrine, dressed in her Blair's uniform, pushed through the door. At eight o'clock on a Monday morning, the room was half full, men and women in suits mingling with shopgirls and blue-collar workers, everyone stretching out the last minutes before the start of the working week. Steed had a newspaper propped on the table in front of him, so engrossed in what he was reading that he didn't look up when Peregrine came in. She stopped where she was and took a moment to study him. For someone who always seemed so stressed, his high forehead was remarkably smooth, although even from where she stood, Peregrine could see lines of fatigue around the detective's green eyes. If he'd only let his hair grow a fraction longer and let it get a bit tousled, she thought, James Steed would look quite at home on a surfboard. Peregrine was just contemplating his lips when Steed glanced up and caught her eye. She wove her way across the café and he half stood as she sat down.

'Good morning, Miss Fisher. Would you like a cup of tea? There's plenty.' He gestured to a large pot of tea sitting in the middle of the table, steam drifting lazily from its spout. 'I also ordered toast.'

As if on cue, a harried waitress dashing past with a laden tray deposited a rack of toast, a dish of butter and a couple of plates and knives on the table and rushed off.

'Just tea, please. And good morning to you too, Detective.'

'Did you find something in the file? You were very cryptic when you phoned yesterday.' Steed put the strainer over a fresh cup and poured Peregrine's tea.

'Sorry. I didn't mean to be.' She added sugar to the cup, watching as Steed slathered butter on his toast. 'I just thought you might need your weekend.'

He paused, toast triangle halfway to his mouth. 'That was very considerate of you. So, what's this all about?'

'Lewis Knox.'

'The storeman?' Steed crunched into his breakfast.

'Why does everybody always ask that?' Peregrine sighed with mock exasperation. 'Yes, that Lewis Knox.'

Steed gestured with his toast for her to continue.

'Barbie's landlady, Mrs. Meadows, said there'd been a white van parked in their street several nights a week for the past few months and—'

'Wait a minute. You went and spoke to the landlady?'

'It's okay. She thinks I'm a friend of Barbie's from the store. And that's beside the point.'

Steed took a deliberately loud bite of his toast.

'The point is that van was the reason why Barbie was signalling to Mrs. Meadows when she got home safely—Mrs. Meadows thought someone was watching her.'

'Probably just belonged to another resident. But'—Steed raised his voice to cut across Peregrine's protest—'how does Knox come into this?'

'The Blair's delivery vans are white and he has access to them. You need to talk to him.'

Steed took another piece of toast from the rack and transferred it to his plate then paused, butter knife in the air. 'I could point out that there are lots of white vans in the city and also that presumably Lewis Knox is not the only one with access to the Blair's vehicles, but I'll cut to the chase. Knox has an alibi for the day of the bridal show: Miss Astor had him running around and he was seen by a number of people. Even if he was fixated on Barbie Jones and sitting outside her home in the evenings, there's no way he could have killed her.'

'That's the other thing I have to tell you.' Peregrine lifted the lid of the teapot, examined its contents, then topped up her cup. 'Violetta looked at the coroner's report, and she says Barbie Jones was killed at least twelve hours earlier than everyone thought.'

Steed stared at her. 'You're not serious?'

She nodded, then took him through Violetta's analysis point by point, also explaining her idea that Dulcie Meadows may have been duped by someone else in a lime green dress and reminding him what one-armed Audrey had been wearing the last time they'd seen the storeman. 'Which means Lewis Knox could have killed Barbie,' Peregrine concluded.

Steed looked at the half-eaten toast in his hand and dropped it back on the plate. 'The whole investigation…' He shook his head.

'But now you know about the timing—and about the storeman—maybe things will start falling into place!'

'I'll talk to Knox, see what he has to say.'

'And I'll go and have a close look at that mannequin in the green dress!'

'Miss Fisher…'

'We can do it together, if you like. You've already admitted you know nothing about fashion, so I'm more than happy to advise you.'

The corner of Steed's mouth twitched but he kept his voice stern. 'If I can't stop you from interfering, I may as well be there while you do it.'

'That's the spirit, Detective!' Peregrine grinned. Then she caught sight of the large wall clock above the counter. 'I have to get to Blair's. Will you find me when you're done with Lewis Knox?' She stood and gathered up her bag.

'I have a feeling you'll find me first,' said Steed wryly.

Peregrine flashed him another smile then hurried from the café.

James Steed remained where he was, staring at the café's steamy window long after Peregrine had disappeared from view. He shouldn't have agreed to let her keep investigating. In fact, that had been part of his reason for meeting Peregrine this morning: to tell her it was dangerous and not her business. To tell her she needed to stop. It was the right thing to do—for a lot of reasons—but...he hadn't.

It wasn't just that he'd been caught up in her enthusiasm, or even because he enjoyed being in her company. Which he most definitely did. It was because Peregrine reminded him of her aunt: a younger, even more beautiful Miss Fisher. She had the same attitude to life, the same disregard for convention and—much as he hated to admit it, even to himself—the same ability to go places and do things he could not. While Steed had helped Phryne Fisher on a number of occasions, what he hadn't told Peregrine was that her aunt had helped him just as much, if not more.

James Steed had always believed in fighting for what was

right. If that meant sometimes going outside the usual chan-
nels, sidestepping Sparrow and his agenda, then that's what he
would do. And if doing the right thing also meant partnering
with Peregrine Fisher from time to time, well...he could handle
that. Couldn't he?

—

As soon as she clocked on, Peregrine was swept up in the organ-
isation and staging of a major new arrangement on the shop
floor. The atrium, a vast area at the foot of the escalators used
for large merchandising displays, was in the process of being
restyled with the latest fashions and products, to be presented
to customers as a walk-through array of *All You Need and More
for 1964!* She was kept busy trotting back and forth, moving
old display stock to sales counters or storage and bringing new
items up for incorporation into the layout. On what must have
been her eleventh or twelfth trip to the basement, Peregrine
rounded a corner on the stairs, her arms full of artificial flowers,
and walked straight into Pansy Wing. Pansy yelped and a cloud
of silk daffodils cascaded across the landing.

'Why don't you watch where you're going?' Pansy snapped.

Peregrine was about to snap back when she remembered
she was supposed to be Penny Foster. 'I'm sorry, Miss Wing.'
She dropped to the floor and began gathering up the flowers. 'I
didn't expect anyone to be standing there.' Peregrine stood and
tipped her head to one side. 'Are you okay? What *are* you doing
here? Can I help with something?'

Pansy flushed and her eyes darted sideways. 'I was just looking for...' She gestured behind her.

Peregrine tilted her head to the other side.

'Must be somewhere else,' Pansy muttered before ducking around Peregrine and hurrying away, the clatter of her high heels echoing down the stairwell.

Peregrine frowned at the retreating figure. What had Pansy been doing? The stairs were empty here, there was nothing to see, no one she could have been talking to... Peregrine moved to stand exactly where Pansy had been and then froze: she could hear voices. Glancing up at the wall behind her, Peregrine noticed she was standing directly below a small grille. Presumably it was there to help ventilation in the basement, but now it was working as a speaker, transmitting sound from the adjacent storage room into the stairwell. Pansy Wing had been eavesdropping.

Leaning back against the wall and closing her eyes, Peregrine concentrated on the sounds drifting through to her. There were two male voices, and it took her only a second to recognise the authoritative baritone of Detective Steed.

'...company van,' Steed was saying.

There was a pause.

'I only drive it for deliveries or when there's errands to run.' Lewis Knox's obsequious whine was impossible to mistake.

'What about at night?'

'I never drive the van at night.'

'And the night before Barbie Jones was killed?'

'What?' Knox's voice cracked.

'The night before the bridal fashion parade: did you take the van that night?'

'N-n-no, I never—'

'Mr. Knox this is a murder investigation, so think very carefully about what you're saying.'

There was a sharp intake of breath. 'Okay, yes. I had it that night. I was taking my girlfriend out.'

'I'll need a name.'

'I'd rather not.'

'Were you seeing Barbie Jones?' Steed's voice was loud with the accusation.

'Barbie? No!'

'Were you following her? Had she rejected you?'

'No!'

'A witness has reported seeing a white van parked outside Barbie Jones's apartment at least twice a week over the past months. Are you telling me that wasn't you?'

'Of course it wasn't me! I have a girlfriend.'

'Then tell me her name so she can verify your story.'

Peregrine had heard enough. She left the listening spot and descended the last few stairs, shoving open the door to the storage room with her hip.

'Detective Steed!' she called as she entered the space.

'Miss Fish—Foster.' Steed didn't look thrilled to see her, but neither did he appear surprised. 'Now is not really—'

'Pansy Wing!' she said.

'What?'

Peregrine dropped her armload of flowers and pointed at Lewis Knox. 'His mystery girlfriend. It's Pansy Wing, isn't it?'

'Really? Pansy Wing? How did you manage to...? Never mind.' Steed turned his attention back to the storeman. 'Well? Is Miss Foster correct?'

Knox cringed away from the detective. 'I can't.'

'Barbie Jones and Florence Astor were murdered and your refusal to cooperate is not doing you any favours. Right now, I have reports of a peeping Tom in a white van outside Barbie's home, and I have you in a white van you weren't supposed to be driving at night. Who. Is. Your. Girlfriend? Or does she even exist?'

'Just tell him.'

The voice came from behind Peregrine.

Pansy Wing shot Peregrine a look as she walked into the storage room. 'I thought you'd work out what I was doing.'

'Miss Wing!' Knox exclaimed. 'The detective was just—'

Pansy cut him off. 'It's okay, Lewis. I'll tell the detective what he wants to know.' She crossed to the storeman and linked her arm through his, then lifted her chin to Detective Steed. 'I'm Lewis's girlfriend. Actually, I'm his fiancée. We've been keeping it secret because Blair's has a no fraternisation policy and doesn't employ married women as models.'

'We're trying to save for a house, and Pansy makes good money,' Knox added, smiling adoringly at her.

Peregrine exchanged an incredulous look with Steed. Pansy Wing and Lewis Knox were an unlikely pairing, but they seemed to be telling the truth.

'I must admit I'm surprised by this,' said Steed, his eyes flicking between the elegant model and the strange storeman.

Pansy's chin came up. 'Why? Everyone around here treats me like I'm a shop fixture, but not Lewis. He's a decent man who's kind and funny and sees me for who I really am, not just a dummy in a dress or something exotic. And he treats me like a queen!'

'In that case, Miss Wing,' Steed nodded politely at her, 'perhaps you can tell me what you were doing the night before the bridal fashion parade.'

'Lewis came over—'

'In the Blair's delivery van,' Knox interjected.

'In the Blair's van and we went out to dinner. Then he brought me home early so I could get a good night's sleep.' She leaned her head on the storeman's shoulder.

Steed studied the two of them, frowning, letting the silence stretch.

'You won't tell anyone about us, will you?' Pansy asked anxiously.

'Not unless it's relevant to my investigation. You can go now, but I might have more questions.'

Peregrine stood back as the couple hurried from the room, then went to join Steed.

'Did you see the look she gave him when he interrupted?' Peregrine asked.

'More to the point, I saw Knox dig her in the ribs. There's something going on there.'

'Even if they were together that night, it doesn't mean they're not involved,' said Peregrine. 'Knox could have killed Barbie after dropping Pansy home.'

'Why? If Knox had no interest in Barbie?'

'Come on, Detective. Lewis Knox is head over heels with Pansy Wing. And what was the one thing holding back her career?'

'Barbie Jones.'

'That's right: Barbie Jones.'

'Could they be in on it together?' Steed mused. 'Could Pansy Wing have been the woman in the window of Barbie Jones's apartment?'

'I like your thinking, but Pansy Wing and Barbie Jones have different shapes. I don't think Mrs. Meadows would have mistaken the two of them in silhouette. Although... Wait! That's it!'

Peregrine abandoned Detective Steed and raced towards the back of the storage room.

Seventeen

Detective Steed caught up with Peregrine in front of the crowd of mannequins.

'Audrey,' she said, gesturing to the one-armed figure.

Steed raised his eyebrows, silently asking Peregrine to explain.

'She's wearing a lime green mini. Mrs. Meadows said Barbie was wearing a lime green dress that last night, but there was nothing like that in her wardrobe. Audrey is about the same size and shape as Barbie Jones.'

'The landlady saw the mannequin!' Steed slapped one hand into the other.

'I think so.'

'But someone still had to flick the lights, someone who knew the signal.'

'Exactly. Someone who'd perhaps sat in a white van parked in the street outside Barbie's apartment.'

'I think Mr. Knox might be more forthcoming if I had him down at the station.'

Peregrine nodded, her eyes still on the mannequin. 'Look at

this!' She scratched her fingers lightly on the shoulder of the green dress, then plucked at the material. When she turned back to Steed, there were a few orange fibres between her fingers. 'I found the same stuff on the back of Barbie's couch, and the coroner's report said Florence had orange fibres under her fingernails!'

Detective Steed bent closer to study the orange strands. 'The light's terrible here. What is it?'

'I think it's hairs from a synthetic wig.'

'What wig?' Steed gestured to the mannequin, bald underneath her large black hat.

'A wig styled to look like Barbie Jones's hair. This is orange and Barbie was a coppery redhead, but I think from a distance and in poor light it would look like her hair. Or close enough, anyway.'

Steed studied the fibres again then pulled a small paper bag from his pocket, holding it out to Peregrine. 'Drop them in there. I'll see what the lab says. So you think what? Florence Astor saw someone with the wig and realised something was amiss?'

Peregrine nodded. 'There has to be more to it than just the wig, but yes.'

'Lewis Knox?'

'It still fits. The van, the mannequin made up to look like Barbie…'

'Where is this wig now?'

She shrugged. 'I suppose it could be anywhere in the store, or he might have got rid of it. We can have a look around here at least.' Peregrine crossed to the closest line of steel shelves and began to search. She worked methodically, going through the first bank top to bottom, moving and lifting items, dragging things into the light for inspection before replacing everything and moving on to the next section. Steed watched her for a few moments then crossed to the next row and started to do the same.

Minutes passed with only the sound of shifting objects and the odd humph or tsk of disappointment. Then Steed called out, 'Where exactly did you find Florence's shoe?'

'Right at the end of the section where you are,' Peregrine called back. She tried to peer through the shelves but gave up, leaving her spot to check what Steed was up to.

She found him facedown on the floor, arm stretched beneath the shelves.

'Can't…quite…' he grunted.

'Hang on.' Peregrine pulled a coathanger from a nearby rack. 'Here,' she said, bending down and handing it to Steed.

'I should carry one of these with me at all times,' he said.

Steed scrabbled around for a moment, then shuffled backwards, bringing the coathanger and an orange-red mop of hair with him.

Peregrine pounced on it, smiling broadly. 'Nice deduction, Detective!'

'Florence lost a shoe here, so it stood to reason she might have been close to this point when she grabbed at the wig.' Steed stood and brushed himself down.

'Look!' Peregrine had placed the wig over one closed fist which she now held up. 'Someone has done a really bad job of hacking a longer wig into a sort of Barbie Jones pixie cut.' She fluffed the synthetic hair with her free hand.

'Are you sure?'

'Completely. You can see that it's roughly the right length and colour.' She wrinkled up her nose. 'But whoever did this has no idea how to cut and style hair.'

'Unlike you,' said Steed with a smile.

'It's that real-life experience we were talking about, Detective.'

Peregrine smiled back at him then turned the wig inside out and peered at the label. '*Hair by Harrison's*. And there's a style number. You know, for a synthetic, this is actually an expensive wig.'

'Does that help?'

'It might. It's not the sort of thing you buy in bulk: especially not in this colour. Which means if it was bought as part of Blair's inventory, there should be a record of a special order—and if it's a one-off, someone would have to specifically request or authorise the purchase.'

'We can find out who wanted a Barbie Jones wig.'

Peregrine's cheeks dimpled. '*We* certainly can. But perhaps, Detective, you won't mind if I see what *I* can find out about the wig?'

Steed hesitated then nodded. 'The sooner I can talk to Mr. Knox the better. Just try to be discreet.'

'Penny Foster is the soul of discretion.'

'I'm sure she is. It's Peregrine Fisher I'm worried about.'

'Let me just…' Peregrine put the wig down on a shelf and stepped forward. 'You're still showing the effects of your horizontal activities.'

Steed tensed as she reached for his face. Peregrine rubbed a thumb across his cheek then straightened the lapels of his jacket.

'Better,' she said, stepping to one side so Steed could get past.

There was a faint crunch as Peregrine's heel came down. She lifted her foot and scanned the floor. A small object, slender and pale, was lying almost underneath the shelves, hidden in deep shadow.

'What is that?' Steed crouched and peered closely, then, pinching it by one end, he carefully lifted the thing from the floor and held it up for Peregrine to see. Heads close together, they stared as he turned it slowly in the light.

'It looks like a finger!' Steed exclaimed.

'It is a finger.' Peregrine put her hand on his and adjusted the angle. 'See? It's a finger broken off a mannequin.'

Instinctively, they both glanced in the direction of the group of shop dummies then back at their macabre find.

'You're the expert. Do they put nail polish on these?' Steed asked.

'Some of them come with their nails tinted. Why?'

Detective Steed transferred the finger to his other hand, then turned the broken end to face Peregrine, exposing a splash of red.

'I don't think that's nail polish, Detective Steed,' she said.

'No, Miss Fisher, I don't either. I think that's blood.'

—

Detective Steed bagged both the broken finger and the wig then ushered Peregrine from the storage room, up the dim stairwell and, finally, out into the fresh air. Once they were standing by the service entrance to Blair's Emporium, he reached into an inner pocket, pulling out a packet of cigarettes. He took one before offering the pack to Peregrine.

She wrinkled her nose and shook her head. 'I didn't know you smoked.'

'I don't. They're just a very handy excuse to loiter around doorways.' Steed lit his cigarette then let his hand dangle, every inch the casual smoker.

Peregrine held up an arm to shield her eyes from the bright sunlight as she studied Detective Steed's face.

'What are we doing out here exactly?' she finally asked.

'Planning the next move while keeping away from what may be a primary crime scene. Although so many people have been in and out of that basement area since Florence... Anyway, it's probably too late for forensics, even if the boss would allow it.'

'What about one-armed Audrey in the lime green dress?'

'Probably safest where she—it—is for now. Besides, if anything happened to Audrey...' Steed grimaced. 'I can't believe I'm talking about an inanimate object like this! The point is, I don't want to rattle Mr. Knox before I talk to him again.'

Peregrine nodded. 'Best give me the wig then.' She held out her hand.

'I'm not sure you should be getting involved. Two women have already been murdered.'

'In case you hadn't noticed, I'm already involved! Anyway, if you've got Knox down at the station for questioning, I'll be perfectly safe. Not only that, it's actually the best time for me to find out about the wig: when he's out of the way and won't know I'm asking about it!' Peregrine wiggled the fingers of her still-outstretched hand.

Detective Steed frowned and looked down at his smouldering cigarette.

'Besides, we've already agreed that I have an advantage when it comes to fashion and style.'

Steed dropped the cigarette onto the cobbles and ground it out with the toe of his highly polished brown Oxford. He'd been keeping the paper bag containing the wig pressed beneath one arm, and now, reluctantly, he pulled it out and handed it to Peregrine.

'Just get the order details and that's it. Nothing else. Call me at the station when you know something. In fact, call me regardless so I know you're okay.'

Peregrine grinned. 'Why, Detective Steed—I didn't know you cared!'

'Of course I care! Between chasing the killer and antagonising Inspector Sparrow, you're a constant source of worry.' Steed tried to sound light-hearted, but Peregrine could see tension in his eyes and the clench of his jaw. She put a reassuring hand on his arm.

'All I'm going to do is talk shop and ask the ladies in the Blair's hair salon for a peek at their sales records. It will be easy. Besides, you might be hot stuff when you come up against gun-toting crooks, but if you set one foot in that place, they'd eat you for breakfast! Believe me, those women are fierce.'

'I'm sure I could manage...'

Peregrine laughed.

'But in this instance I will step aside.'

Peregrine gave his arm one final pat, then, with a spring in her step, she disappeared into the cool interior of Blair's Emporium. Detective Steed checked his watch. There were more than four hours remaining before the store closed. Plenty of time for Peregrine to chat up the hairdressers and still be home by nightfall. Plenty of time for him to drag Lewis Knox down to the station and give him the third degree.

He settled his hat lower on his brow and followed Peregrine inside.

—

Peregrine stuck her head into the Blair's hair salon several times throughout the afternoon, but each time all the chairs were taken, every dryer was humming, and the air was heavy with the scent of sharp chemicals mingled with sickly sweet hairspray. Finally, half an hour before closing, her persistence was rewarded. Only one client was still in the salon, sitting with her head under a dryer's clear dome. Elsewhere in the salon, a couple of assistants were busy sweeping and tidying, while two other women—who looked to Peregrine like the senior stylists—were balancing the till. They all looked up when she entered, took in her Blair's uniform and drab pigtails, and went back to what they were doing.

Peregrine pocketed her glasses, straightened her back and put a bit of pizzazz in her walk as she crossed to the desk.

'Can I…help you?' The older of the two women, her bleached hair teased and back-combed to within an inch of its life, arched one perfectly plucked brow.

Peregrine rolled her eyes and sighed heavily. 'I must look a fright! I was almost too embarrassed to come in here with my hair all…' She used the back of her hand to dismissively flip one of her pigtails then leaned forward conspiratorially. 'I'm trying to grow out the worst perm you've ever seen.'

Instantly the two women began to cluck. 'Do you want me to take a look, honey?' The blonde started around the desk, one hand already reaching for Peregrine's head.

'I don't want to trouble you with that now; I'll make an appointment for another time. There is something you can help me with, though.' Peregrine pulled out the wig and arranged it over one hand.

'Oh my stars!' The hairdresser reeled back in horror.

'I know.' Peregrine shook her head. 'One of the VIP customers up in ladieswear was complaining about the quality of the wig she'd bought. She was kicking up a real fuss, so I was given this and told to arrange a replacement. Now, I have a bit of salon experience—nowhere near your level of course—and it's perfectly obvious the customer has tried to cut and style it herself. Not that I could say anything in front of her, of course!'

The blonde picked at a lock of acrylic hair disdainfully. 'It looks as though she's gone at it with a blunt knife!'

'Or sheep shears!' her associate chimed in, her voice high-pitched and nasal.

Peregrine grimaced. 'Hideous! Anyway, I need to find out the details of the original order so we can get a replacement.' She flipped the wig inside out.

The blonde frowned. 'I don't recognise that colour—do you, Shirl?'

'Nuh-uh.'

'It's a Harrison's and the style number is here.' Peregrine turned the wig so the two women could see for themselves.

'Hang on, honey.' The blonde moved back behind the desk and pulled out a ledger. 'Order book,' she explained. Opening the book to somewhere near the middle, she licked her index finger and began to leaf through it slowly. Peregrine leaned across from the other side of the desk, trying to read upside down.

'I don't see it, Shirl, do you?' The blonde looked at her associate who was also leaning in, her long black hair brushing the pages.

'Go one more time, Annette.'

Blonde Annette licked her finger again and carefully went back through the book, commenting on each entry.

'No, no, that was for Mrs. Broadbent... Nup... Ooh, that one was lovely... No... Nope...' Finally she looked up at Peregrine. 'It's not here. No wonder Shirl and I didn't recognise it! Either it was a special order put in by another department—in which case you'll need to go to management to check—or the old cow bought it somewhere else and tried to return it there first. That shop told her what to do with her ruined wig and now she's trying to pull a fast one. The ones with the most money are always the cheapest!'

On the other side of the salon, one of the associates turned off the dryer and Annette's words fell loudly in the sudden silence. Peregrine and the two women glanced cautiously at the customer, but the woman appeared oblivious.

Peregrine tucked the wig back in its paper bag. 'I bet you're right—it's probably not even from Blair's. But you should have seen this woman stack on a turn!'

'Check with management, but I'm positive it didn't come from us. We're really strict about the order book. Everything in triplicate: one for the customer, one for us, and one for management. If it's not in here'—she tapped a long fingernail on the ledger—'we never saw it. Now, shall we see what we can do with your hair?'

'Next time. I'd better get up to management before everyone goes home. Thanks again, ladies!'

Peregrine hurried from the salon and across to the elevators. It was just after five, but hopefully Mrs. Hirsch would still be at her desk.

Eighteen

In the interview room at Central Police Station, Detective Steed stood and placed his fists on the table, leaning forward, forcing Lewis Knox to shrink back into his chair.

'Mr. Knox, I know you're hiding something. But because I'm a reasonable man, I'm going to give you one final chance. Tell me what happened the night Barbie Jones died.'

Knox shook his head miserably. 'I took the van so me and Pansy could go out. That's it.'

Steed slammed the palm of one hand down, hard, making Knox jump.

'Rubbish! Is Miss Wing involved? Is that it? Were you in it together? Did she ask you to kill Barbie?' Steed prowled backwards and forwards behind the table, his eyes never leaving the storeman's face.

Sitting in the corner, Constable Connor waited, pencil poised, to record Knox's answer in her impeccable Pitman shorthand.

Knox gaped at the detective like a goldfish before finally finding his voice. 'No! Pansy would never ask… She has nothing

to do with… I mean, neither of us has anything to do with…'
Knox buried his head in his hands.

'With Barbie Jones's murder? Is that what you can't bring yourself to say? And Florence Astor?' Steed had stopped his pacing and
now he crouched down so he was at eye level with his suspect.

'Look at me, Mr. Knox. Lewis—can I call you Lewis? Look
at me.'

Slowly, reluctantly, Knox raised his head until he was eye to
eye with the detective.

'Lewis, I'm going to be straight. Things are looking bad
for you. We have the white van at Barbie's place. We have you
taking a van of the same description from Blair's on the night
of Barbie's murder. You claim you were with Pansy Wing, but
she's not what we call an independent witness; as your girlfriend, she's biased. Although that won't stop me from dragging her in here and questioning her. So we have you in the
van with no solid alibi. And we also have the mannequin—the
one you referred to as Audrey—wearing a lime green dress—
just like the dress Barbie was wearing when she was last seen
alive.' Steed stood up suddenly, making Knox yelp, and half
turned his head towards Fleur Connor. 'What else do we have,
Constable?'

Fleur looked up from her notes. 'Motive, sir,' she said calmly.

'That's right. Thank you, Constable. Whether Miss Wing
was involved in Barbie's murder or not, she's your motive.
Getting Barbie out of the way means Miss Wing's career takes
off, doesn't it, Lewis?'

Steed pulled out the battered metal chair from his side of
the desk and sat down opposite Knox, folding his hands on the
table. 'Two murders, Mr. Knox, and enough evidence to lock
you away for a very long time. Is there anything you'd like to say

before I formally arrest you? Before I get Miss Wing in here and tell her in great detail exactly what you've done?'

Lewis Knox groaned, dragged his hands through his hair, then pulled off his glasses and frantically rubbed his eyes.

Steed waited, leaning back in his chair as though he had all the time in the world.

From her place on the other side of the room, Constable Connor watched, hardly daring to breathe.

Knox put his glasses back on and mumbled something.

'What was that?' asked Steed, his voice suddenly gentle.

'I needed the money,' Knox whispered.

Steed sat up straight. 'You killed Barbie Jones for money?'

'No!' Knox shouted, then his voice returned to a whisper. 'No. I needed the money so I promised I wouldn't tell...' He squirmed uncomfortably in his seat.

'Promised who you wouldn't tell what?'

'I took the Blair's van every Tuesday and Thursday evening and returned it the next morning, but it wasn't for me.'

'Then who?'

'Mr. Blair.'

'Just to be clear, do you mean Terence Blair?' Steed tried to keep his tone neutral but couldn't entirely hide his surprise.

Knox nodded. 'He was paying me—cash in hand—but part of the deal was that I couldn't tell anyone; it had to be secret.'

Steed glanced across at Constable Connor, but she just shrugged.

'Perhaps you'd better explain from the beginning. Just what was Terence Blair paying you for?'

Knox drew in a long shuddering breath. 'I'd take the van those nights and park a couple of streets away from the store. Then a bit later, sometimes ten minutes, sometimes half an hour, Mr. Blair would come and we'd swap cars.'

'What was he driving?'

'A Rolls-Royce Silver Cloud! Two-tone!' Knox smiled for a second. 'Beautiful car.'

'And then?'

'I'd take his car for the night—keep it safe; he didn't like leaving it out on the street—and next morning we'd swap again, and I'd drive the van back to Blair's.' Knox's voice was slowly gaining strength as he warmed to his story.

'Why? What was the point of all this?'

Knox shot a glance at Constable Connor then lowered his voice again. 'Mr. Blair had a bit on the side.'

'Pardon?' said Steed.

Knox looked at the policewoman again, and Steed rolled his eyes.

'She's an officer of the law. Constable Connor won't be shocked or offended by anything you have to say.'

Fleur Connor nodded encouragingly.

Knox wet his lips. 'Mr. Blair was having an affair with Barbie Jones,' he said loudly.

'And the van?' Steed prompted.

'The Silver Cloud was too distinctive. He didn't want anyone to find out about the mistress, so he came up with the idea of swapping his car for the van. He was paying me twenty quid a week, and I needed the money—Pansy and me are saving—so...' Knox shrugged. 'Pansy didn't know anything about it, and I never thought...'

'So on the night Barbie Jones was killed, the night before the bridal fashion parade, you swapped cars with Mr. Blair as usual?'

'Yes. Well, actually, no—not as usual.'

'Explain,' said Steed.

'A few days earlier, when we were swapping cars, Mr. Blair told me it wasn't going to happen that night, on account of the bridal parade the next day. Then I got a note telling me to bring the van to the usual place, but just to leave it. Put the keys in the wheel arch, go home, and collect it the next morning. Left me an extra tenner for my trouble.'

'And that's what you did?'

'Yep. Caught the tram home, and in the morning the van was exactly where I'd left it.' Knox shrugged. 'I thought maybe Mr. Blair had a change of heart about letting the likes of me cruise around in his Roller. Besides, who am I to judge? The van belongs to him anyway, and he was paying good money for our little arrangement.'

'And Miss Wing?'

'Like I said, she didn't know anything about any of it. She was just covering for me earlier when she told you we'd been out in the van. I swear!'

Steed folded his arms, tipped his head to one side, and assessed Knox. The story was plausible, except for one thing. 'What about the mannequin? Audrey?'

'All I know is she went missing, and then she turned up dressed but without an arm.'

Steed stood suddenly, sending his chair screeching across the floor. 'I'm going to have to verify your story,' he said. 'You can go. For now. But don't try to leave town, and don't discuss our conversation with anyone. You're not off the hook here, Knox. Even if everything you say checks out, I can still charge you with withholding information and hindering an investigation.'

Steed crossed the room, and pulled the door open. 'Go on.' He jerked his head in the direction of the hallway. 'And remember what I said: don't mention this to anyone—especially Mr. Blair.'

Lewis Knox stood slowly, his eyes darting between the detective and the policewoman, then he scuttled around the table and out the door.

Constable Connor stood, smoothed down her skirt and looked at Detective Steed. 'Don't try to leave town, sir?'

The corner of Steed's mouth twitched. 'It had the desired effect, Constable.'

'And now?'

'Now I'm going to phone Terence Blair and ask him to come down here immediately.'

'What if he refuses?'

'If he refuses, I'll offer to send around a couple of uniforms in a marked car to collect him.'

Nineteen

When Peregrine stepped from the elevator, Joyce Hirsch was still behind her desk, but the typewriter was covered and her handbag and gloves were lined up on the edge of the blotter, ready to go.

'Oh, Mrs. Hirsch—I'm glad I caught you!' Peregrine hurried across the thick carpet, already pulling out the orange wig and giving it a shake.

The older woman glanced pointedly at a clock mounted above the bank of filing cabinets. 'Is it something urgent? I was just on my way.' Joyce Hirsch emphasised her words by pulling on her coat.

'Well, it is, rather, but it should only take a moment.' Peregrine put a pleading note in her voice.

Mrs. Hirsch hesitated, her hand hovering near the switch of her desk lamp. Then she sighed. 'All right then, but I've only got a few minutes to spare. If I miss my train, then I won't make the connection, and it's dreadfully inconvenient.'

'Thank you! I need to know who ordered this wig.' Peregrine held it out for Mrs. Hirsch's benefit. 'I've checked with the girls in the hair salon and it didn't go through their books. You can see what a mess it is.' She shook the chopped mop. 'Definitely not good enough to be seen on the shop floor of Blair's!' Peregrine was banking on the idea that Mrs. Hirsch wanted to get home and wouldn't want to hear an elaborate story about an irate customer.

She was right.

Mrs. Hirsch tutted at the sight of the wig then turned to her filing cabinets. 'Special orders are all in here.' She tapped the top of one cabinet. 'Last thirty days all in the top drawer, filed by date of purchase, newest at the front.' Mrs. Hirsch slid her glasses down her nose and regarded Peregrine over the frames. 'Do you know when the order was placed?'

Peregrine dropped the wig onto the desk, where it fell in the pool of light cast by the lamp. 'I think it was recent, but I'm not entirely sure.' She brushed past a large rubber tree in a brass planter, its thick leaves casting wild shadows up the wall, and joined Mrs. Hirsch in front of the array of steel drawers.

The older woman sighed again. 'If it's older than thirty days it will be in here.' She tapped the next drawer down with a knuckle. 'Filed under the wholesaler's name.' She looked up at the clock and inhaled sharply. 'Is that the time already? Perhaps we could look tomorrow? Ever since Miss Astor…well, I really don't like being in the store at night anymore.'

Mrs. Hirsch edged towards Peregrine, clearly used to having junior staff get out of her way, but Peregrine stood firm.

'Would you mind if I took a look, please, Mrs. Hirsch?' Peregrine asked. 'I promise I won't mess up your files. It's just that I hate going home and leaving work undone.'

Joyce Hirsch glanced at the clock again then back at Peregrine's face. She nodded briskly. 'I wouldn't usually allow it, but you seem sensible and I've always tried to adhere to the principle of never putting off until tomorrow what you can do today. Besides, we working girls have to look out for one another.' She gave Peregrine a conspiratorial wink.

'Thank you!' Peregrine immediately backed up, allowing Mrs. Hirsch to squeeze past.

'Turn off the lamp when you leave, dear,' said Mrs. Hirsch, buttoning her coat.

'Yes, Mrs. Hirsch.'

'And don't stay too long.'

'I won't.' Peregrine put a hand on the top drawer, eager for the secretary to leave. 'Don't let me keep you—I'd hate for you to miss your connection!'

'Heavens!' Mrs. Hirsch bustled over to the elevators and jabbed the button. When the doors opened she stepped into the car. 'Good night, dear,' she said as the doors slid shut.

Peregrine tugged open the top drawer, pulled out the first manila folder she encountered and put it on the desk next to the discarded wig. She flipped the folder open and squinted at the top sheet for a moment, then remembered she was still wearing Penny Foster's glasses. Impatiently she yanked them off and dropped them in her pocket, then sat down in Mrs. Hirsch's chair.

She scanned page after page, astounded that so many special orders had been placed in just the last thirty days. Many of the items were for window displays, with an abundance of decorations for Christmas, still months away. She got to the end of the file with no luck.

'Rats,' Peregrine muttered. She slapped the file closed and straightened up, suddenly aware the building had grown quiet and dark around her. Security lighting must have been switched on, but either the fixtures were very sparsely placed or a number of bulbs were broken, because the executive floor of Blair's Emporium was now full of shadows. Far away at the end of the hall, Peregrine could see a feeble yellow light, but between the desk where she sat and the door to the stairwell was only a blackness so thick it seemed almost solid. She shivered, then reminded herself there was nothing to worry about; at that very moment, Lewis Knox was sitting in Central Police Station getting the third degree from Detective Steed.

She swivelled the chair around to face the filing cabinets, replaced the recent orders folder, then opened the next drawer and rifled through the alphabet to *H*. She moved the new folder into the light, opened the cover and there it was, right on top: Hair by Harrison's, with a style number and description. Peregrine picked up the wig, now warm from sitting under the light, and turned it inside out to check the number. As she did so a faint smell wafted through the air. She brought the wig up to her nose and inhaled deeply.

'Strange.' Peregrine frowned and sniffed the wig again. 'I know that scent from somewhere. Lemony.' Still frowning, she checked the number. It matched the order—which specified a shoulder-length copper-orange wig in modacrylic—so Peregrine turned her attention to the client.

'This makes no sense.' Peregrine shook her head and read the details again.

The wig had been ordered for Maggie Blair.

'Why would Mrs. Blair…?'

Then she caught sight of the scrawled signature executed by the person who'd approved the purchase. Not Maggie Blair. And now that Peregrine thought about it, it was unlikely Mrs. Blair had the authority to make wholesale purchases from suppliers.

She looked at the signature again, tilting the page back and forth in the lamplight. It definitely said Blair, but the first initial was so florid and looping it was impossible to decipher. Peregrine dropped the purchase order onto the desk and leaned back in Mrs. Hirsch's chair, staring at the wig, as she tried to work out the truth behind the murders of Barbie Jones and Florence Astor.

Minutes passed.

Suddenly she sat forward, snatching up the telephone. The switchboard was closed for the night and she had to hit various buttons before she finally heard the echoing burr that signified an outside line. Peregrine punched in a number she'd been careful to memorise several days ago. She needed to talk to Detective Steed. Now.

Twenty

Ordinarily, a ringing phone in the detectives' room at Central Police Station at that time of evening would have been pounced on within seconds, but at that moment the place was in an uproar. It took James Steed a few beats even to realise his phone was ringing, and by the time he'd managed to cross the room, grab the receiver, fumble with it and drop it, then finally get it to his ear, there was no one on the line. Cursing, he hung up and turned back to the cause of the disturbance.

Terence Blair was not a happy man.

'Mr. Blair.' Steed tried for calm, but Terence Blair was too busy ranting to notice.

'Blair!' Steed barked in his steeliest police voice.

The other man shut up, but only to draw in a breath. From his red cheeks to his blazing eyes, it was clear he had plenty more to say. Before he could start shouting again, Detective Steed opened the door to his boss's office.

'Shall we talk in here?' he asked, though it wasn't really a question. Hopefully Terence Blair would calm down a bit in the private and somewhat more comfortable surrounds of Chief

Inspector Sparrow's personal domain. Blair stared at him for a moment, mouth curled into a snarl and chest heaving with fury, before stalking across the room and into the office. Steed closed the door quietly behind them. Neither man sat down.

'As I said, I'm sorry I had to ask you to come in, but this is a murder investigation and one that impacts directly on your store. The sooner we can clear things up, the better it will be all round.'

Blair pointed an angry finger at him. 'I will be reporting you to your boss. Then we'll see if things are better for you!'

'That's your prerogative, but Chief Inspector Sparrow isn't here at the moment. So, for now, how about you tell me all about your affair with Barbie Jones?'

Terence Blair gaped at him. 'That's not... How...?' Then he collected himself. 'I specifically—'

'Yes, *specifically*,' Steed interrupted. 'Why don't you tell me about your little arrangement with the Blair's van and why you changed that on the night Barbie Jones was murdered?'

'Van? What van? Blair's has several vans, but I have managers and drivers who are responsible for—'

'Perhaps I should mention that I've already had a lengthy conversation with one of your storemen. Lewis Knox?' Steed leaned his shoulders against the closed office door, folding his arms across his chest.

Terence Blair's hands curled into fists. 'Knox!' He almost spat the name. 'That money-grubbing little...'

'In all fairness, he was doing a good job of keeping your secret until I told him that if he continued to insist he was the one driving the van that night, then he was the one I was going to charge with murder.' Steed crossed one ankle over the other.

'Well, *I* wasn't driving the van that night! And I told that mouth breather I wouldn't be needing it, so not to bother.'

'Where were you, then, Mr. Blair?' Steed asked quietly.

Terence Blair's chest puffed and he smirked at the detective. 'As it happens, I was dining with the mayor. He's a good friend of mine. Perhaps you'll catch a glimpse of him when you're back in uniform and standing on the steps of Town Hall for ten hours at a stretch.'

Steed regarded him coolly. 'Naturally I'll have to confirm your whereabouts. Since you're such good friends, you wouldn't happen to have the mayor's phone number, would you?'

Blair's face began to redden again.

'No? Never mind, I'm sure we can track it down. If you wouldn't mind waiting here a few minutes longer.' Steed straightened up and opened the door. 'Oh, and Mr. Blair'—he stepped into the outer office—'I'm sorry for your loss.'

Blair looked momentarily blank, but as Steed slammed the door he was gratified to see the man's face transformed once again by a look of incredulous fury. After a second's hesitation, the detective twisted the key in the lock. It wasn't likely to make Blair more cooperative, but it made Steed feel a bit better. Besides, Inspector Sparrow was probably going to crucify him anyway; he might as well make it worthwhile.

When Steed turned around, Constable Connor was standing several feet away, looking at a stack of files on one of the desks, but with the distinct air of someone who, moments earlier, had been glued to the other side of the door. Despite the late hour, her uniform looked immaculate and not a single blonde hair had escaped the confines of her regulation bun.

'Constable,' said Steed.

'Sir?' She looked up, her expression one of polite enquiry.

'See if you can find an after-hours phone number for the mayor.'

'Yes, Detective.' Constable Connor pivoted smartly and headed for reception.

Behind him, Terence Blair began to pound on the locked door. Steed closed his eyes, pinching the bridge of his nose. It had been a long day and it wasn't over yet.

On his desk, the telephone began to ring again. This time, he deftly plucked the receiver from its cradle.

'Central Police. Detective Steed.'

'Detective, it's Peregrine Fisher. I tried earlier but I guess you were busy.'

'Things were a bit hectic,' said Steed dryly. 'I'm glad you're home safely. Did you manage to find out anything about the wig?'

Peregrine hesitated. 'Actually, I'm still at Blair's.'

'You're what? Miss Fisher—'

'It's fine. Mrs. Hirsch had to go but she showed me where to look in the files.'

Steed was silent.

'Anyway,' Peregrine resumed, 'do you want to know what I've found? Because it doesn't make sense.'

'What I want is for you to be at home.'

'That's very domestic of you,' said Peregrine tartly.

'Fine. What have you got?'

'The wig—which, by the way, was originally a full-length piece—was ordered over a month ago for Mrs. Blair. But I've never seen her wearing a wig.'

'She wanted to revive her modelling career,' Steed reminded her. 'Maybe she thought looking like Barbie Jones would do the trick.'

'That is not how modelling works, Detective,' Peregrine responded. 'Believe me, looking like Barbie Jones would be the absolute last thing Mrs. Blair would want to do.'

'What if she knew about the affair and thought it might make her more attractive to her husband?'

'If she made herself up as a much older version of her incredibly attractive and vivacious rival?' Peregrine snorted.

'Point taken.'

'Anyway, Maggie Blair didn't sign the purchase order, one of the Blair men did. The problem is, I can't make out whether the initial is a C or a T.'

Steed glanced over his shoulder, reassured to see the door to Sparrow's office was still firmly closed.

'Take the paperwork home with you; I can stop by and collect it from your house later. But please, leave now. You shouldn't be alone in that store.'

Fleur Connor returned to the detectives' room and caught his eye. She waved a piece of paper at him then came over, placing it in the centre of his desk blotter. 'Mayor's phone number,' she mouthed silently. Steed nodded his thanks.

'Miss Fisher? Are you still there?'

'Yes, I'm here. Did I mention that the wig has a smell? Sort of a lemony cologne smell. I can't quite put my finger on it.'

'Probably hairspray or hair oil or something,' Steed said impatiently. 'Would you please—'

'Hang on! I just had an idea! When I first came in for my job interview, Terence Blair was at his desk on the other side of the office signing things. I bet if I check the out-tray on his desk there'll be something I can use to compare his signature with!'

'Miss Fisher! I don't want you snooping around!'

'It will take me five minutes, tops. I'll be in and out!'

'Miss Fisher!'

But all Steed got in response was a clunk as Peregrine hung up, followed by the steady beep of the disconnect tone.

Slowly, Steed replaced the receiver of his own phone. He picked up the slip of paper Constable Connor had left him and put it down again. He didn't like it. Peregrine Fisher was one of the most capable women he'd ever met, but... Steed looked up to see the constable watching him from the other side of the room. She raised her eyebrows at him.

'Constable Connor, I've got to step out for a moment.'

Her eyes seemed to get wider and she gave a minute shake of her head.

'You're not going anywhere, sonny Jim. You've got some explaining to do!'

Steed's shoulders stiffened and he turned slowly. Standing behind him, with a face like thunder, stood Chief Inspector Sparrow.

Twenty-One

Peregrine picked up the purchase order and tucked it into her pocket, then returned the folder to its rightful place among Mrs. Hirsch's files. She started around the desk, grabbing the wig as she moved. The acrylic mop had sat close to the lamp for some time now and the lemony smell rose up again, stronger than ever. This time, as Peregrine breathed it in, the memory came back with a rush: she knew what the scent was, and she knew where she had last encountered it. It was the French cologne Colin Blair had been wearing when she'd had her job interview.

Peregrine stood in the darkened office, her shadow made long by the desk lamp, piecing together the elements of the case. She could see it now, understand the how and why of everything that had happened. A faint noise jolted her back to the present and she froze, straining her ears and trying to work out what the sound was and where it had come from, but silence had descended once again.

It was time to go. She could call Detective Steed from a phone booth or wait until she got home; either way, Peregrine was suddenly very keen to get out of Blair's Emporium. But first, she decided to do what she had planned and compare the signature on the wig order against Terence Blair's. With the scent of Colin's cologne still lingering in the air, she was sure the two would be different, that it was Colin who'd placed the order for the wig, but Peregrine knew she needed stronger evidence than just her memory of a fragrance.

At that moment there was a faint click and the door to the inner office swung wide. A shadowy figure loomed on the threshold then moved forward slightly. The light from the desk lamp wasn't designed to reach so far across a room, but illuminated by its outermost traces was a face.

'Colin!' Peregrine gasped.

'Miss Foster?' Colin Blair remained in the doorway. 'What are you doing here?'

'Sorry, Mr. Blair! I didn't know you were working late. I was just—that is, Mrs. Hirsch asked me to...' Peregrine's voice trailed away. Colin Blair was staring at the orange pixie-cut wig in her hand.

'Oh dear, Miss Foster, oh dear. In the reference she gave you, Miss Astor did say you showed a lot of initiative. But this'—he nodded in the direction of the wig—'this is a problem.'

Colin Blair advanced slowly into the room and Peregrine felt the hairs on the back of her neck rise.

'Mr. Blair, I—'

'That's quite enough, Miss Foster.' Colin's voice was quiet, full of menace. 'I'm terribly sorry, but I'm afraid I'm going to have to terminate your position.'

Peregrine slammed her hand on the base of the desk lamp. As the light blinked out, shadows leaped forward, shielding her as she bolted for the stairs.

Twenty-Two

Steed stood manfully, trying not to flinch as Chief Inspector Sparrow raged. Constable Connor had melted into the woodwork on the other side of the room and remained standing, trying not to draw attention to herself. She needn't have worried; the inspector was completely focused on James Steed.

'I don't know what you think you're playing at, Steed!' Sparrow yelled, his face inches from Steed's own.

'There was—'

'I'm not finished! I gave you an order! I told you to arrest that Astor woman and wrap up the case, but the second I turn my back you go off half-cocked and now look what's happened!'

'Sir, if you'd just listen—'

'All you had to do was clean up the mess you'd made and keep your bloody head down, but what did you go and do?'

'I—' Steed tried again.

'Don't interrupt!' bellowed Sparrow. He stood, breathing heavily.

In the sudden silence, Detective Steed opened his mouth to speak, but Sparrow silenced him with the jab of a finger.

'I got a call telling me you'd brought Terence Blair in for questioning.' Inspector Sparrow's voice was quiet, his words uttered through clenched teeth. 'Please tell me, Detective, that I have been misinformed.'

Steed swallowed and moistened his lips, but remained silent.

The inspector's mouth twisted into a smile, but his eyes were like flint. 'Well, Detective? Have I been misinformed?'

'New evidence came to light based on a revised time of death for Barbie Jones,' Steed said, with as much authority as he could muster.

Inspector Sparrow frowned and looked away, catching sight of Constable Connor, who quickly put her head down and snatched up the nearest piece of paper.

'I'm at a bit of a loss here, Detective. A revised time of death? Would you care to enlighten me on one or two points?' Inspector Sparrow held both hands in front of his chest, tapping his fingertips together.

Silence grew around the two men until Steed cleared his throat.

'Sir,' he rasped.

'Who revised the time of death?'

'An independent consultant who reviewed the pathologist's report,' Steed said confidently.

'The report, yes, the report. And who authorised this independent consultant to look at a police file? Because—and correct me if I'm wrong—those things are, what's the word...Constable!' The Inspector barked the final word, making Steed jump.

'Yes, sir?' Constable Connor replied, without moving from her place near the far wall.

'You do all the filing. Can you remind Detective Steed what we call police files? There's a special word that means we don't share them around.'

'Classified, sir,' said Connor.

Inspector Sparrow snapped his fingers. 'That's it! They're bloody classified! So why are we sharing them with every Tom, Dick, and Harry, Detective?'

Steed stared at his boss.

'Request from the Coroner's Office, sir.' Constable Connor took a couple of steps towards the men. 'Some problem with their system so they were conducting a review of all cases.'

Steed looked at her and flashed a silent thank you, but the inspector scowled, his gaze flicking between detective and junior officer. Finally it settled on James Steed.

'I suppose you should fill me in then, Steed.' He folded his arms. 'And it had better be good.'

'The evidence shows Barbie Jones actually died much earlier that we'd first thought—probably about twelve hours earlier. Naturally that meant we needed to review alibis.'

'Oh, naturally,' said Sparrow. 'Go on.'

Steed stood ramrod straight as he told the inspector everything—or, rather, a version of events that included all the information uncovered to date, while avoiding any reference to Peregrine Fisher or the Adventuresses' Club. Throughout Steed's monologue, Inspector Sparrow nodded politely, his eyes never leaving the detective's face. When Steed finally finished speaking, the inspector placed a thoughtful index finger on his chin, resting his elbow in the palm of his other hand.

'That's very impressive, Detective. But I notice you failed to mention why Mr. Terence Blair has been brought into the station like a common hoodlum.'

'Hardly like a—' Steed began, then changed course when he saw the look on his boss's face. 'He was conducting an affair with Miss Jones. The night of her murder coincided with one of their weekly assignations.'

'And yet you tell me he was dining with the mayor that night. *The mayor.*'

'Which we've only just found out since—'

'Do you know how important Terence Blair is?'

'Now we have that information there are just a few loose ends to—'

'Do you know the trouble you've caused?'

'I was just on my way out to gather some remaining evidence, and then I'm sure—'

'Listen, Detective,' Inspector Sparrow began.

He was interrupted by the sound of someone hammering on his office door.

'Sparrow!' Terence Blair roared and hammered again. 'I want a word with you!'

The inspector's jaw dropped and he stared at Steed. 'Don't bloody tell me you've got Blair locked in there!'

As Inspector Sparrow strode across the detectives' room, Steed snatched up his hat and made for the door. He was half-way into the hall when Sparrow noticed his retreating figure.

'Steed! Where do you think you're going? Steed!' Inspector Sparrow took a step towards him, but then Terence Blair pounded on the office door again. With a growl the inspector turned back to his office. Steed would have to wait.

As Sparrow was fumbling with the lock, Constable Connor edged her way cautiously across the wall until she too was able to bolt down the hallway. Steed was just backing out of the car park when she charged through the door of the police station.

'Sir!' she called.

Steed rolled down his window.

'I thought perhaps you could use a female PC. You know, in case anyone needs their hand held.'

Steed rolled his eyes. 'Get in.'

Constable Connor didn't need a second invitation. She jumped into the passenger seat and just managed to get the door closed as Steed accelerated out into the street.

Twenty-Three

Peregrine burst out of the stairwell on the ground level, then hesitated for a moment, unsure whether to head for the front of the store and hope to get out that way or try her chances escaping through the rear exit. The problem with the back door was, not only would Colin Blair expect her to go that way, but if the security guard was there she'd really be sunk. Peregrine knew there was no way she could convince a Blair's employee she was under threat from the boss's son and, if Colin turned up, he'd easily be able to talk the guard into believing it was she who was the problem. Behind her, she heard the sound of footsteps pounding downwards at a rapid pace, the noise echoing through the stairwell. Peregrine closed the door then ran towards the shop floor.

It was quite dark here. Displays and counters loomed, indistinct shapes in the faint glow spilling through the windows from the street. At least it was enough to show Peregrine which direction to take. Suddenly she found herself at the back of the huge *1964!* display, right next to an array of camping equipment. A large torch had been placed close to a sleeping bag, the silver of its tube gleaming in the dim light. Peregrine scooped it up, surprised by the weight of it in her hand; someone must have actually put batteries in it, presumably so customers could see how powerful it was. She hefted it. It wasn't very long, but if Colin Blair got too close, it would do a bit of damage. Peregrine hurried further into the display, through a mock lounge room, past a selection of record players and into a crowd of mannequins dressed in the latest fashions. Some were in business suits, some attired demurely to appeal to older customers wanting something for a garden party or day at the races, but most were dressed in styles designed for young men and women, from higher hemlines and bright colours to Italian knits, bold patterns, and Beatles-inspired collars.

Peregrine pulled up short with a gasp. Audrey was directly in front of her, now with a new arm, but still wearing the lime green mini—exactly the same dress as the one she'd last seen in the storage room. Exactly the same as the one Barbie Jones's landlady had described. A blonde wig styled in a bubble flip covered the mannequin's head but Peregrine, with a quick glance behind her, ripped it away, swapping it for the orange pixie-cut version she'd carried from the office. Yes. From a distance the mannequin could definitely pass as Barbie Jones.

'Miss Foster?' Colin Blair called from the darkness. 'Where are you?' His tone rose and fell, an eerie singsong that seemed to come from everywhere and nowhere. Peregrine suddenly remembered something: her aunt's gun. Thank God she'd kept her promise to Birdie! But as she pulled it out the gun caught on the edge of her pocket, dropping from her hand and skittering away, the sound echoing through the vast, empty store. There was a faint squeak in the darkness behind her and to the left—the leather soles of Colin's handmade shoes on the polished floor as he turned towards her. Peregrine had to move. Now.

Cursing silently, she abandoned the gun and crept in the opposite direction, ending up in a sportswear display. On one side of her stood a dummy on waterskis, her arms outstretched to grip a thick wooden handle connected to nothing, and on the other a male figure in tennis whites, looking for all the world like Randy the squash pro. At the sight of it, Peregrine had to stifle a giggle as nerves almost got the better of her. She gave herself a mental shake and kept moving. Another footstep, much closer this time, sent Peregrine ducking behind a surfboard, held upright by a male dummy in Bermuda shorts and a Hawaiian shirt.

'Is that you, Miss Foster?'

There was a sudden pounding of feet, followed by a loud crash. Peregrine, her back pressed to the board, eased her head around the edge. In the dim light she could see Colin struggling to his feet, a mannequin clad in a black-and-white dress lying on the floor. He'd crash-tackled a dummy.

Peregrine didn't know how long she could keep playing this cat and mouse game, so she decided to go on the offensive. Colin was still in her sight line and she watched as he ran a hand across his temple, smoothing down his hair, then stooped and reached into the shadows. When he straightened up, Peregrine could see he was holding a cricket bat. Colin began to turn a slow circle, the bat swinging in his hand.

'I know you're in here, Miss Foster!' Colin yelled, his voice raw with sudden fury. 'I *will* find you! The longer this takes, the worse it's going to be!'

Peregrine pulled Penny Foster's spectacles from her pocket as she watched Colin Blair, gripping them tightly as he continued to turn, waiting until he was looking the other way.

'You're very devoted to your mother, Colin,' she called softly, instantly pulling her head back behind the surfboard. At the same time, she threw the glasses away to her right as hard as she could. They clattered loudly as they hit the terrazzo.

Peregrine heard Colin rush towards the sound and she went in the opposite direction, moving as quickly and quietly as she could. Among a group of mannequins dressed for an after-five soiree, she found a free-standing cocktail bar, complete with an ice bucket, cocktail shaker, and an array of different glasses. Peregrine took refuge behind its padded green front.

Straining her ears, she tried to pinpoint Colin's location. It sounded like he was still heading away from her. After listening for a few moments, Peregrine decided he was far enough away that she could call out again without revealing her exact position. 'Do you think your father was neglecting his wife?' she asked, trying to project her voice without raising the volume.

For a second the vast room seemed to hold its breath.

'Neglecting? *Neglecting?*' Colin's voice was shrill. 'He was *cheating* on her! Cheating on *my mother*! He was humiliating her.'

It didn't sound as though he was moving as he talked, so Peregrine took another chance.

'You had to act.'

'I followed him. Watched him swap with Knox—his Rolls for the van—and followed him to that tawdry little apartment. And then I saw him with that—that *gold-digging slut* Barbie Jones.'

Peregrine stayed crouched behind the bar.

'I kept an eye on her—on both of them—here and outside her apartment.'

Colin's voice seemed to be getting closer, which meant Peregrine needed to move again. Still crouching, she reached for the top of the bar and grabbed the first thing that came to hand. It was the cocktail shaker.

'Then I found out Barbie was pregnant.' Colin sounded calmer now, but it was an eerie calm, filled with menace. 'She was pregnant and she expected my father to abandon his wife. For her! A harlot and her bastard! I couldn't take that chance. It would have broken Mother.'

'How did you lure Barbie to the store that night?' Peregrine asked, then lobbed the cocktail shaker high and to her right. She was careful not to throw it too far: now that Colin had a vague idea of the direction she had taken, the noise had to come from somewhere fairly close by.

It must have landed in one of the display vignettes—perhaps the mock lounge room?—because instead of glass shattering on a hard floor, the cocktail shaker hit with a dull thud.

'Barbie Jones was easy in every sense of the word.' Colin sounded as though he was still nearby, but his voice was slightly indistinct. Peregrine hoped that meant he was looking towards the cocktail shaker's resting place as she crawled swiftly away, the torch clamped awkwardly between her teeth.

'I told her that Father wanted to see her backstage where all the wedding dresses were being kept; I said he had something to ask her. The stupid slut got all excited. She was sure he was going to propose. I just sat back and waited for her to turn up.' His voice had become a little fainter as he talked.

Peregrine found herself among an arrangement of suitcases and mannequins dressed to embark on a world tour. There wasn't much cover, so she made herself as small as possible behind an artistically stacked set of matching luggage.

'Did you like the wedding cake?' Colin called out suddenly. 'I had to make sure Father got the message about his

254   *Katherine Kovacic*

dear intended. I'd always planned to dress the bitch in white, so that everyone could enjoy the irony, but putting her on the cake was a last-minute stroke of inspiration. *I* thought it made quite the impact.'

There was a crash, followed by a second or two of silence.

'I thought that was you, Miss Foster! Never mind. There's nowhere for you to go. Just like poor Miss Jones. I should have known when Harvey White threw her out that she'd be trouble. But she tricked me with her crocodile tears. Still, *I* tricked her! And that old landlady turned out to be very useful. Their signal gave me a brilliant idea, a way to make it look as though Barbie was alive hours after I killed her. I knew Father was dining with the mayor, so I sent a note to that simpleton, Knox, telling him to leave the van and make his own way home. Offered him a bonus. Then all I had to do was put Barbie's dress on the dummy, pose it in the window, flick the lights and bingo! Barbie's home! I did have to give Mother an extra pill—I was sure she wouldn't mind, given the situation—and then I spent the morning of the fashion parade surrounded by police officers. I was rather proud of how I created the perfect alibi.'

'No kidding,' Peregrine muttered, then clamped a hand over her mouth. She risked a peek around the edge of the luggage pile. In the dull light emanating from outside the store she could see Colin only as a shadowy outline, although the pallor of the cricket bat, still in his grasp, was easier to see. He was moving slowly in her direction, pausing every few steps to peer at the displays, look behind objects and, once, prod one of the dummies.

Peregrine had to end this. Her hidden circuit of the *1964!* exhibit had brought her back in the direction of the mannequin in the green dress and Barbie Jones wig, but she needed to get closer. She needed to find her aunt's gun. Colin had fallen for the noise distraction twice; he was unlikely to be so stupid a third time.

Double bluff, she thought.

The topmost piece on the luggage pile was a vanity case, which Peregrine carefully lifted from its place. Holding it about a foot above the floor, she chanced another look in Colin's direction. He was currently poking the cricket bat at something, but definitely getting nearer.

'Why did you kill Florence?' Peregrine spoke without turning, then let go of the vanity case. It hit the Astroturf base of the display with a soft but clearly audible whump.

She heard Colin take several rapid steps in her direction then stop. Silence. Peregrine held her breath.

'Miss Astor...' Colin's voice was so loud it sounded like he was standing directly in front of the luggage display. 'Unfortunately, she saw me returning the mannequin to the storeroom. I'd left the dress and wig on it. I made some light remark to try to pass it off, but Miss Astor said'—he switched into a whiny falsetto—'*That dress is a one-off I made for Barbie! What are you doing with it?*' Colin continued in his normal tone, 'And then her face changed. She clearly realised there was only one way I'd have Barbie's precious dress, so...'

There was a strange slapping sound. It took Peregrine a moment to realise Colin must be smacking the cricket bat into the palm of his opposite hand.

'Oh, Miss Foster, do you really think...?' Colin's voice began to recede and Peregrine slowly exhaled. It had worked. Colin thought she'd thrown something from another location.

'Obviously I couldn't have her ruining my plans. I pulled an arm from the mannequin and...' The slapping sound started up again and Peregrine had to bite her lip as she thought of Florence's last minutes.

Cautiously she eased herself into a crouch and peered over the top of the suitcases. Colin was still moving away, making a thorough search as he went. She had to get in position now. There was no chance she could fool him again. Peregrine watched as he took a wary step into one of the display areas. Bent almost double, she crept closer to the Barbie Jones mannequin, keeping to the deepest shadows. Colin was still talking, his voice smug and satisfied, clearly delighted with the way he had managed everything. His callousness filled Peregrine with anger, but at least his torrent of words covered any sound of her movement.

'I knew the police already suspected her—Father had told me as much, and he presumably heard it from one of his well-connected cronies—so I thought a tragic guilt-ridden suicide would fit the bill nicely. The elevators are parked in the basement level every night. All I had to do was roll her onto some packing plastic to keep things tidy, drag it into the elevator and up we went to the third floor, where I wedged the door open, pulled her out and sent the car back down. I'm sure you know the rest.'

Peregrine had made it to within a few feet of the mannequin, but there was no sign of the gun. She tucked herself into a small gathering of store dummies staged in a garden tableau; it didn't give her much cover, but hopefully her plan would work. It *had* to work. She took a deep breath and lined up the torch, pointing it towards the plastic-and-plaster version of Barbie Jones, thumb ready on the switch.

'When I found the broken finger and Florence's shoe, I thought it must be Lewis Knox,' Peregrine said quickly. 'But you had to order the wig yourself. If you'd asked a shop assistant, that would have left a trail, and you and your father are the only other people who can place an order.'

Colin was striding in her direction, his head swivelling left and right as he tried to home in on the sound of her voice. When he was a dozen steps away, Peregrine snapped on the torch, spotlighting the Barbie mannequin.

Colin staggered back, gasping with shock. Peregrine flicked the light from side to side. There! A flash of gold. The gun, just beyond the mannequin, too far to reach.

'And there was your cologne, Colin—on the wig and at Barbie's apartment.' Raising her voice, Peregrine added, 'You left so many traces of yourself, it was only a matter of time before things caught up with you!'

With a howl of rage, Colin lunged at her, swinging the cricket bat wildly at her head. Peregrine leaped backwards, pushing one of gardening mannequins into him and knocking over an artificial tree in the process. It slowed him down, but only for a moment, then he was after her again. She flung the torch away and made a dive for the gun, throwing herself to the floor, her hand closing around the pearl handle.

Peregrine rolled onto her back and fired once into the darkness.

The shot went wide and hit the shoulder of the waterskiing dummy, sending her into a spin on her pedestal. As the mannequin came around, Colin Blair was running forward, and the outstretched arms swung straight into him, the wooden water-ski handle smacking into his face. Hard.

Colin went down.

Peregrine scrambled to her feet, keeping her gun trained on the prone form. She had just taken two cautious steps closer when suddenly the overhead lights blazed into life.

'Police! Don't move!' Detective Steed bellowed as he ran across the shop floor, gun drawn, face grim. He came to a stop next to Colin's inert body. Keeping his gun pointed at the man, Steed gave him a nudge with the toe of his polished shoe. Colin Blair groaned and started to move.

'Stay where you are. Hands where I can see them.' Steed checked to make sure there were no weapons within Colin's reach. 'You're under arrest for the murders of Barbie Jones and Florence Astor.'

'Thank goodness the cavalry's arrived!' said Peregrine dryly, as she tucked her revolver away.

'Are you all right, Miss Fisher?' Steed asked, risking a glance in her direction.

'I think I've lost my job in retail, but otherwise, yes, I'm okay.' Peregrine smiled, then she nodded towards Colin, who had lifted his head a fraction and was looking about. 'You should...'

'Of course.' Steed transferred his gun to one hand and reached around to the small of his back, fumbled for a moment and came up empty.

'May I, sir?' Constable Connor stepped forward, a pair of handcuffs dangling from one finger.

'Oh, yes. By all means, Constable. It will be good practice for you.'

'My thoughts exactly, sir,' she replied politely. The policewoman turned to Colin Blair. 'Hands behind your back,' she said, her tone flinty, entirely unlike her usual voice.

Peregrine raised her eyebrows and exchanged a look with Detective Steed, whose surprised expression must have mirrored her own. They watched as Constable Connor slapped the cuffs on smoothly and hauled Colin Blair to his feet.

'What happened, Miss Fisher?' With the situation under

control, Detective Steed re-holstered his gun and looked around at the partial wreckage of the *1964!* display.

'The usual.' Peregrine shrugged and walked over to join him. 'A man was explaining to me how smart he was, and I politely disagreed.'

Steed opened his mouth to answer, but as he looked at Peregrine's face, words failed him. All he could do was exhale and shake his head. 'You really are quite extraordinary. Most women who'd just been through—'

Peregrine stopped him with a hand. 'In case you haven't noticed, I'm not most women.'

Their eyes locked.

'Excuse me, Detective!' Constable Connor's voice was loud and all business. She was holding Colin Blair by one shoulder and the handcuffs. 'What would you like me to do with the prisoner?'

Suddenly there was a commotion at the main entrance to Blair's Emporium. Seconds later, Terence Blair appeared, Chief Inspector Sparrow a couple of steps behind.

'What on earth—' Terence Blair began.

'Here's your killer, sir,' Detective Steed interrupted, addressing himself to the chief inspector. 'There's means, motive, opportunity, and a considerable amount of evidence.'

'And a confession!' Peregrine added, earning herself a filthy look from Sparrow.

Fortunately, the arrival of several uniformed policemen caused the inspector to refocus his attention on securing the evidence—particularly the wig and Colin's cricket bat weapon—and issuing instructions regarding the transport and detention of the suspect. Sparrow appeared oblivious to Terence Blair, who was loudly threatening the chief inspector and his men with everything from high-powered lawyers and the mayor to tabloid newspapers and a permanent ban on their wives shopping at Blair's Emporium.

'As for you, Sparrow,' Terence Blair snarled, 'there's a small matter of our agreement.'

The chief inspector, in the middle of issuing a directive regarding the Barbie Jones look-alike mannequin, spun away from the officer he was addressing and in three short strides was standing toe to toe with Terence Blair. Peregrine and Detective Steed watched for a moment as the two men conversed in furious whispers, interspersed with one or two hard finger jabs to the inspector's chest. When Terence Blair waved an angry arm in their direction, Peregrine stirred.

'Perhaps now would be a good time...' she said, taking a couple of slow steps backwards.

'You read my mind, Miss Fisher.' Steed also moved back, his steps matching hers. 'High time we got out of here.'

Twenty-Four

Several days later, Peregrine was lying facedown on her banana lounge, strategically positioned to make the most of the afternoon sunshine. Clad in a pink-and-white gingham bikini, she intended to work on her tan while recovering from the drama of her encounter with Colin Blair. Peregrine had been surprised to find she had a lot of emotions to deal with, and this was the first chance she'd had to really think about recent events: from her inheritance and the people she'd met, to Inspector Sparrow's vendetta, and the death of Florence Astor. Her life had changed forever.

On the table to her left sat a newspaper and a tray holding two tall glasses and a jug, the latter beaded with condensation. Peregrine had made the Pimm's punch earlier in the day, after deciding that chopping the necessary fruit was a good way to practise her knife-wielding skills. Overall, it had been a successful exercise.

Peregrine rolled over, picking up a wide-brimmed sun hat from the crazy-paved patio and placing it squarely over her face. The Budgiwah caravan park and back beach felt like they belonged to another person's life.

A small scuffing noise reached her ears, standing out from the sound of the breeze and the distant hum of traffic.

'I wondered when you'd turn up,' she said from beneath her hat.

'How did you...?' James Steed stood at the edge of the patio, sunglasses in one hand and a large black garment bag slung nonchalantly over his shoulder.

'Sit down, pour a drink.' Peregrine gestured to the table at her elbow and a second banana lounge, which lay just beyond. The hat still covered her face.

Steed crossed the patio, then hesitated.

'For goodness' sake, you're blocking the sun! Sit down, Detective Steed.'

Steed put the dress bag on the end of the banana lounge, dropped his sunglasses on top of it, then cautiously sat down. It was even lower than he'd thought, causing him to drop awkwardly at the last second. The lounge wobbled dangerously and almost tipped over, only prevented from doing so by some frantic scrabbling on Steed's part. Beneath her hat, Peregrine remained quiet, pretending not to notice the detective's discomfort. He fidgeted for a moment, trying to find the least precarious position, and ended up sitting sideways, feet firmly on the ground and knees high.

Peregrine pulled the hat from her face and smiled at him. 'Is this a social call? I mean, it's Saturday afternoon, and I think this is the first time I've seen you without a tie.' She turned her head, casting a pointed look at the jug of Pimm's. 'At least pour me one, would you?'

Steed leaned over, filled two glasses with the fruity cocktail and handed one to Peregrine, who sipped gratefully.

'It's mainly a social call,' he said, sniffing his own glass suspiciously.

'Mainly. I thought you'd wrapped up the case.' Peregrine shaded her eyes with a hand to look at him more closely.

He gestured to the newspaper that lay on the table. 'You've seen the headlines.'

Peregrine rolled her eyes. 'I've seen Sparrow claiming all the glory for himself. The way that reads, he single-handedly unravelled the mystery, captured Colin Blair, and wrested a confession from the disturbed young man.'

Steed grimaced. 'I'm sorry you didn't get any credit, but Inspector Sparrow…'

Peregrine waved his words away. 'I'm not worried about getting credit or not. But I do want to know about the large wad of money your boss palmed from Terence Blair.'

Steed thought for a moment. 'Based on events that occurred in the Central Police Station in the hours immediately following the arrest of one Colin Blair, I believe I can assure you that an unnamed chief inspector was allegedly obliged to return an unknown item, widely considered to be a roll of cash. Allegedly,' he said, his tone expressionless, eyes fixed on a point above Peregrine's head.

She smiled again, wider this time. 'Detective! I think that's the first time I've really heard you speak police. I like it.'

Steed returned her grin. 'Just don't mention it to Inspector Sparrow. Needless to say, I'll deny telling you anything.'

'Needless to say.' Peregrine took another sip of her drink. 'So, even though the case has been finalised, you said this is *mainly* a social call. Why are you sitting on my patio on this lovely afternoon, Detective Steed?'

Steed's smile faltered and he placed a gentle hand on the garment bag. 'I have something for you,' he said quietly.

Peregrine frowned. She put her drink down and sat up. 'What is it?'

Steed looked at the ground beneath his feet then back up, meeting Peregrine's puzzled gaze.

'When we went through the crime scene at Blair's—I mean the storeroom and area where Florence Astor was working—we found this.' He patted the bag softly.

'I remember. That garment bag was hanging on the end of the rack. It was one of the things that wasn't there when I spoke to Florence the night before...' Peregrine stopped and abruptly turned her head away, staring at the trees, the garden, nothing in particular.

James Steed waited.

After a minute, Peregrine took a deep, ragged breath and brought her focus back to him.

'It's from Florence,' Steed said.

Peregrine stared at him, bewildered.

'It's a dress. Florence Astor made you a dress.'

'Me? But how do you know it was meant for me?'

Steed fished in the pocket of his shirt. 'Because there was a note pinned to it.' He pulled out a folded piece of paper and passed it over to Peregrine.

She took it slowly, held it for a moment, then opened it out and read. *For Peregrine Fisher, investigator, Adventuress, friend. Because every woman needs a little black dress.* Peregrine kept staring at the note, dashing a quick hand under her eyes.

'That's what she was making,' she whispered.

Abruptly, Peregrine swung her legs to the ground and stood up. She reached for the garment bag, leaning across the still-seated detective. Steed's eyes widened in surprise, but Peregrine, her thoughts on Florence and the dress within the bag, seemed oblivious.

'I'm going to try it on,' she said, hurrying towards the house.

'I'll leave you to it.' Steed struggled to his feet.

Peregrine stopped and turned, one hand on the sliding glass door. 'Please don't. Stay. There's no fun trying on a new dress when there's no one to show it to.' She didn't wait for a reply, vanishing into the dim interior.

She was gone a long time. Long enough for James Steed to walk the length of the patio a dozen times, drain his glass and, after debating with himself, pour another. And long enough for him to wonder—not for the first time—what he was getting into if he continued to associate closely with a woman named Miss Fisher.

Steed was standing at the edge of the patio, admiring the garden and enjoying the sun on his face when the sound of the sliding door heralded Peregrine's return.

'What do you think?' she called.

Steed swung around and stopped, staring.

Peregrine had taken the time to restyle her messy ponytail into a *Breakfast at Tiffany's*-inspired up-do, her face framed by several soft tendrils of hair. She stood in the doorway, one arm extended up the frame and the other hanging by her side, then stepped out onto the patio, her high heels tapping sharply.

'Stunning,' breathed Steed.

'It is, isn't it?' Peregrine turned a slow three hundred and sixty degrees to show off the short black dress, pausing for an extra second so Steed could fully appreciate the elegant cowl back.

Steed cleared his throat. 'I've never seen anything like it.'

Peregrine sashayed over to join him at the point where steps led down to a perfectly manicured lawn. They stood side by side, arms almost but not quite touching, aware of their proximity. Several minutes passed in silence.

'Miss Fisher.' Steed spoke with sudden urgency as he turned to face her.

'Detective.'

They were only inches apart, staring into each other's eyes.

'I wanted—' he began.

'Knock knock!' came a disembodied call from inside Peregrine's house.

Steed took a step back. The spell was broken.

'Peregrine? Where are you?' The voice came closer, and was now clearly identifiable as belonging to Birdie.

Peregrine caught Steed's eye and gave a wry shrug, then she turned back to the house. 'Outside on the patio!' she called.

'I should...' Detective Steed pointed to the side gate and began edging in that direction.

'You don't have to,' said Peregrine.

Birdie appeared at the still-open sliding door.

'There you are! And Detective Steed too! Hello, Detective.' Birdie flashed a broad smile at them both.

'Miss Birnside.' Steed nodded politely then hurried over to collect his sunglasses. 'I was just on my way.'

'Not on my account, I hope.'

'No, not on your account. Miss Fisher... Thank you. For everything.' Steed walked backwards for a few steps before turning smartly and disappearing around the side of the house.

'Sorry.' Birdie stared after his retreating figure. 'Didn't mean to interrupt anything.'

Peregrine sighed and shook her head. 'It was nothing that can't wait.' She gave Birdie a quizzical look. 'What are you doing here?' Peregrine went to collect her drinks tray. 'Not that I'm unhappy to see you,' she said over her shoulder. 'In fact, I couldn't be happier. I just thought you'd have better things to do on a Saturday afternoon.' She tucked the newspaper onto the edge of the tray, grabbed the handles, and carried it back towards the house.

'Oh, I was just in the neighbourhood!' Birdie said breezily.

Peregrine stopped in front of her, the tray between them.

'Really?' she said, one eyebrow raised sceptically.

Birdie's eyes flicked about and her gaze landed on the newspaper. She snatched it from the tray, almost causing Peregrine to lose one of the glasses.

Birdie slapped the back of her hand on the headline. 'Blast that Sparrow!' she fumed.

'At least now that Florence's name has been cleared I don't have to give him that film or any of my aunt's other files.'

'Oh, he'll still be after them, don't worry about that!' Birdie gave the newspaper a shake, and to Peregrine it looked as though she'd rather be shaking the inspector, preferably by the neck.

'I know, but it will be so much more entertaining now the balance of power has tipped back in our favour!'

Birdie smiled approvingly. 'We just have to keep it that way.'

'And I just have to find the film. Come on, let's go inside.'

Before Peregrine could take a step, Birdie pulled the tray from her hands. 'Let me take that,' she said, her voice suddenly loud. 'You go first. I'll be right behind you.'

Peregrine took a few steps then looked back at Birdie, frowning suspiciously. 'What are you up to?'

'Up to? Nothing! Go on, in you go.' She tipped her head, indicating the open door.

Peregrine complied but stopped almost as soon as she was over the threshold; she needed to give her eyes a moment to adjust from bright sunlight to the darker interior. Behind her, she heard Birdie slide the door closed and the gentle clink of glass as the tray was put down somewhere.

'Let's go and sit on the sofa.' Birdie gave her a gentle shove in the direction of the lounge room.

Once again, Peregrine did as she was told, sure that she was being set up, but unsure why or what to do about it.

Entering the lounge, Peregrine was even more confused. 'Why's it so dark in here? Did you shut the curtains, Birdie? Is there a problem? Is someone *spying* on me?'

'*Surprise!*'

A chorus of voices erupted from around the room and an unseen hand pulled open the curtains, flooding the room with light. Peregrine stood, her mouth open in amazement as Violetta, Samuel, and an assortment of Adventuresses appeared from their hiding places.

'What?' Peregrine continued to stare as Birdie came up and put an arm around her shoulder.

'Someone told me you needed a housewarming party,' she said quietly.

Peregrine pulled Birdie into a hug, briefly meeting resistance before Birdie relaxed and returned the gesture.

'I'm only sorry we didn't get a chance to have a party before...' Birdie's voice wavered.

'Me too,' Peregrine murmured. 'Me too.'

Birdie increased the strength of her hug then released Peregrine. 'Let's show Peregrine how the Adventuresses party!' she shouted.

Violetta came forward, arms outstretched to Peregrine. She grabbed her by the hands and stood back, holding Peregrine's arms out wide and taking in the black dress.

'Is that one of Florence's creations?' she gasped.

Peregrine nodded. A tear glinted briefly in the corner of her eye, but she blinked it away.

'*Tu sei bellissima!* You look beautiful, Peregrine.' Violetta let go of Peregrine's hands and pulled her into an embrace. 'Welcome to your home. Welcome to the family!'

'Thank you, Violetta.' Peregrine hugged her back.

'Now! Music!' Violetta let go and moved off into the crowd, weaving her way over to the record player.

Peregrine remained where she was, looking at the happy faces, hearing the laughter. She closed her eyes and realised that for the first time in recent memory she felt content. When she opened her eyes again, Samuel was smiling at her.

He was standing over at the cocktail cabinet, glasses and bottles lined up, garnish, jiggers, strainers, and muddlers laid out as though he was preparing for surgery. He called out a greeting then held a bottle aloft, waggling it invitingly. Peregrine laughed and nodded. Then, remembering last time, she went to join him to see what he was making.

'I'm going to invent something in honour of the occasion,' he said.

Rock'n'roll music suddenly filled the room, and Peregrine was surprised to see that not only was the very prim and proper Professor Violetta Fellini dancing the Watusi, she was really good at it. Clearly there was more to Violetta than just science.

Samuel said something that Peregrine didn't hear. She shook her head and pointed to her ear.

'I said'—Samuel leaned in close—'what happened to the goddess?' He nodded towards the end of the cocktail cabinet.

Peregrine stared at him, thinking she'd misheard. 'What did you say?'

Samuel shook his head and mouthed, '*Never mind.*'

'No!' Peregrine grabbed his sleeve. 'What did you say?'

'What happened to the goddess?' he yelled.

'I can hear you, you don't have to shout,' said Peregrine. 'I just wasn't sure I heard you right. What goddess?'

Samuel's raised voice had caught Birdie's attention and she appeared on his other side. 'Is everything okay?' She had a handful of nuts and popped a couple in her mouth.

'I just noticed Phryne's goddess is missing.' Samuel pointed to the empty space on the end of the cocktail cabinet.

'Huh. So it is,' said Birdie.

'Stop!' Peregrine held up her hands. 'Would one of you please explain? What goddess?'

Birdie frowned at her. 'A small statue of the goddess Isis. Your aunt kept it there. Said she liked it because Isis had incredibly strong powers; she resurrected her dead husband, you know.'

Peregrine, eyes wide, abandoned them abruptly and ran across the lounge and into the den. She emerged moments later carrying the small statue.

'That's it,' said Samuel.

'Yes.' Peregrine was staring closely at the statue, turning it this way and that. 'I think this *is* it. Because that's what it said in my aunt's notebook. She compared Madame Lyon to a goddess who guards secrets! Aha!' Peregrine was holding the statue upside down and now she dug a fingernail into one corner. The base came away, revealing the statue's hollow core.

And something else.

Peregrine turned the statue over and shook it. A small roll of film fell into the palm of her waiting hand.

Birdie, Peregrine, and Samuel stared at it, then at each other.

'That's film from the miniature movie camera I made for your aunt!' Samuel exclaimed.

Peregrine put the statue to one side and carefully unrolled a few inches of film, holding it up to the light. Then, as Birdie and Samuel crowded round, she unrolled a bit more.

'Is that...?' asked Samuel, tilting his head almost ninety degrees to the right.

'The Chief Commissioner of Police? Enjoying some of Madame Lyon's more...exotic skills? Yes. Yes, it is,' said Birdie. 'Definitely a side of him I've never seen before.'

Peregrine unrolled another inch of film. 'Ew! I did not need to see that.'

'What are you looking at?' Violetta, flushed and slightly dishevelled, had joined them without anyone noticing. She examined the strip of film and gasped. 'Is that Inspector Sparrow?'

'Impossible to be sure from that angle,' said Peregrine. 'But the commissioner seems to be in almost every frame.' She let go of the end of the film and it curled back into a roll. 'Now we know why Sparrow was so keen to get his mitts on this.' With careful hands, she tucked the film back inside the statue and replaced the base. 'Isis has kept it safe for this long; she may as well hold on to it.'

'Perhaps I should make a copy?' suggested Samuel. 'Additional insurance?'

'If you can stand to look at it long enough.' Birdie had poured herself a double shot of whisky and downed it in one go.

'Let's forget about Sparrow for one night,' said Peregrine. 'We'll have plenty of time to deal with that.'

'An excellent suggestion! Samuel! Where are these drinks you're supposed to be making?' Birdie set her tumbler down with a clunk.

'Actually, I think this calls for champagne! I took the liberty of selecting something from the cellar earlier.' Samuel matched his words by thumbing the cork from a bottle of Piper-Heidsieck, sending it towards the ceiling with a satisfyingly loud pop. He filled four hollow-stemmed glasses, passing them out and taking the last one for himself.

'What shall we drink to?' asked Violetta.

Birdie raised her glass. 'To the Fisher women, Phryne and Peregrine. Remarkable women, Adventuresses extraordinaire, treasured friends!'

Peregrine, Violetta, and Samuel brought their glasses up in response.

'Treasured friends!'

ACKNOWLEDGMENTS

Writing Peregrine has been such a joy! Deb Cox, Fiona Eagger, and Mike Jones at Every Cloud Productions—thank you so much for entrusting me with your marvellous heroine. Thanks to the Allen & Unwin team, particularly my wonderful publisher, Annette Barlow, and editor, Courtney Lick, for all your hard work, feedback, and enthusiasm. Thank you also to Ali Lavau for your editing prowess.

Finally, special thanks to Sisters in Crime Australia for all the support you continue to give to women crime writers.

ABOUT THE AUTHOR

Katherine Kovacic has written short stories, true crime, and crime fiction. Her debut novel, *The Portrait of Molly Dean*, was

Photo © Rebecca Taylor Photography

shortlisted for the 2019 Ned Kelly Awards for Best First Fiction and is the first of three books in the Alex Clayton Art Mystery series.

Katherine frequently lives in her head with her characters but generally maintains a physical presence in Melbourne.